Book 7 in the SEE.

C000175313

HIDING

JESUS

A NOVEL

Jeffrey McClain Jones

HIDING JESUS

John 14:12 Publications

www.jeffreymcclainjones.com

Cover Photo from Shutterstock

For Penny, who contributes even more in inspiring enthusiasm than she does in expert proofreading.

Chapter 1

What You Do When You're Bored

Matilda Hawkins flopped onto her bed and adjusted the thin white cords to her earbuds among her dangling braids. Justin Timberlake was there with her. She nodded as he sang, "It's just Justin." Or did he say, "It's just destiny?" The phone rang before she could scroll back and find out.

"Hello."

"Tildy. Whatcha doin'?"

"Hi, A.J. Nothing."

"I think I'm gonna switch to being Annabelle."

"Really? Annabelle. Okay. Why?" Tildy rolled to her back and kept the wireless telephone pressed to her ear, one earbud still plugged in her other ear. But Justin was waiting on pause.

"A.J. sounds like a boy's name."

"Hmm. I guess."

"You think Annabelle sounds too White?"

"White?" Tildy's mouth quirked involuntarily. "But ... you *are* White."

"I know, but ... well ... that's just so boring."

"You think it's boring being White?"

"Life in the White suburbs, you know?"

"Hmm." Tildy considered starting Justin Timberlake in one ear while listening to A.J., aka Annabelle, in the other. "You think Justin Timberlake is bored with being White?"

Annabelle snorted a laugh. "I googled him. He's from, like, the suburbs. White suburbs."

"Googled?" Had that become a—what was that—a verb? Tildy wondered what Mrs. Fredericks would say about such an abuse of   grammar.

Annabelle sighed. "Maybe it's just me. Maybe I'm just bored with *everything*."

"Well, maybe boring is a good thing. Boring is better than having lots of drama." Tildy checked the digital clock radio next to her bed. Her grandma would be home soon. Grandma might bring some drama. Tildy forced herself not to go there. "What are you doing for that short story?"

The sound of a big breath filled the phone line, riding on the cables hung beside those boring suburban streets, and then jumping somehow to this phone with no wire. "It's easy for you." A.J.'s voice came from a rumbly place in her throat. "You're always imagining stuff. And that's a good thing, of course. Especially for writing a short story."

"Does that mean you don't know what you're writing about?" Tildy allowed herself a private grin.

"Yeah." A.J. was clicking something against the phone. "I could write about being bored."

"Well, Mrs. Fred *said* write about what you know."

"Are you writing about your mom? Or maybe about your dad?" A.J. sounded strangely hopeful about those ideas.

"My dad is basically fiction, so that would be a pretty short story."

"Mm-hmm. I guess I could write about my part-time dad. Like, the one that shows up just before I go to bed and on most weekends."

"Write what you know."

"It would be more fun to write about an imaginary dad. Or maybe just an imaginary man that hangs around more than mine does."

"That sounds creepy."

"Not if it was Justin Timberlake."

"Ha. He's not old enough to be a dad."

"Not my *dad*. I'm gonna marry him, dummy."

"Well, good luck with that." Tildy was getting a little bored with A.J. *and* Annabelle. She wanted to get back to Justin. At

8

least his music. She wasn't really wanting him to show up at her house. "I should start writing."

"Yeah. Me too, I guess."

After hanging up, Tildy wondered if A.J. said that stuff about being bored with being White just to make her feel better for *not* being so White. She stood up and checked her reflection in the window above her desk. It was a mirror with the suburban night behind it. No, she was not so White. She was the Black girl. That's what kids at school saw. Even if her mom was White.

The garage door opened with its mechanical hum. Grandma was home. Her White grandma. A minute later, Grandma's shout confirmed her arrival. "Tildy? You in your room?"

Tildy couldn't remember her Black grandma. She had met her. She had even stayed with her for a while, apparently. But that was when she was really little. Tildy had long wondered whether she would see that grandma more if her parents had gotten married.

But she really did have to start writing that short story. She pulled her chair out and flipped a spiral notebook open. She snatched a ballpoint from her backpack and dropped it on the blue-lined page. "Yeah. In here." She might have sounded as bored as A.J., but that was an act. It's what was expected. If she sounded bored, then her grandma wouldn't suspect she was up to anything bad. Getting caught talking on the phone with A.J. was less bad than being caught watching old sitcoms on TV or surfing the internet.

Grandma's voice was closer. Probably at the end of the hall. "Okay. I'll get supper started. Come talk to me about your day."

A command performance. Tildy was better behind the curtain than out front. She checked her nails for signs of black from painting theater flats in the auditorium last week. She remembered to extract her other earbud and stuffed it into her pocket with her MP3 player. Grandma was no fan of Justin Timberlake. Or any good music, for that matter.

"How was your Sunday afternoon, sweetie?" Her grandma was still wearing her big puffy gray winter hat, like her head was a giant mushroom growing out of her shoulders. She tugged the hat off as Tildy stared at it.

"The usual. What about you? Sell any million-dollar houses today?"

"Oh. That reminds me." Grandma cast a glance toward the boxy gray computer hunkered in the corner of the family room. "Oh, I'll check email later." She dropped her mobile phone on the counter near where Tildy stood leaning on the doorframe. The silver-and-gray candy bar spun slightly as Grandma let it go. She finally snorted a laugh. "No, dear. No million-dollar sales today. Though there is a nice place in Naperville that has two offers." As usual, Tildy's grandma swirled. Hurricane Carolyn.

Tildy wondered about Grandma's glance at the home computer. "Are people making house offers by email now?"

"Sometimes. Sign of the times, you know."

"I need an email address, remember?"

"Are you planning on selling some houses?" Her grandma didn't look at her, which meant she wasn't taking Tildy seriously.

Tildy had already set up an email address. She was just checking if she could go public with it yet. A more receptive moment would maybe come before bedtime. The eye of the storm.

"I should get back to writing my story for English." Something A.J. had said was stirring in Tildy, spinning more slowly than the winds off her grandma, but nudging her to move nonetheless.

"Oh, okay. Sure. I'll call you when it's ready." Grandma pulled a plastic bag of food from the freezer. Some sort of stir fry thing. Those were usually not too bad.

Tildy drifted toward her room over the shag rug in the hallway, probably the oldest carpet in the house. Her sock feet treated it gently, considering its old age. Tildy was sure her grandma would tell a home seller to replace that carpet before listing this house. What was the saying about the baker or the shoemaker or someone and their kids not getting taken care of?

As she drifted, Tildy rode an idea that was growing more visible on the surface of her thoughts. She could write her short story about a ghost that shows up in a house, in a girl's bedroom, even. But she was trying to figure out how to make that not too creepy. Mrs. Fredericks would send her to the counselors again if she wrote a story about a creepy guy showing up in her room. Though, actually, it had been Mr. Khor that sent her to the counselor.

Anyway ...

Justin Timberlake was not the guy. Even if he was young and cute. It would still be on the creep spectrum to have him show up in her room, even as a ghost. Maybe a really old guy would be less creepy. But there was a thing about dirty old men too, right? That wasn't a thing she knew about, of course, and definitely would *not* try to google on the computer in the family room. Annabelle, on the other hand, might google that. It was the kind of thing her friend did when she was bored.

"The ghost who showed up the day I was bored." Tildy tried that title aloud. It was long, but maybe she could adjust it as she started to write. Sitting at her white-painted desk, she scrawled words for about half an hour before Grandma called from the kitchen.

"Supper's ready!"

A page and a half of the story done, Tildy was glad for the break. She was hungry. The sweet, savory aroma of the warmed-up stir fry was driving that point home. She hadn't eaten an afternoon snack.

She entered the kitchen without remembering to pull the earbuds out.

Grandma grimaced at those white wires hanging from Tildy's ears. Tildy's mother had given her the MP3 player. An off brand, but it held enough songs for Tildy to block the outside world for a few hours.

"You're not listening to that rap music, are you?"

By *that rap music*, Grandma surely meant the dirty stuff with lots of X-rated words in it. Tildy didn't like that kind of music. Talk about creepy. "No, Grandma. Just pop songs. Love songs."

"You're too young for love songs, Tildy. You're still a girl."

Could her grandma make it so? Could she forbid Tildy from becoming a young woman, even a teen? Her words were weights slowing Tildy, like those ankle weights she tried in gym class. *I don't need anyone slowing me down.* She didn't say that aloud. No use arguing with Grandma.

Maybe she could write a story about her other grandma—her Black grandma. She could make her a profound and inspiring woman like Maya Angelou or someone like that.

"Tildy? Hello!"

Tildy snapped out of that field trip into her imagination. "Huh?"

Her grandma was reaching for her hand. Time to say grace for the meal.

Time to pay attention to Grandma for a while. "Oh, sorry. Go ahead."

Grandma said the standard thank you for the food and the day, and then they took turns scooping chicken stir fry onto their plates. There were about four varieties of this frozen meal that her grandma liked. Tildy didn't mind them. Except the one with asparagus in it. Her opinion that asparagus should never be frozen was proved each time Grandma served that one.

"So, did you say you were writing a story?" Grandma scooped and scraped, scraped and scooped, until her fork was loaded with a full bite.

Tildy chewed and swallowed. Reaching for her water glass, she nodded. "Yeah. It's for Mrs. Fredericks's English class."

"I remember those days." Grandma swallowed and started searching her teeth with her tongue. "My daddy used to give me ideas for stories. I could never come up with 'em on my own. But his ideas were always good to get me started. Though I doubt any of my stories were particularly good."

Tildy studied her grandma for a few seconds. She was not really an old lady, even if it was hard for Tildy to picture her as an eleven-year-old getting story ideas from her dad. Grandma had dark hair that she colored whenever that white stripe started showing down the middle. And she had dark eyes like Tildy's mother. And like her father too, come to think of it. Grandma was probably about fifty or fifty-five. Tildy had surely heard the right number sometime recently, but she couldn't remember right now. Right now, Grandma's makeup was showing the wear of the day, the powder cracked around her eyes and her lipstick covering only the outer edges of both lips.

When her grandma's brow hunkered for a second, Tildy stopped staring. She stabbed the last slice of chicken on her plate. As she chewed, she regretted her indiscretion. She liked to make the meat last to the final bite, not leaving only veggies. She wasn't going to become a vegetarian anytime soon, no matter how many movie stars bragged about their conversion.

"I heard from your mom today." Grandma cleared her throat after she said that. Not a good sign.

"How did she sound?"

"Oh. Well, you know. She's still working on it. One day at a time, they say."

Tildy scowled at her grandma. "What's that supposed to mean?"

Grandma glanced toward the dining room. "I suppose it just means that it takes time." She lowered her gaze to Tildy's plate, then to her hands, and finally up to her face. "Some people never even try."

"Like my grandpa?" As soon as the last syllable hopped from her mouth, Tildy froze.

Blinking hard four or five times, Grandma's lips twitched. "Yes. Like your grandpa." She took a deep breath. "That's probably where your mother got it from."

13

The way her mother had told it, Grandpa had been a mean drunk. "Mean drunk" was exactly how she said it. But Tildy's mom wasn't a drunk. She drank, probably, but it was drugs that got her sent away. Was that the same thing as her grandpa, really? Tildy didn't seek clarification from her grandma. She had surely said too much already. "So, she didn't say anything about when she would get out?" That was probably a safe question. Safe because Tildy already knew the answer.

Grandma took a deep breath and settled her fork onto her empty plate. "No. No word about that." She hung there for a second, probably trying to decide how much to say.

Tildy knew most of what her grandma said was edited for her "little ears." Tildy was actually glad she *had* little ears. Jimmy Carlson had huge ears. And his parents wouldn't let him grow his hair long enough to hide that fact. She reached up and touched her right ear. When her grandma scowled at her, Tildy adjusted to pulling a few of her braids away from her face.

Grandma stood from the table, dragging her plate off the edge. She seemed suddenly weary, as if Tildy had made a long day even longer. But surely it wasn't all Tildy's fault. She could shuffle most of the blame to her mom. Grandma's own daughter. *She* was making every day longer for both her mother and her daughter. One day at a time? One freakishly long day at a time.

Imagining little wavy lines following her grandma to the sink, Tildy blinked those away and headed back toward her room. She could see her grandma lifting her phone just as Tildy hit the hallway. Checking messages? Was Grandma using texts for her work now, or just voice messages?

Tildy let go of the quest for an approved email address for another day. And she wouldn't even put a cell phone on her wish list. That was just for rich kids. Right along with those iPods the girls at school had. The popular girls.

Thinking of those girls squeezed Tildy, shrinking her like when Aunt Barbara hugged her hard from the side. Crushed and fumigated with cigarette smoke, it was hard to breathe with Aunt

Barbara around. Tildy shuddered at the memory of that moment when it was up for grabs whether she would stay with Aunt Barbara or with Grandma. A wriggle like having a dog thrashing a rag doll shook her at the time.

She stopped herself from slamming her bedroom door, even leaving it open an inch to comply with the law of the house. Grandma's rules. Looking at the spiral notebook on her desk, she wondered if she could just type her story on the computer. Mrs. Fredericks preferred that, though she couldn't make it a rule. Teacher's rules. Poor kids couldn't do that. The poor kids in her school were mostly Hispanic. The few poor Black kids were refugees from Somalia. Or most of them, anyway. Random thoughts. Her head was whirling like she was still caught in Hurricane Carolyn. Maybe she would always be caught in that hurricane, even after her mother got back from rehab.

For a second, she thought she couldn't possibly return to writing her story about the ghost of some old person visiting a lonely little girl. Then she remembered how easy it was to use her anger in painting those black flats on the stage at school. Angry strokes of darkness. Real blackness, not the coffee-and-cream brown of her skin. That same anger could fuel some writing. It could be a story about a visit from a man who could save her from her horrid life.

She pulled the wooden chair away from the desk, the chipped paint along the left edge catching her eye as it always did. That chip was so tired. No—she was the one who was tired of looking at it. Tildy pulled open one desk drawer and then another until she found the white correction fluid. She would correct her chair, cover the two-inch rhomboid of pinkish red that shone through where the antique white had been chipped.

Sitting on the floor on her knees, she thought about who could save her from her horrid life. Probably no one. Not her mom, of course. Not her grandma. Not Aunt Barbara and her two noisy kids. Not even Justin Timberlake. She snorted at that thought as she stroked the clumpy little brush over the red-and-pink paint. The correction fluid would probably just chip too, but at least she could make the gash go away for a little while.

A fleck of the pure white correction fluid shone clear on her brown skin just above the first knuckle on her right pointer finger. She dipped the brush in the bottle again. Stroking that little tool over her finger, she turned the tip of it white all the way to the second knuckle. Then she stood and grabbed a tissue. She wiped most of the correction fluid off—the part that hadn't dried.

The ghost would be all white. Dead white. That's what she decided as she sat in her chair, careful not to let her jeans touch the correction fluid on the seat.

She plugged her earbuds in again and pulled her MP3 player from her jeans pocket. She pressed the play button and welcomed Justin back into her room, into her head. Though not into her story.

Chapter Two
Be Careful Who You Talk To

That night, Tildy dreamt about an intruder. Then he wasn't an intruder. Then it was her dad, but she couldn't see his face. And then he was gone. Somehow it turned into some alien hiding in her closet like in *Monsters, Inc*. But it wasn't a monster. It wasn't even a ghost. It was a guy.

He sort of slipped out of her closet and pretended it wasn't unusual for him to be in there. He stood by her dresser and smiled at her. Then he turned toward the box of her found art still packed on top of the dresser—what her mom called her "Tildy Treasures." Grandma would certainly call it junk. The guy seemed to be appreciating the things in that box. Somehow he had unfolded the flaps on top before she noticed him there. Or maybe he didn't need to loosen the interlocking flaps to get inside the box. How did he do that?

It became a growing concern, a looming problem. How could that guy open her box of found art without even unfolding the top? That was unrealistic. This story had to be realistic even if it was fiction. Even if it was a dream, it had to be realistic. Otherwise Mrs. Frederick would give her a bad grade.

Somebody cackled from the hallway. Tildy's door was closed, which was against the rules. The cackler pounded on the door. "Let me in. Don't lock me out of your room."

But Tildy knew the door wasn't locked. She could see the button wasn't pushed in. And anyway, her grandma had those little metal clips she could push into the door handle from the outside if she wanted to, one was stashed above Tildy's door. But maybe Grandma had lost those.

That was when the guy by her dresser pulled a small brass thing out of the box. It was a wire. It was the key clip for opening the door. Her grandma wouldn't be able to get in. But maybe that wasn't her grandmother knocking. It was someone evil. Her grandma wasn't evil. Just bothersome sometimes.

The man or ghost or whoever by her dresser was looking at Tildy and then at the door like he wanted permission. Permission for what?

The person in the hall pounded on the door much harder. And harder. And louder.

"Tildy. Tildy!"

She awoke with a start. It was cold in her room. Her grandma was peering in the door. "You were having a dream, dear."

"What?"

"I heard you whimpering. You were having a bad dream."

Whimpering? Tildy didn't whimper. At least she didn't in her waking life. She didn't remember whimpering in the dream either. She looked at her dresser. The box was still on top of the antique white chest, ghostly in the night, a slice of yellowish light cutting into one edge of it. "Sorry."

"Oh, don't worry about it. I was just making sure you were okay."

Tildy checked the clock. It was 11:37. She had been asleep for about two hours. Had Grandma still been awake? Tildy checked for signs she had awakened her grandma. It was hard to tell with the light coming from behind her. "Okay. Good night." Tildy tried to sound rational—or at least awake. Maybe reassuring her grandma against fears that Tildy was losing it. Losing something.

"Good night, Tildy." Grandma hesitated a second before pulling the door closed to within half an inch. Then she turned off the hallway light.

As Tildy fell asleep, she started looking for the path back to that dream. Despite the reported whimpering, she wanted back

18

in. Who was that guy by the dresser? It wasn't just that he had figured out how to open the box. He knew other things too. He knew where the key was. Even if he seemed to need Tildy's permission to open the door.

She slept without returning to that dream, of course. She didn't expect most people could do that.

When she woke in the morning, she was still thinking of that dream. Maybe her grandma waking her in the middle of it had tattooed it on her brain. How old would she have to be before Grandma would allow her to get a tattoo? Probably lots older than her mom. She had several tattoos Tildy knew about.

With those thoughts, Tildy slipped from under her covers and hit the button to prevent her alarm from beeping. As usual, she was up before the alarm. Maybe the alarm needed her to wake it. She was so reliable. Or maybe it was the anticipation of the alarm that woke her. Didn't Mr. Khor teach them something about subconscious powers in the brain? That would be more like a superpower. The human alarm clock. She dragged her feet through the shag carpet on the way to the bathroom.

An hour later, A.J. greeted her as Tildy approached the bus stop. "Yo. You look like a train with that steam comin' outta your stack." A.J. let out her own cloud of vapor as Tildy shuffled over the ice and snow toward her. The year 2003 had arrived frozen like one of Grandma's dinners.

"You been watchin' *Thomas the Tank Engine* again?"

"Yeah. Benny loves that stuff." A.J. rolled her eyes so the blue parts disappeared under her purple fleece hat for a brief rotation. "He's such a useful engine." She imitated the narrator pretty well for an eleven-year-old girl. Then A.J. switched to her regular voice. "How's your story?"

"Angry."

"What?"

"I'll probably have to fix it before I turn it in, but I got lots of words done when I went like full fury on it."

"Like the fires of Mordor?" A.J. bugged her eyes.

"Well, maybe not *that* furious."

A.J. retracted her head into her scarf like a shy turtle. "Huh. I don't really get it, but whatever. I got mine started. I bet it's really lame. I tried to write a love story about this famous pop star and this girl who runs into him at the mall."

"Literally runs into him?" Tildy stood shoulder to shoulder with A.J. by the curb as the bus rounded the corner two blocks away. She bounced a couple times to get the feeling back into her feet, careful not to bump the two boys waiting ahead of them.

"Actually, yes. She's looking at her MP3 player and playing one of his songs and, like, crashes right into him outside a store."

"A record store?"

"Hey, yeah! I should make it a record store."

Tildy snuffled two columns of white steam out her nose as she bounced, and flapped her elbows. This would be the perfect day to slip past the big eighth grader and be first on the bus. Sixth graders were gonna die as the eighth grader rescued himself from the deep freeze. He would probably just watch out the window as she and A.J. breathed their last steamy breaths.

Though it was warmer on the bus—no wind for one thing—it was still freezing. A.J. huddled close with Tildy.

"I had a weird dream last night about some guy coming to visit me in my room." Tildy surveyed the riders on the bus to see who was missing.

"Justin Timberlake?"

"No. Not him. And not really a ghost, like in my story. And my grandma woke me up 'cause I was, like, talking in my sleep." She didn't share everything with A.J. Not every vulnerable moment. She hadn't known A.J. that long.

"Sounds creepy." A.J.'s voice vibrated with her shivers.

"I guess that's what bothers me about it, though. 'Cause it wasn't creepy. It was, like, welcomed or comfortable or something." Tildy slowed again at the edge of her trust for A.J. "It was like I knew him, and he knew me really well." She sighed a long cloud of vapor into the rumbly air of the bus. It was a fainter cloud. The bus was warming up, either from the heater or the dozens of kids in their coats and hats huddling together.

At school that day, Tildy did finally warm up. She was even able to change into her gym uniform without it feeling dangerous. The gym was no warmer than any other creaky old room in the school, but they were shooting baskets and running after their misses as soon as they came out of the locker room.

Tildy chased a wild miss by Bethany Miller and nearly ran into Darla Davis. "Oh. Sorry." Tildy gathered the dark brown basketball and held it to her chest.

Darla puckered her lips and shook her head, only venturing eye contact for half a second.

To Tildy, there seemed to be more than a near crash by the baseline behind that look of disapproval. "What?" She didn't know Darla well. Unlike most of the kids in the class, Tildy had just arrived in this school district in the fall.

Darla shook her head more vigorously and focused on Bethany, who flashed her blue eyes wide and snickered as she arrived on the scene.

"What?" Tildy tried again, but was beginning to think maybe she didn't want to know what.

As the other girls huddled, a boy bumped into Tildy and scampered away, distracting her for a moment.

When she looked back, Darla had a hand up to her mouth. But Tildy clearly heard the words "drug addict."

A hot flood rose to Tildy's head. She stepped toward Darla and Bethany and then realized it was too dangerous. Getting closer to them and what they were saying felt threatening.

"You calling Tildy a drug addict?" Jason Bowerman had taken a jump shot and landed right next to Tildy.

Again, Darla spoke into her hand. "Not yet."

"What's your problem?" Tildy boiled over.

"Nothing." Darla turned fully toward her. "You're the one whose dad left her because her mom is a drug addict."

"Typical," Bethany said in the background.

"Typical of what?" Tildy was still planted on the baseline.

"Uh-oh. Cat fight." Jason made a theatrical display of distancing himself from the three girls.

"How ...? What are you ...?" Tildy wanted to deny the facts. Darla didn't seem to have them straight. But she clearly knew something. How would she know about Tildy's mom? Even A.J. only knew her mom was away for a while, getting her stuff together. No specifics. A.J. had never demanded details. She had met Tildy's mom when she was still living with Tildy and her grandma. And Mom had been sober that day, as she usually was around Tildy. But maybe A.J. had guessed. Still, A.J. didn't hang out with Darla or Bethany. They were rich girls from a completely different neighborhood.

"You don't know sh--." Tildy blurted a phrase she had heard from others but had never used before.

Unfortunately, Mr. Enriquez heard it. "Tildy?" Mr. Enriquez was one of the cool teachers, but he wouldn't be able to ignore her use of bad language. Not so loud and clear in the echoing gym. "Come here, girl."

Being called away from Darla and Bethany felt like deliverance. Tildy was still feeling danger around them. Like *she* was dangerous. Who knew what she would do to stop them from talking about her and her mom? Tildy dropped the basketball and took a deep breath.

"I've never heard you talk like that before." Mr. Enriquez had raised his eyebrows about halfway, maybe only half surprised. He spoke low enough that the dribbling, shooting, and shouting gave Tildy some cover.

"Sorry. She just said something really mean about my mother." The excuse slipped out like a reflex block. As soon as she said it, Tildy regretted such a pitiful plea for sympathy. Even though what she said was true, in middle school you weren't supposed to tell the teachers everything. Not if you wanted respect from the other kids.

Mr. Enriquez sent his dark eyes toward Darla and Bethany, who were huddled over a basketball like a pregnant woman and her commiserating friend. Which one was the pregnant woman? Tildy shook that thought off.

"All right. Take a seat and cool off a minute. Then stay clear of Darla."

That solution could work, given that the teacher was the one who divided up teams for scrimmaging. Surely he would put them on separate courts.

The word Tildy had said was not a capital offense, but punishable for sure. Tildy was getting off easy, probably because of what she told the teacher about Darla insulting her mother. Niggling her conscience was the fact that Darla was right. Tildy's mother *was* a drug addict.

What did Bethany mean when she said *typical*? Sitting on the bench at the side of the court just gave Tildy a chance to stew over what had happened. That wouldn't cool her down. When she looked for Darla and Bethany, she saw Mr. Enriquez talking to them. But he was doing it in a sort of casual way from ten feet, not huddled in a serious confrontation. Tildy was glad for that less-intense intervention. Mr. Enriquez was probably not asking for details about Tildy's failure of a mother. He was just warning Darla in the generic way teachers often did.

Tildy turned her eyes away when Bethany looked toward her. That left Tildy scanning the class to show she was disinterested in Bethany and her kind. This school was divided, with kids coming from a variety of neighborhoods. Darla and Bethany surely came from the newish housing developments with massive homes selling for hundreds of thousands. But maybe they lived in the nice older homes worth twice that. Tildy had learned some of the numbers—and the attitudes that went with them—from her realtor grandma.

Had her grandma told someone about her wayward daughter? Who would she tell? Someone at church? Surely not a real-estate client in a ritzy neighborhood.

Mr. Enriquez blew his whistle and drew the students to the center of the near court. There were three full courts in the big old gym. He made a quick wave for Tildy to join them.

She rose slowly from the varnished wooden bench and glanced at the folded bleachers behind her, as if they might be more interesting than the kids staring at her as she rose. She wanted to shout more profanity, but that would just bring more staring.

One problem with being one of the rare dark-skinned kids in the school was the constant staring. As if these White people had never seen a real live Black kid before. Never mind that she was half White herself. Never mind.

The staring had faded in most of her classes during the fall, but this was a new semester and a new gym class. There were two boys in the class who were as brown as her. One looked Indian, as far as she could tell. The other might have been half Black like her. She didn't know either of them, though someone in the class would surely assume she did.

It was hard to play basketball with what felt like a super tight band around her chest. It was hard to breathe under the weight of what Darla had said. Harder still to run and defend under the pressure of what Tildy feared about her mom's disgrace being common knowledge. It was impossible to have fun.

She was good at basketball. She had played on a girls' team when she was in fifth grade, before she had to change schools to live with her grandma. But she wasn't used to playing while trying not to cry.

When one of the bigger boys tried to dribble right through her as if he assumed she would just get out of his way—which she would never do—she found good reason to cry. Crashing to the shiny wood floor, Tildy banged her right elbow sharply while trying not to hit her head. Pain shot up through her hand like an electric charge. Her right arm seemed to explode with the impact.

The teaching assistant had been watching—at least the final crash landing—and blew her whistle long and loud. Tildy had already noted that the college girl helping Mr. Enriquez was hard on the boys and protective of the girls. The football move by that clumsy boy provoked the longest and loudest whistle Tildy had heard in this class—or maybe on any basketball court. "You okay, uh, Tildy?" The assistant was still learning their names. She seemed slower at it than Mr. Enriquez.

Tildy was crying. And she hated that she was crying. This was typical. This was what she didn't want to be—a victim. Not a victim of the bully boys. Not a victim of the rich White girls. Not a victim of her mother's addiction. But not wanting all that only intensified the tears. Tears of pain. Tears of frustration.

On the way home on the bus, Tildy stuffed all those staring faces into a closet where she couldn't see them. The pain in her arm had dulled, though the bruise would surely live on to tell its story. Long sleeves would come in handy there. But Tildy was still stinging from those overly concerned eyes on the basketball court. Even the guilty bowed head of Eddy Marcos, the boy who fouled her, stung. She didn't want to be looked at or thought about like that at all.

"Can you bend it now?" A.J. was leaning against the window looking at Tildy's arm.

Tildy held that arm straight. It seemed to hurt less when it was straight. There was swelling just above her elbow where most of the impact had happened. Apparently most of the shock was from banging a nerve. The smack hadn't done as much damage as the electric pain had insisted. That's what the nurse said. "It's okay. Just a bruise."

"Did anybody say you should get an X-ray?"

"Mrs. Copple was talking about that, but my grandma said she would take me later if it didn't feel better."

"They called her?"

"Yeah. I guess they have to call ... someone."

"Not your mom ... I guess."

Tildy turned toward A.J. "Did you tell Darla or Bethany or one of their friends something about my mom?"

"Who? Like what?"

She snorted two slightly steamy breaths. It was probably better for A.J. to hear it from her than from Darla. "That my mom is in drug rehab?"

"She is? I mean, no. I didn't even know that. Is that really where she is?"

Certain that A.J. wasn't that good an actor, Tildy relaxed a bit. Her one good friend at this school had not betrayed her. At least not yet. Now Tildy had to decide how much more to say. "Yeah. That's where she is. Drug rehab." Tildy had lowered her voice, glancing around to guess if anyone could hear her. "I really don't want anyone to know about that."

"Yeah. I get that." A.J.'s voice was hushed. "I won't tell anyone."

Those were the right words, but there was a look in A.J.'s eye. Suspicion? Was that what Tildy saw? Would it be suspicion of Tildy, or just about her mother?

Tildy recalled A.J. telling her about a house up the street, just two blocks from Tildy's grandma's, that had been raided last summer. Some guys were selling drugs, maybe even cooking them in the house. The details were scarce and muddled. And her grandma had refused to confirm or deny. Grandma was, of course, upset at what that news would mean for property values in their housing development of middle-class three- and four-bedroom homes.

Tildy spoke low and steady. "She's not, like, a drug dealer or anything. She just has this addiction that has to do with drugs. Some people drink. Some do other things. My mom just got caught in drugs." Tildy was arguing against what she imagined A.J. was thinking.

"Sure. Of course. I didn't think she was a dealer." But A.J.'s voice faltered right through her denial. Maybe she hadn't thought Tildy's mother was like those people in that crack house or meth house or whatever, but she was thinking something.

The tightness around Tildy's lungs was back. Maybe she would just stop breathing. Maybe she would just stumble off the bus and lie down in the snow and stop breathing. How long would it take to freeze to death? How much would it hurt?

"Don't worry, Tildy. I won't tell anyone. I won't say anything."

Again, her friend was saying the right things. But the fact that A.J. *needed* to say it was stifling. That Tildy could not escape her mother's addiction and her father's abandonment was smothering. A rising rush in her ears alerted her that she was holding her breath. She couldn't breathe. At least not easily. Worse, she didn't *want* to breathe.

"Are you okay?" Maybe A.J. could see Tildy changing colors.

Tildy loosed her breath and thumped her head against the back of the seat. The bus was nearing their stop. She would breathe for now. For a little while longer, at least.

At home alone, waiting for her grandma to arrive, Tildy spread peanut butter on crackers and focused on a question. A question she would ask her grandma ... or not.

Had Grandma told people about Tildy's mother and her addiction?

Testing her arm by bending it slowly distracted Tildy from that question. Would she have to get X-rays? She dreaded sitting in the emergency room with her grandma. Or maybe at the immediate care. Would they have X-rays there? She wasn't afraid of an X-ray. She just didn't feel like spending her evening in a medical facility, waiting and waiting.

As she crunched the peanut butter laden cracker, Tildy hit the message button on the answering machine.

"You have two messages."

She played them. One was from a window sales company, the other from Grandma.

"Tildy, call me if your arm is hurting more, and I'll come right home. But I have some calls to make and probably another showing around six. So, if you're okay, I'll be home a bit late. Warm up what's left of that chicken stir fry if you're hungry."

As the message ended, Tildy spoke out of her sticky, dry throat. "*If* I'm hungry? I'm a kid. I get hungry at suppertime." Who was she complaining to? She was alone. A sob tried to escape her throat, but it was too stuck from peanut butter and crackers.

She headed for the sink and ran a cool glass of water. A long, glugging drink, and she was free to cry. But she didn't want to cry. No more than she had wanted to bawl on the gym floor. For some reason, she recalled the look of that brown Asian kid as the teaching assistant helped her to her feet. Pity. That's what was written on his slender face in black eyebrows and pursed lips.

Tildy didn't want his pity. She didn't want to be stared at. Not at school. But she wanted her grandma to see her and to know she was hungry. She also wanted Grandma to not tell everyone about her mother, the drug addict, or about the lazy and selfish man who was her father.

"Typical." She echoed Bethany. Was it because Tildy was Black? At least Black in Bethany's White-girl eyes. The drug-addicted mother, the missing dad. Was that typical? Maybe Bethany assumed Tildy's mother was Black. Black like her. Like Tildy, not an addict "yet."

Her eyes fell on the drawer by the sink with the knives in it. But maybe those sharp scissors in her room would work better.

Chapter Three
And What If You're Not Alone?

How many times had her grandmother said it? "Be careful, you could seriously cut yourself with those things. They're sharp."

Yes, they were. Tildy sat on her bed with the super-sharp scissors open, her thumb testing the blades.

"Don't do it, Tildy."

She stopped breathing again. This time to listen. Did someone say something? And what was she doing with the scissors?

Cutting had just jumped into her head. She had heard of girls doing it. There was that one girl on TV who said it made her feel better—that's why she did it. Tildy hadn't believed that weepy girl and had changed the channel. Was Tildy thinking about it now because she wanted to feel better?

She really didn't want to be alone. Would cutting herself bring her grandma home? Was that all she wanted, her grandma to come home? She could call Grandma's cell phone and tell her the pain in her elbow was getting worse. Then she would come home.

But not only did she not want to spend the evening in a waiting room, she couldn't locate any kind of hope in her grandma being there. At school, she didn't want people to look at her. At home, she wanted her grandma to know ... to know what? To know she would be hungry after school? To know she was in more pain than just in her elbow?

Maybe cutting herself would show Grandma about her pain.

"It would do that, but it would also do lots of other things."

She was sure she had not said that to herself. She had not spoken. But it felt like someone else had.

"Tildy, I'm right here." It was a man's voice.

"Dad?" A sob followed that word. Not because she thought it really was her dad talking to her. It was just a desperate burst. He wouldn't be there. He wouldn't know any better than her grandma about how much pain Tildy was in.

"Tildy, it's me. Jesus."

The flood of warmth that came with those words was the only thing that kept her from screaming and running from the room. It was like a campfire on a cold night. She could run off into the dark to get away from the flames, but she wanted the warmth.

"Jesus?" The real Jesus? The one from church and after-school program?

"I'm right here."

"I can't see you."

He seemed to fade into view right next to her dresser. Right where that man in her dream had stood.

This time she did scream. And she jumped toward her door. But something stopped her. And it wasn't him. It was her.

She looked back at him.

He was smiling. A sympathetic smile.

And she felt a sort of gravity pulling her into that smile. That gravity came from the sympathy. Here was someone who could see her. Someone who knew she was hungry. Someone who knew she was lonely. It was all there in his eyes.

She shook her head. "But this is impossible. No one can see your face. Or they would, like, drop dead right away."

Jesus laughed. Or at least the Jesus smiling at her in her imagination laughed. Clearly if it had been the real Jesus, she would be dead. Or something. Maybe she would be a saint. Or maybe she *was* dead. Maybe she *had* cut herself, so bad ...

"No, dear. You're still alive. I stopped you from cutting yourself."

"Oh." She looked away. "Sorry about that."

"You're sorry? I'm sorry. What do *you* have to be sorry about?"

"You're sorry?" Her questioning inflection wedged against a sob. She was crying again.

Jesus stepped toward her. That campfire flared brighter. Closer. He paused. And his pause seemed to ask for permission. Jesus was asking for permission ... from her.

It felt like pure insanity, but she rushed to him and grabbed him, right there in front of that ugly old dresser. She grabbed him and held him, and he held onto her. And the heat of that fire got inside her. The warmth of his presence ran deeper than hugging, saturating her heart. She breathed. She sobbed. The tightness was all gone. She cried hard. Harder than she had ever cried in her life.

And he held on and just stood there. Solid. Strong. In no hurry to go anywhere.

But it only took a minute, or something like that, for her to start wondering again. *How can this be? This is impossible.*

"Who says it's impossible?"

She pulled away and looked at his face. He looked just like the Jesus she had always imagined. In her imagination, she had always cheated a little against the pictures she saw at her grandma's church. *Her* Jesus was dark, at least a bit darker than the White Jesus in the Sunday school papers. She saw a video online once where Jesus had black hair. He looked like he was from some country over there, a foreign place. A place where people had dark brown eyes like Tildy's and black hair like hers. He wasn't brown, but he was darker.

"I must be imagining this."

"Because I look more like you want me to look than the pictures?"

She hadn't even said those things, and he was answering. And now she became aware that she was still touching him. She had her hands on his waist. She backed up. This was crazy.

31

"I can go invisible if you would rather. But I will never leave you."

That was two things. Maybe more. "Invisible?"

The air around her seemed full, as if saturated. More than just a hundred percent humidity. More than the wall of noise in the utility closet behind the stage at school. Full. Full of ... him.

"You know what I'm thinking?" She paused, closed her eyes, and snorted at herself. Was that all she could think to say?

He was smiling again when she opened her eyes. He leaned one arm on top of her dresser. "Of course, Tildy. I know everything about you. And I care. I care, and I will never abandon you."

A shiver flared from her spine outward. Her hands shook, and her knees wavered. He was ... Jesus was ...

Then everything went black. Tildy was out.

She could hear before she could see again, but she knew she was lying on her bed. And she was fully dressed. And her light was on, so it wasn't night. But she didn't have her earbuds in. Tildy sorted those things without grabbing hold of the real thing. The big thing.

"I will never leave you."

This time it wasn't like someone had spoken aloud. It felt like the words came from inside her. And those words made her think of that time when she was eight and prayed that Jesus would come into her heart. Was this what it meant to have Jesus in her heart? Why didn't she hear him before?

Maybe this was happening because she was going to hurt herself. Or at least she had been thinking about it. Was she really going to do it? She shuddered at the thought and opened her eyes. Maybe it sort of made sense. She was feeling so crazy that she was thinking about cutting herself. And then that craziness produced this hallucination. Total craziness.

"I know it's not what you're used to, Tildy, and it won't always be like this, but I can appear to you again when you're ready." That seemed more like a voice.

She turned her head. She couldn't see him, but it sort of seemed like he was hiding in her closet.

That thought started laughter. *His* laughter.

Tildy sat up. It was like she was hearing him now but not seeing him. He was laughing.

Huh. But the question was not whether Jesus laughs, the question was whether she could actually see him and hear him. Talking. Laughing. Whatever. Should she be seeing? Hearing? Was that allowed? Tildy couldn't remember anything about that from church or the after-school program she had gone to at that other church.

She sat on her bed looking at the closet. What if, instead of monsters, she had Jesus hiding in her closet? That started Tildy laughing. She laughed until she was crying again. But this was different. These tears felt good. The flow of it was so good she dropped the questions about seeing or hearing Jesus. She could think about that later. Right now she just needed to laugh and cry and let the two get all mixed together.

By the time the tears and the laughs had run out, she felt inspired. Maybe she had just imagined Jesus coming out of her closet, but it made her feel like writing. She had a new idea for her story, the story about the ghost who showed up to make everything right for that girl. What if the ghost was actually an ancient holy man, not just a random stranger? She would probably have to keep Jesus out of it, but it felt like she needed to write about something like what had just happened. And she felt permission to do it. Not permission in words, not even in her head. But she felt like it would be good for her to write. Even if it was just a made-up story for English class.

A story about a girl who was desperate and then met this ghostly stranger who told her true things about herself.

Tildy wrote until her grandma came in the front door, not even stopping to warm up supper for herself.

Hiding Jesus

Chapter Four
Who Can She Tell About This?

"Tildy? Did you have supper?" Her grandma was opening the closet door and setting her keys on the shelf near the closet. A familiar soundtrack.

But her arrival set off new feelings. It wasn't the frantic fear of her grandma getting home before Tildy could close the email window on the computer. This time, Tildy froze at her desk, wedged between all the things she could not tell her grandma. There was the story she was writing. There was the fact that she had forgotten to eat supper. There was what happened in school today—everything that happened in school. And that left the really big thing.

"Tildy? I suppose you have your music too loud and can't hear me." Grandma was getting closer.

Tildy liked to write with her music in her ears, but she had forgotten to do that. She hadn't even turned on a pop music station on her clock radio. "Uh, no. Uh, no, I was just doing homework." That was barely the discarded wrapper of an answer.

Her grandma appeared at her door. "Are you okay?"

The slightly sweetened sincerity of her grandma's question nearly started Tildy crying again. She could feel her face flush. "Oh, sorry. I was just ... just getting into this story I was writing."

"Well, I guess that's good. How's your arm?" Grandma scanned the room as if she smelled something. Sensed something.

Tildy glanced at the closet. "It's ..." She hesitated because she didn't know the answer. She flexed her elbow and found it stiff. She pressed on the back of it and found it dully sore, but better than at school. "It's getting better, I think." She stopped herself from another check of the closet, the door half open.

"Are you okay? You seem ... strange."

Barking a small laugh, Tildy closed her eyes for a beat. "Gee, thanks. I'm strange, even to you." What started as a joke reawakened the feeling of being stared at in gym. "People think I'm strange at school. Probably because I'm Black." As soon as she said it, she wondered why she did.

The blank stare on her grandma's face stacked regret on regret. What did Tildy expect her grandma to do? But maybe it was just enough for her to know.

"I mean ... there are ... there are other ... *minority* kids there, aren't there?" Was Grandma unable to say *Black*? But she was the White grandma. She, of all people, couldn't think of her granddaughter as simply Black.

Tildy really wished she hadn't said anything when she saw that startled animal look on her grandma's face. She tried for reassurance. "Well, there's not so many other ... But I don't wanna talk about that." And that reminded her of how many important things she didn't want to talk about with her grandma. She glanced at the scissors, still sitting on her desk, ignored as her short story captured her focus.

"You wanna use the computer tonight to type your story?" It was a good question, good enough to lead them away from all that unfinished business.

"Sure. After we eat, I guess."

"Yes. I'll get something going. Maybe Italian tonight?"

"Sounds good." Tildy loved pasta. And she didn't have any worries about her weight. Her grandma didn't either. She seemed wiry and lean, though Tildy had no idea what Grandma weighed or what she should weigh.

Now they were both drifting away from the crisis roiling around them. Tildy floated into the smooth water out in the middle where they didn't have to bump into anything sharp or hard. And where they wouldn't have to bump into each other.

They did bump into each other, literally, when supper was over and Tildy carried her plate to the sink. She had answered all her grandma's questions about what happened in gym. She had not told her everything, of course, just focused on the boy fouling her and the elbow bang. She included Eddy's apology and her weepy trip to the nurse's office. Her grandma knew the story from there.

But Tildy's restrained answers bothered her more than Grandma's questions. In the pauses, Tildy worried about not telling her grandma what happened when she got home from school. The counselors would surely say a girl should tell an adult when she has thoughts about hurting herself. She might have even heard that in an assembly at school or somewhere. And of course you should tell a grown-up when a strange man shows up in your bedroom. That was a no-brainer.

Maybe she should just admit to Grandma that she was going nuts. Not just because of cutting. Tildy had really believed that Jesus himself was ... where? In her closet? She snickered at herself as she powered on the PC in the family room. Then she stopped snickering. *Was* he in her closet? Did she really believe she had seen him? Touched him?

No. He was just inside her head.

"And in your heart."

That was an inside voice. But not what grown-ups mean when they say, "Use your inside voice." No, this was really inside. Inside her.

She tried answering, talking low without moving her lips. "Am I going crazy?"

"You don't have to use your mouth, Tildy. You can just send me your thoughts. Think of them as silent prayers."

"Do I start with 'Dear heavenly Father,' like the lady said in Sunday school?" She didn't really think of that as a question for Jesus to answer. It was more like something from her Sunday school packet of info slipping out and landing at the feet of her imaginary friend. Asking Jesus into her heart had been like that.

Just part of what they said at church. Did that Sunday school stuff make sense? Did it make more sense to her now?

He wasn't answering now. Had she asked him a question? Maybe not. Maybe that was why he didn't answer. He knew when she was really asking and when she was just babbling. Mental babbling.

She snuffled another laugh at herself. It was more doubtful than amused. Not the hilarious and weepy laughter from before. This was a tired laugh. She realized then that she was very tired. She wasn't going to get anything done on the computer.

Tildy looked at the clock above the fireplace. Seven forty-five, almost. Maybe the long hand was tired too, struggling to climb up to the twelve. She shook her head at her own strange imagination. No wonder Grandma thought she was strange.

Was Grandma ashamed of Tildy's dark skin and eyes and her kinky braids? Tildy had never put that question together before, but it had been with her, of course. Maybe not inside her like that Jesus voice, but knocking at the door.

"Behold, I stand at the door and knock." Another scrap from Sunday school or the after-school program at that other church.

A knock from the kitchen made Tildy jump. She was losing it. She didn't want to type on the computer. What did she want? She couldn't go to bed this early. She didn't want to be in her bedroom alone. Not with that man in the closet.

This time she snickered between her teeth. This time it wasn't nervous laughter, but relief. If the only thing haunting her closet was Jesus, that Jesus she had seen and hugged, then she had nothing to fear.

She started to rest her elbow on the computer table so she could prop her head on her fist, but that really cranked up the pain. The combination of bending her arm and pressing it onto the desktop was too much. She straightened it and touched behind her elbow again. The blower on the furnace startled her as a blast of warm air filled the space beneath the computer. "I'm a mess." She shook her head and pushed away from the computer.

"Did you say something, dear?" Her grandma had snuck up on her.

Tildy tipped her head and raised her eyebrows as well as a little grin. "I don't think I can work on the story anymore. I'm suddenly really tired."

"Oh. Well, you had a hard day."

"Yeah." And her grandma didn't know most of what was hard about it. Tildy's hard day was like one of those icebergs that's bigger below the surface than the part you can see.

"I'm gonna watch some TV. Wanna join me?" Grandma reached for the remote.

It was sort of like surrendering. Giving up on doing anything really important. But Tildy was too tired to do anything constructive or to talk about anything as important as thinking about cutting herself or having Jesus visit her after school.

The people on the TV show were even more messed up than Tildy. The cops were after them, for one thing. Despite A.J.'s possible fears and Darla's little prediction, Tildy didn't have to worry about the police. No one had seen her with those scissors. Except Jesus. He wouldn't tell, would he?

Breathing was difficult again. But this time it wasn't tightness in her chest. Her head felt like she was wearing a pillowcase over it. She barely kept her eyes open until nine o'clock. It was the earliest she usually went to sleep, but this seemed like a good day for an early bedtime.

"Let me know when you're ready, and I'll come say good night." Her grandma was wearing that sympathetic grin again, though she seemed distracted by the previews for the upcoming show. She was probably tired too. Getting a call from the school nurse must have loaded more stress onto her normally stressful day.

Each step of getting ready for bed seemed to require pushing off for momentum, like ice skating on a big rink where her friends were way out in the middle. She had to push off to get dressed, to brush her teeth, to put her stuff together for school the next day. Then she stood by her bed thinking she should call her grandma to come say good night. But she was having second thoughts about going to bed. She could put her robe on and try to watch another show with Grandma instead. But that seemed even harder. Her feet were rooted in the carpet.

"You ready?" Grandma startled her again.

"Oh. Yes. I guess I am." She smiled apologetically. "Is it possible to be too tired to go to bed?"

Grandma stepped into the room and stopped right next to Tildy. For a second, it looked like she might wrap Tildy in a hug. But she stopped short and just patted her on the cheek. "Your arm okay? I worry that I should have taken you for X-rays."

Tildy slowly flexed her right arm. She was left-handed, so it hadn't been a factor in writing the story. Writing had erased the pain for over two hours. Maybe typing wouldn't have been so easy. "It's okay. I bet it won't hurt so much in the morning."

"I hope so. Sometimes things like that hurt more the next day."

Shrugging at that bad news, Tildy lifted the corner of her blankets and climbed into bed. It wasn't so much of an uphill climb as it used to be, but it was harder than she could remember it being the night before. And that probably wasn't just about one stiff arm or the incredible tiredness. She was climbing over the feeling that she was forgetting something. Something she should have taken care of before bed.

Those worries erased whatever her grandmother said while she pulled the covers up to Tildy's chin. She usually didn't do that. Was she tucking Tildy in?

Not until the light was out and the door closed all but a slice did Tildy roll her eyes at her grandma tucking her in. Grandma had tucked in the cousins the last time they stayed over, but they were six and eight. And they needed tucking. Maybe even restraints, like they put on people in a mental hospital. She had seen that on TV.

Tildy suddenly worried that her mother was being restrained where she was. Maybe that was why she hadn't talked to Tildy since Christmas. Only then, in the fading end of the strangest day she could remember, did Tildy face that big ugly monster. Why had her mom not talked to her for so long?

It usually had to be arranged with her grandma so Tildy would be waiting by the phone when her mom called. Grandma had said she talked to her oldest daughter over the weekend. It was easier for Grandma. She had a cell phone she carried with her all the time. That fact had made it easy for the school nurse to reach her too.

Tildy turned onto her right side, but the pain in her elbow reversed her turn. Now she was looking at the closet door. The light was off in the hallway, but a dim tan light collected from some more distant part of the house was slicing the darkness right next to the closet.

Of course Jesus was not hiding in her closet like in *Monsters, Inc.* Had the guy in her dream come out of the closet? She couldn't remember clearly. Was the man in the dream the same person?

Person? Was Jesus a real person? Someone who could hug you? Someone who could tell you he cared about you and ...? He said he would never leave her.

"Are you there?" She didn't speak aloud, remembering his advice about silent prayer.

"Yes, dear. I am here. I am always here."

"Not in my closet though?"

He laughed. And maybe she even *heard* him laugh with her right ear, the one not pressed into her pillow. Or maybe Jesus was inside her. Jesus was in her heart and laughing.

If Jesus could laugh like that, all peaceful and happy right inside her heart, then maybe Tildy wasn't so bad off after all.

Except for believing that Jesus had actually hugged her in her bedroom that afternoon. A chill ran up her spine. But settling herself from that chill led right into settling down to sleep at the end of a very tiring day.

Chapter Five
Not Sure She Can Face It

When Tildy awoke, she knew it was Tuesday. And she knew she would have to go to school. No holiday. No teacher training day. She flexed her right arm, finding it easier to close it all the way, her right hand even touching her shoulder. It seemed less swollen. But she could still find that sore spot on the back, probably an impressive bruise. She still hoped to avoid a trip to the emergency room. Though maybe that would be better than going to school. She flexed her arm open and folded it back to her shoulder, testing the sore spot with two fingers of her left hand. She took a deep breath.

"I can go to school with you."

There it was. That inside voice. Internal voice. That spook haunting her head. She thought about her story. She knew Jesus wasn't a ghost. In fact, she didn't really know anything about ghosts. Real ghosts. It was just a story for sixth-grade English. Not real in any way. Though it did feel good to write about the kind man visiting the girl in the story to tell her everything would be all right.

"Is that what you want?"

He hadn't gone away.

"Do I want you to come to school with me, you mean?" She at least remembered to whisper. That seemed most appropriate for discussing whether Jesus should accompany her to school. Before yesterday his question wouldn't have stirred hope like it was doing now. Today she really felt she needed him with her at school if she couldn't get out of going all together. Tildy returned to fingering the sorest spot on the back of her elbow. It was a dull pain, like a bruise. Probably just a bruise.

43

"It's not broken."

Something about that felt even more sketchy than all her previous interactions with this Jesus voice. He was offering medical information, a sort of diagnosis.

"The Great Physician, you know."

She had heard that phrase in her grandma's church, she was pretty sure. It felt sort of like part of her brain was reviewing all her church and Bible teaching. That was a weird thing to do.

"But not weirder than seeing Jesus come out of your closet."

Tildy snapped her head to her left. She held her breath. He was there. Not just a voice. "Did I want to see you?" It was so much like talking to herself that Tildy wasn't sure whether the question was for Jesus or herself. She suspected the answer was yes. She did want to see him. But she also wondered how her brain seemed to be dashing in four directions all at once.

"Tildy? Are you up? How are you feeling?" With each phrase, Grandma's voice came closer to the bedroom door.

Simultaneously, Jesus stepped backward into the closet. Not fast. Not dashing like Tildy's brain. But he slipped out of sight just as Grandma entered.

She pushed the door open, and Tildy snapped her head toward the foot of her bed. Clearly her neck had not been injured in the crash yesterday, but her head was definitely spinning. It was a cliché, of course, but Tildy was literally feeling the room rock and spin.

"You okay? You look a little ..." Grandma didn't finish. Maybe she didn't want to call her *strange* again. Maybe she couldn't describe how Tildy looked any more than Tildy could explain how she was feeling.

A brief possibility staggered into view. Tildy could stay home because of whatever was wrong with her head. But she hadn't actually banged her head in gym, so she couldn't imagine the scenario where her spinning brain equaled a day off school. She struggled to sit up without putting too much weight on her right arm.

"Your arm still hurts?"

Tildy hadn't really been trying to make that obvious, but it must have been pretty clear since Grandma noticed. Or maybe she was just super worried about not going to the emergency room. Tildy felt the back of her elbow one more time. If she had really broken something, wouldn't the pain be sharper? It just felt like a bruise. She pushed the sleeve of her pajama top up and lifted her arm for Grandma to see.

"Oh, it's blue now. Can you move your arm?"

Tildy flexed in demonstration. "Yeah. I don't think anything's broken." A gust of betrayal tossed some regret that she was giving up so easily on skipping school. But there was a quiz in math she wanted to get over with, so there was that.

"Okay. Just let me know if that changes. You gotta get up now and get moving."

Tildy did. She showered and dressed and sorted her braids and ate her cereal while still being jostled by all those cross winds. Part of her wanted to see A.J. to make sure she was still her friend. Part of her feared that revealing her mother's addiction had ended her only true friendship in this neighborhood.

As testimony to how messed up the day had been, Tildy realized she hadn't listened to her music once yesterday. She shook her head at the thought and wondered if she could get any new stuff from A.J. She had Avril Lavigne music Tildy was still waiting to get. Acquiring a copy of that music about a skater guy was more likely than getting her grandma to buy her a skateboard. Dropping her bowl in the kitchen sink, Tildy headed to the bathroom to brush her teeth. Just ten minutes till the bus. She moved fast. Speed helped her cut through those cross winds.

Standing on the corner alone for almost a minute brought back lots of those stormy blasts from the day before, the newest fear being that A.J. wouldn't talk to her anymore. What had Jesus said about going with her to school? She didn't ever finish that conversation with him. At least she couldn't remember it getting resolved.

A purple puffy coat appeared at the end of the block, a long pink scarf flapping in the wind. *Here she comes.* Tildy tried to watch A.J. without looking like she was staring, without looking anxious.

"Don't worry, Tildy. I have you." The Jesus voice was out in the cold, but still inside her.

And Tildy actually relaxed her shoulders a little as A.J. slowed to a stop in front of her. "How ya doin', A.J.?"

"A.J.? Who's A.J.? It's Annabelle to you, bit--." Her friend, formerly known as A.J., cocked her head coquettishly.

Tildy laughed, probably a bit too hard.

The two brothers now joining them at the stop looked suspiciously at her under their parka hoods. The bus rounded the corner.

"Good timing, boys." Tildy was feeling strangely bold.

One of the brothers grunted. The younger, Peter, spoke to her. "How's yer arm? You didn't have to get a cast?"

Tildy looked more closely at him as Annabelle climbed the steps in front of her. "No. It's not that bad." She started up the steps. "How did you know?"

"Kyle Granger's in your gym class. He said it was a major crash."

She nodded and followed Annabelle to a seat. "Yeah. I'll survive though."

"Cool."

Hmm. That was by far the longest conversation she'd ever had with Peter. His brother James was an eighth grader. No words had fallen from that great height to Tildy yet. She wasn't holding her breath.

For a change today, she wasn't holding her breath at all. What really happened yesterday?

"So, you get that story written?" Annabelle plopped a spiral notebook in her lap and flipped the top of her mitten/glove open so she could write.

"Pretty much. I didn't get it on the computer though. Too wiped by the time I got a chance."

"Yeah. It was a tough day yesterday."

"Did I freak you out with what I told you?"

Annabelle found the page she was looking for and started with quotation marks, then paused. "Of course not. We're friends. We listen to each other's problems, and we don't judge."

That sounded good. Where had Annabelle picked that up?

"Are you serious about *Annabelle*?" Tildy knew she should let her friend get to work, but she wanted to make a grateful gesture.

"I think so. Let's give it a try, anyway."

"Okay. I'll get the word out, Annabelle."

"Thanks. No big deal though."

"No. I'll be cool about it."

Annabelle wrote the line about being cool after the quote marks.

Tildy watched, but opted for showing her coolness by not commenting, as if she wasn't reading over her friend's shoulder.

While Annabelle wrote with her blue ballpoint pen, occasionally breathing on it to keep it warm, Tildy wondered why she had been so depressed yesterday that she thought of cutting herself. Was that real? It seemed so far from reality today. But what had changed overnight?

Well, a lot had changed. She had either gone entirely insane, or she had seen and even touched Jesus in her grandma's house. The insanity part might make sense since she was thinking about cutting herself when it happened. Maybe a little crazy had grown up quickly to become full-grown crazy.

But he felt so real. He was warm. He was clever and friendly and ... Of course those facts just meant she was even crazier.

Wouldn't it be more sensible to think she had only seen a very faint ghost of Jesus? She shook her head and snorted.

"What? You don't think that's a good thing for her to say?" Annabelle looked at Tildy with wide eyes.

"Oh. No. I wasn't paying attention. What did you write?"

"I can just be your secret, not-famous friend."

"This is the rock star talking to the mall girl?"

"No, it's *her* talking to him."

"Oh, yeah. That makes sense. So she's saying they could be friends even if she's not famous. Or is it like she's saying he needs some friends that aren't famous?"

"Hey, that's good. Yeah." Annabelle crossed out a line above the part she had just read aloud.

Tildy grinned quietly. Her ghost story was maybe more grown up than Annabelle's fan-girl boyfriend story, but Mrs. Fredericks probably wouldn't mind either one. She liked ghost stories. She'd read the class one last semester around Halloween. Tildy could still recall the warm smile with which the teacher read that story while leaning against her desk. Mrs. Fredericks wasn't as cool as Mr. Enriquez, but she was good to have as an English teacher.

Today Tildy was looking forward to meeting the new art teacher. She was totally new to the school, and no one knew anything about her. Art was the other class she and A.J. — Annabelle—had together. Annabelle's artistic work was like her writing. Girlish and cute, but not very adventurous. That was okay. Tildy could have a friend like that. At least Annabelle was cool about Tildy's mom. And she was cool about her music.

"Hey, do you have that Avril Lavigne music you got over Christmas? Can you put those MP3s on a disc like you said?"

"Oh yeah. I forgot. Sure. I'll do that tonight." Annabelle didn't even look up. She was straightening out some of her printed letters, maybe planning to show the story to Mrs. Fredericks before handing in the final. Tildy didn't plan to do that, but lots of things had happened yesterday that she hadn't planned. Hopefully today would just be another boring old day at school.

Chapter Six
I Can Defend You, My Girl

"She was mouthing off about you and how you cried in gym, and I told her I would sock her if she didn't shut up." A.J. was pretty tough. She was a good athlete and played soccer and other sports. As Annabelle, she certainly wouldn't want *tough* to be the first thing people said about her, but Tildy suspected Darla cowered at the threat of a sock from either A.J. or Annabelle.

"Thanks, girl. I know you got my back." Tildy grinned gratefully. They were in the art room for their first class with the new teacher. They had endured a substitute for the first week of school. Apparently the new teacher had moved from somewhere else.

A tall and slender woman came out of the supply closet carrying a stack of pads and dropped them on the long table at the front of the room. She was beautiful. Long arms and legs, wearing all black down to her leggings and her zip-up boots. But the most remarkable thing about her was her skin. It was brown. She was just a little lighter skinned than Tildy, and she wore her black hair in an Afro with gold highlights along the top.

Tildy almost squealed. Then she slowed down to worry that this was just another substitute.

The woman cast her gaze over the room, a small, amused smile on her face, a sparkle in those dark eyes. Then she turned to the blackboard behind her and wrote in a flowing script,

Ms. Sullivan.

"Hello, young artists. I am Ms. Sullivan. I'm your new art teacher." Her voice was strong and confident, and she seemed both young and in charge. Not like a substitute.

Tildy stared.

Annabelle bumped her. "Close your mouth." She giggled in whispers.

Tildy closed her mouth, then licked her lips. Art was her best subject. She wanted to be an artist someday. A real artist. Not just a sixth-grade artist the way a teacher might say it. In September, Tildy had turned in a paper to Mrs. Fredericks that was supposed to be a story, the first fiction writing assignment for her new English teacher. Tildy had elaborately illustrated the story of a girl lost in an enchanted wood. There weren't many words. The four-page story was more drawing than writing.

"You are a very talented artist, Tildy, but this is English class. What I want you to do for me is practice drawing with words. Paint me a picture with words. You never know, your life as an artist may be greatly enhanced someday by being able to articulate ideas about your art."

Tildy hadn't even considered substituting drawings for words in her latest story for Mrs. Fredericks. The notion of painting with words was all she needed to start at least trying to create interesting stories for English class. The respect Mrs. Fredericks expressed for Tildy's art made complying super simple.

Ms. Sullivan recruited two kids to pass out sketch pads and soft pencils as she took the attendance. She lingered over each name and asked about nicknames. That got some snickers from some of the usual miscreants. That was Mr. Khor's word—*miscreant.* It fit Billy Waltham perfectly.

"Matilda Hawkins."

Billy or someone near him snickered.

"Tildy, please."

"Tildy. Very good. No problem, snickering naysayers notwithstanding."

Not exactly sure what all that meant, Tildy savored the eye contact with Ms. Sullivan. This woman was going to be her favorite teacher. She just knew it. "Thank you." She tried an encouraging smile. A new teacher needed encouragement, didn't she?

Two names later, Ms. Sullivan said, "Annabelle Jamison."

"A.J." Someone in the front row spoke at half volume.

"Annabelle." Tildy and Annabelle said it simultaneously.

"I wanna start going by Annabelle now ..."

Tildy could feel her friend glitching over whether to add more explanation for the transition.

"Okay, got it. Annabelle it is."

Now they had Ms. Sullivan on their side. She seemed a substantial ally for Annabelle's cause. And for Tildy's too. What was her cause? The cause of becoming an artist. That was a pretty big cause.

As Ms. Sullivan continued through the attendance, and Tildy received her new pencil and sketch pad, she savored the familiar smells and the taste of a much better day. It was more than the difference between gym and art, always a step up for her. Something was better *inside* her.

She could see now how Jesus had saved her from totally screwing up this very good day. If she had cut herself last night, she would surely have missed out on Ms. Sullivan's first day. But maybe that was all random. Not really connected.

By the time her lunch period ended right after art, Tildy was feeling pretty good. Grandma had packed her the cream cheese and tomato sandwich she loved. And Mrs. Fredericks's English class was next. Not bad.

Then a cloud rose from the horizon. Jeremy Bagheli stared at Tildy as she walked all the way from the top of the stairs to Mrs. Fredericks's door.

Most days Tildy would have kept quiet, but she was feeling strong. "What are you looking at?"

He turned to the boys next to him for half a second. "Just wondering how much you charge." Then he snickered and loped down the hall.

"Wha—?"

Annabelle was catching up to Tildy just then. She craned her neck to follow Jeremy and his crew down the hall. He was a pretty popular seventh grader, but not someone Tildy would ever want as a friend.

"How much I charge?" Tildy crumpled a squint and shook her head.

"What?" Annabelle twisted her neck again.

"I have no idea."

Seated in class, a slip of notebook paper appeared magically on Tildy's desk before she could tell Annabelle the weird thing Jeremy said. The note probably wasn't magic. Mike Mahler sat behind her. He might have slipped it in there.

Tildy unfolded the paper as Mrs. Fredericks entered the room and set her water bottle on the desk.

"Darla Davis is spreading nasty rumors about you. I know there not true. Just thought you would want to know." His scribbles were hard to decipher, but Tildy got the gist of it. She turned her head and received a freaky, wide-eyed glare from Mike.

He was a good guy. Maybe boyfriend material someday, when that was a thing for Tildy. But she hadn't thought much about Mike, really. Was he standing up for her? Had he challenged Darla's false claims? Were they false? Hopefully it wasn't more of the truth about her mother. But what did it matter what Darla said? Tildy glanced at the note again. *Nasty rumors.*

Anabelle was saying something about her story. She apparently hadn't seen the note.

Tildy wasn't inclined to share just yet.

Then a brain circuit connected Mike's note to what Jeremy had said in the hallway.

Mrs. Fredericks was turning the overhead projector on, showing the first page of a short story. Tildy checked to see if she needed to pay close attention. She doubted it.

What had Jeremy said about what something costs? What did she charge?

She lost pretty much that whole English class. Tildy was glad she didn't need more inspiration for her short story. It seemed such inspiration was the purpose of Mrs. Fredericks's lesson that day. That was what Tildy had gleaned. She had spent the time, instead, trying to figure out how Jeremy's weird question might fit with Darla's rumors.

Unable to resist any longer, she wrote on Mike's note, *"What kind of rumors?"*

A minute later, when Mrs. Fredericks turned toward the story on the screen, Mike's reply came back. *"Inapropriat about your mother and about you."*

Inappropriate? It was the word the teachers used about sex stuff. PG rated and beyond should not be discussed in school. That was certainly what Mike meant. Darla was saying sex stuff about Tildy and her mother? Why? Well, just to be mean. But …

Some of the kids seemed totally obsessed about sex already, even in sixth grade. Tildy didn't get the fascination. She thought quite a bit about how cute Justin Timberlake was, but she had no interest in anything … inappropriate. Darla was probably one of those oversexed sixth graders. Darla probably had her own inappropriateness she was dealing with.

"You don't need to go there, Tildy. I will take care of you." Jesus was in her head again, right there in English class.

The bell rang.

The next class, Social Studies, was a blur too. And, since Annabelle wasn't in her study hall, Tildy didn't have anyone to talk to about what was happening. She had shown the weird note from Mike to Annabelle after English, but Annabelle's response was confusion … until the end of the day.

Annabelle scooted up next to Tildy on the way to their bus. "Darla takes the number forty-six bus. We can catch her on the way."

"And do what?"

"Make her stop talking trash about you and your mother."

Before Tildy could ask how they would accomplish that, she spotted Darla treading down the curving sidewalk to the buses. She was gabbing with Brianna Price.

"Stop Annabelle, Tildy." This time the Jesus voice was urgent.

Tildy startled and flung her sore right arm out in front of Annabelle. When she looked at her friend, she found Annabelle with her fist raised and murder in her eyes.

"What? Let me ..." Annabelle tried to push past Tildy.

Just then one of the vice principals stepped from between the buses. He was closer to Darla than Tildy and Annabelle were, and would have had a front row seat to Annabelle smashing in Darla's pink braces.

"Oh." Annabelle swore under her breath.

"Yeah. Let's get on our bus." Tildy turned away from Darla's bus to where theirs was waiting.

"Why did you stop me?"

"Good thing I did. Mr. What's-his-name would have given you detention for the rest of your life."

"Mr. Garibaldi. Baldy for short."

"Yeah. Him."

"But why did you stop me like that? You weren't even looking at me. It was like you knew I was gonna smack her in the side of the head and that Baldy was gonna see the whole thing."

"Yeah, it *was* like that, wasn't it?" Tildy tried to access the recording of those words from the Jesus voice. It had been urgent. Like, "Stop her now," or something. Just in time too. "Huh."

"Are you, like, starting to be like Legolas? Like, seeing what's gonna happen in the future?"

"Legolas? Is he the elf one? The cute one?"

"Right. Not the hairy old dwarf."

"Legolas. I could be him."

"Yeah, but I'm not being the dwarf." Annabelle led the way up the steps into the bus.

Tildy tried not to laugh too hard at her shorter friend.

It was much warmer on the bus than outside, and less damp. Tildy pulled down the zipper on her light blue coat and pushed her white fleece hat off her forehead.

When they settled into a seat, she was still replaying her intervention to stop Annabelle. "I don't know exactly what happened. It was like there was this voice that warned me, 'Stop Annabelle before she punches Darla' or something."

"A voice? A voice that knew what I was gonna do?" Annabelle was looking out the window. "You should put that in your ghost story."

"Yeah. It's not really a ghost story in, like, the scary way they do those, mostly. It's more sort of inspiring." She pulled her hat off entirely, her braids falling against her coat. "So actually that voice fits pretty well in there."

"Hey, that could be the 'voice of reason' Mrs. Frederick was talking about today."

"I missed just about everything Mrs. Frederick said today."

"You were worried about that note from Mike?"

Tildy puckered for a second. "You think Mike likes me? Is that why he told me that?"

"Could be. He's kinda cute. And real nice."

"You think boys like him care that I'm Black? At least half Black?"

"If he likes you, then he doesn't mind." Annabelle spoke sleepwalker-like, as if surprised by the question.

It *was* pretty surprising. Tildy didn't often talk about race with Annabelle. They danced around it, mostly. "You know, Jewish people say you're only really Jewish if your mother is Jewish."

Annabelle shook her head in a shivery way. "I won't tell you what my dad says about Jews."

"Better not. But I was thinking maybe because my mother is White, then I'm really White."

"Well, since you're half and half, you can probably choose, right?"

Tildy breathed a big sigh, no cloud of vapor blocking her view of the seat in front of her.

"Or why not be *both,* to be exactly what you are? I mean, look at Ms. Sullivan. She's so cool. And I bet she's, like, half and half."

Tildy smiled. She had forgotten all about Ms. Sullivan. She glanced at her backpack where the nine-by-twelve sketch pad peeked out. "She is pretty cool, isn't she?"

"And I could tell she liked your drawing the best."

"You think so? I thought she was being pretty neutral and careful about not saying too much, like how dumb Billy's drawing was."

"She probably expected that from him after he started screwing around with the attendance."

Tildy turned and smiled at her friend, recalling attendance in art class. "Annabelle."

"That's my name. Don't wear it out."

Chapter Seven
Guess Who's Waiting at Your House

Tildy said goodbye to Annabelle in front of her house, accidentally calling her A.J. again. The girls were under strict orders to go home to their own houses directly after school. Hanging out would have to be on the phone or arranged with the parents, Grandma standing in. For a couple seconds, Tildy had been tempted to break that rule and invite Annabelle in. Mostly because she was afraid of what she'd find in there.

As she unlocked the front door, she tried to figure out if she *was* afraid Jesus would show up again. The idea of telling anyone she had seen him gave her a stomachache, but maybe she was more worried that he *wouldn't* be in the house. He would surely want to know how things went at school. But then, he would already know, wouldn't he?

She walked to her room while still pulling off her coat. "Are you in here?" Her voice cracked. She started to turn and leave, fleeing her stupidity.

But he stopped her. "I'm here whenever you are." Again, he seemed to come out of the closet. Maybe he had seen *Monsters, Inc* and was just messing with her. "No need to twist yourself around, girl. Just ask me. I'll tell you everything."

She was breathing hard. "What exactly did Darla tell those kids about me and my mother?" Was that really the most important question? It was the first one she could get out of her mouth.

"You don't need to know the exact words, but she claimed your mother had other problems besides her addiction, and that she was doing certain illegal activities. Darla claimed you were just like your mother."

"Am I?" She dropped her coat on the bed. "I mean, she *is* my mother."

"We inherit a lot from our parents, but we get to choose what to do with our inheritance."

Tildy laughed. She still needed to decide how she felt about talking to this man in her house, in her bedroom. Once she paused to ask herself that, she noticed a deeply peaceful pool inside, right about where that stomachache had been a couple minutes ago.

This was just like a dream. In her dreams, she wasn't always scared when she thought she should be. Like she was disconnected from the fear part of herself since she was asleep. But she was awake now. She was standing in her room.

And this Jesus guy was standing there smiling at her. He seemed to know she was working things out in her head and stood waiting with no dent in his happy face.

"If I told someone I saw you, they would put me in a nut house."

"We don't like to call it a *nut house* these days." Jesus scowled very briefly.

"We?"

"Us hallucinations."

Tildy noticed a thrilling little chill tingling her back. Everything this hallucination said seemed so good and true. Even his jokes. Maybe he really was Jesus. But he was maybe a bit too funny to be real.

His smile seemed to turn warmer, his eyes a bit more at rest. "Are you gonna work on typing your story? I think your elbow is ready." He nodded toward her right arm.

"You know about that?" She snorted. "Of course, you ..."

"I know everything about you—even what hasn't happened and what might happen."

"You knew A.J. would hit Darla and get in trouble?"

"Annabelle, if you please." He grinned. "Yes. And I knew she wouldn't get any satisfaction out of hitting Darla. If she knew Darla like I do, she wouldn't even consider hitting her."

"What? Why?" Tildy shifted her weight from left to right and then decided to just act normal, including getting a snack.

"Go ahead. I'm not confined to your bedroom."

"Like you were sent here for some punishment?" She led him out to the hall, her knees a little spongy.

He didn't look around like it was the first time he had been in the house. "Nope. I'm free to roam the house, but I don't wanna scare your grandma."

"Yeah, she would call the police. Strange man in the house."

"I'm always in her house. She believes in me. She invited me in."

"Into her house?"

"Into her heart. Like you." He leaned against the counter next to the stove and watched as Tildy opened the fridge.

She pulled out a yogurt and hesitated.

"No thanks, dear. I'm fine."

She laughed and just stood there staring at him with her mouth open. When she forced her jaw shut, she remembered seeing Ms. Sullivan for the first time.

"You and she are going to get along famously, as your grandfather liked to say."

"My grandfather?" Her mother's father had died of something related to alcoholism a few years ago. That was the grandfather she thought of. He and Grandma were not living together at the end, and Tildy had only seen him about once a year. He didn't get along so well with her mom.

"You're surprised I knew him?"

"He wasn't very nice to my mom and my grandma."

Jesus nodded but didn't say anything for a few seconds.

Tildy pulled a spoon out of the drawer and started prying at the foil lid on the yogurt. "And he was the one who started the drinking and addiction that's screwed up my mom so much."

"It doesn't help to think of your mother as being screwed up. She's in pain. She's learning new ways to deal with her pain."

"She *is* pretty screwed up though." Tildy checked with him out of the corner of her eye, wondering what he would do about her insisting on saying that.

Again, he nodded but didn't speak.

"So, do you, like, think all people are good?" She didn't expect that was right, at least not from what she had learned in church. But this Jesus seemed pretty mellow.

"All people are created in the image of God. The blueprint is good. Very good. But that blueprint gets marked up and crumpled along the way." He shrugged. "All people were designed to be good."

"But then they screw up. Like my dad."

"What do you know about your father?"

"He left my mom."

"Do you know why he left?"

"My grandma said he's an irresponsible father."

Jesus nodded for a second but spoke up this time. "Remember what Darla said about your father?"

Darla? Tildy had the spoon upside down in her mouth. Darla did say something about her father. Something about him leaving. She pulled the spoon out. "He … he left because my mom is a drug addict."

"That was a big part of it. Your mom wasn't getting the help she needed. She wouldn't listen to him when he told her he was willing to work an extra job to pay for her rehab. She felt condemned by him when he suggested it."

"Felt condemned?" Tildy remembered a time she came home and found her mother high on something. Or maybe it was really *low*. She was crying and saying how she felt condemned by everyone. Everyone including her boyfriend, Tildy's father? "Then why did he disappear?"

"Disappear? Your father didn't disappear. Your grandma's lawyer got the courts to order him to stay away."

"What did he do?"

"He tried to take you. He didn't trust your mother to take care of you."

"What? I don't remember any of that."

Jesus waited a few beats. "I'm telling you all this, Tildy, because the hate you feel for your father is coming back on yourself. You wanted to cut yourself yesterday because of self-hate. It's a spillover from the hate you've been fed toward your father."

"What? What are ..." Tildy plunked into the nearest kitchen chair, which scraped on the tiles as she wedged herself in.

"I don't want you to hurt yourself, Tildy. I don't want you to hate yourself. And you have no reason to hate your father."

"But ..." Alarms were blaring in her head. She couldn't possibly take the word of this Jesus hallucination against her grandmother and her mother. That would be crazy. But something about what he was saying sounded familiar. When she was six, there had been something about the police. And a lady in a suit had asked her some questions. Tildy told the woman what her grandma told her to say. What was that?

"It didn't feel right to you at the time." Jesus seemed to be tracking with Tildy's thoughts again.

"I didn't understand what was going on. I didn't know what they were talking about. I remember going out to eat with my dad. And he packed a backpack for me. But then there was something I didn't understand. I just agreed with my grandma because she was so upset." She looked at Jesus for the answer even though that still felt risky. "What did he do? What did my dad do?"

"It was wrong. He was desperate. He shouldn't have taken you. But he didn't feel like he could afford a lawyer at the time. And he didn't want you dragged through the courts."

"He didn't?" Tildy's chest had hollowed out. She sat holding the spoon in one hand and the yogurt in the other, both resting on her lap.

"He sends money every month. He's helping pay for rehab for your mother as well as clothes and things for you. The MP3 player. The braids."

"What?"

"You didn't know, of course. And you haven't done anything wrong. The grown-ups are responsible. Not you." He leaned forward just a little. "And all of them genuinely want what's best for you. All of them."

"Wait. My dad sends money? So my grandma knows where he is?"

"She could find him if she wanted to."

"She said she didn't know where he is."

"You haven't asked for a while."

Tildy shook her head slowly. "No, I haven't. I could tell they didn't want to talk about him. And I thought he didn't care about me—that's why he left."

"He sends money to help raise you instead of spending it on lawyers to try and get custody of you."

Tildy was floating.

"He knows you live with your grandma now. And he knows that's safer than living with your mom, the way she was on her worst days. So he's not fighting for custody right now."

"My grandma lied to me."

"I don't want you to focus on that, Tildy. Your grandma loves you. She wants to be sure you're taken care of. She didn't trust your father. She was afraid he would take you away if she let him visit." He pulled out a chair and sat across the table from her. "I just don't want you to hate your father. That makes you hate the part of you that came from him."

"The Black part?"

"The father's part. It's hard not to hate yourself if you hate where you came from."

"Jesus." Tildy didn't usually swear, and she wasn't sure just how she meant it when she said his name this time. Her head was so muddled.

He seemed to ignore whatever that was. "You also don't need to hate your grandma. She didn't do it to hurt you. She did the best she knew. But I wanted you to have more of the story."

Tildy noticed the yogurt and spoon. Setting them on the table, she looked across at Jesus. "Is this why you came to see me?"

"I became visible because you were thinking about hurting yourself. Your parents have both been praying for you, and your grandmother and her prayer group too." He lowered his head at her and found that sly grin. "Prayer works."

Tildy laughed at him yet again. "You don't seem as serious as I expected. If I ever would have expected ... It's hard to know when you're being serious about things."

"Even if I see irony in pointing it out, that doesn't mean I'm not serious about prayer."

"Irony. Mrs. Fredericks really likes irony."

He smiled in the way one does at the end of a workday, ready to go and do something fun for a change. "I should let you get to the computer. Your grandma will be home in about forty-five minutes. It would be good to make some progress before that."

"So you're, like, my homework coach now?"

"Whatever you need, my girl. Whatever you need."

Chapter Eight

What to Say to Grandma?

Jesus went invisible, or maybe just faded back into Tildy's overactive imagination. Exactly where he was seemed strangely less important, however, in light of what he had told her. Part of the strangeness was the feeling that it might not be right for Jesus to tell her those things about her dad. But then, if he really was Jesus ...

Her yogurt container in the trash bin and spoon in the sink, Tildy followed a fit of craziness—a new fit of craziness—into her grandma's "office." It was only an office in quotation marks because it had been Tildy's mother's room when she lived there.

Tildy recalled times her grandma had carefully ferried mail through the house. At the time, Tildy just assumed it was business stuff and her grandma wanted to keep her business private. What does an eleven-year-old need to know about her grandma's business, after all? But what if it wasn't just her grandma's business? What if it was Tildy's business too?

She bumped her knees past the corner of the bed that had been her mother's and would presumably be hers again when she got out of rehab. Tildy slipped past questions about when that would happen. She could see a stack of mail on the desk/table next to the wall. Trying to keep them in order and even maintaining the angle of the envelopes, Tildy bent at the waist and peered at each business-sized item. Electricity. Water. Bank. Credit card. Generally not interesting. Though maybe if she looked closer she could see evidence of what Jesus said about checks from her dad.

65

"This isn't a good idea, Tildy."

She spun toward the door. No visible Jesus, just a voice. *"This?"* She didn't say it aloud. And she wasn't really questioning what he'd said. A skittering fear that she needed to get out of that room animated her limbs. She let go of the stack of mail, straightening it to the way it lay before. Then she hurried out of the room, rubbing her knees roughly against the bed to get by it quickly.

In the hall, she started to breathe again. Then she stepped into her room. No Jesus, but his words still filled every room she entered. Words about her father. Her dad had not just run away from her. He had not left her without a fight. That's what Jesus was saying.

What would her grandma say? What should Tildy say to her? "Hey, Jesus told me you were lying to me ..."

"That's not the best way to start, Tildy. You know that." She said that to herself without imitating Jesus's voice, but it *was* what she imagined he would say ... if he was real.

Was she just telling herself all this to make herself feel better? The whole Jesus appearing in her room and in the kitchen? And where else? It seemed like he had spoken to her when she was at school.

She wandered out of her bedroom to the family room, stopping at her backpack propped against the wall. She left the backpack there, but pulled out the spiral notebook for English class. Thinking about what Jesus had said, or even about her sanity, made her tired. Her story seemed a safe place to hide from all those questions. And hadn't Jesus suggested she could work on that story? Had he? Someone had. Maybe part of Tildy was just getting more responsible, more grown up.

More like Jesus? Hmm.

It wasn't easy to set aside the weirdness of that day. It had, in fact, been even weirder than the day before. Who would have thought that possible?

Her story about the ghost of a wise old man coming to reassure the scared and frustrated girl seemed like a sort of frame on her real life. *Real* had become as slippery as a new bar of soap. Was Jesus real? Was her dad real? Well, she knew both of them were more real than an old ghost coming out of a girl's closet. As she waited for the computer to finish booting up, she wondered about her story. What was the girl in the story confused or upset about? Just that her mom didn't understand her? That was what it seemed like so far. Mrs. Fredericks would want more. Maybe not all the gory details, but specifics. That's what she always said.

How about the girl was upset because she found out her grandma—no, her mom—was lying to her about her father? Would that be too obvious? Too real? The teacher said to write about what Tildy knew. Did Tildy also want Mrs. Fredericks to know? Actually, yes. Not the gory details about Tildy's life, but yes, she did want her to sort of know. Some of it.

Tildy wouldn't include the part about cutting. That would start the sirens going. She didn't want that. Those were gory details. And then there was her mother's addiction. Very gory.

Somehow she actually got some work done. Tildy was a pretty fast typist. She entered almost four out of the five pages she had written so far. Then her grandma came home.

"Hello, Tildy. Homework, I hope." Grandma stretched her neck as she walked toward the front closet. She had opened the electronic garage door just as Tildy was thinking about checking for the latest fan news about Justin Timberlake. Instead, she had saved her story one more time.

She felt an impatient warmth rise with her grandma's suspicion about what she was doing on the computer. "Yes, homework ..." But Tildy stopped herself. It occurred to her that Jesus was listening. *Huh.* Even if he wasn't really showing up in her house or talking to her at school, he probably *was* listening. She softened her voice. "I got most of my story into the computer. I wanna finish typing it and print it to take to school for Mrs. Fredericks to look at before I finish writing it."

"That sounds like a very advanced way to do a story. In my day, we just brought in a few pages of notebook paper with loopy writing on it."

"You guys actually wrote cursive, didn't you?"

"Cursive? Yes, that's right."

"Huh." The wistful note in her grandma's voice dampened some of the fire Tildy had been building for when she came home. Amid the thickening smoke, she returned to the question of what to say. Maybe a clever question. Well, not *too* clever. That would give her away.

She finished typing while Grandma cooked. When she finally printed what she had, she noted that her stomach might not have room for food on top of all those fists. A brief temptation to skip supper, saying she had no appetite, stalled her as she headed to her bedroom.

When Grandma called for supper, Tildy wandered to the kitchen slowly.

"You're not hungry?" Apparently her grandma saw that slow walk.

"Kinda, but my stomach feels a little weird."

"Can you eat? Are you sick?" That deep wrinkle between her grandma's eyebrows showed up, almost like a scar. Like her worrying was a wound.

Tildy thought about that. Jesus had said her grandma just wanted to take care of her, to keep her safe. Her daughter was in drug rehab, and the daughter's boyfriend had tried to take her granddaughter away. All that might leave a scar.

At the table, pushing her mac and cheese and peas around on her plate was occasionally interrupted by a small bite. Tildy was a little hungry.

"Is something bothering you?" Grandma was still displaying that cut between her eyebrows.

Tildy looked at her and let one of those fists loosen. "I've been thinking about my dad. Is there any way to get in touch with him? Do you know where he is?" It wasn't carefully planned, but it was a big part of what she wanted to hear her grandma answer.

After a deep breath, Grandma started pushing the remnants of *her* macaroni around too. "What made you think of that?"

"I miss him. I miss having … I just wonder what he's doing. I wonder if he thinks about me."

Maybe her eyes just blinked, but Grandma's whole face seemed to reset. Her cheeks turned red, then her nose. Then the rims of her eyes. She took another deep breath. "I don't know. I don't know how much he thinks about you." She blinked a lot. "I mean, I expect he *does* think about you. I know he still cares about you."

"Really? You do? How do you know?"

"He … he sends money to help support you."

"He does?" Tildy worried how dishonest she was being, pretending not to know. But what else was she going to do? She wasn't going to tell Grandma that Jesus had come to talk to her. She could feel her head shaking, like her hands did when she tried to do one more pull-up in gym. It was suddenly hard work to keep her head upright. Maybe what she really wanted was to flop facedown on the table and weep.

Grandma pushed her chair back an inch. "I didn't know if I should tell you. I didn't want you to get caught in the middle. But I think it is good for you to know that he does think about you. I know he's making a financial sacrifice to send that money. I don't think he's rich." She glanced at the kitchen window as if she had heard something outside. But maybe she just her listening to herself say what she had resisted saying all this time.

"I'm glad you told me. It hurts to think that my own dad doesn't care about me." One of those fists was in Tildy's throat now. She didn't mean to cry. And it didn't feel like she was especially sad now. Maybe more relieved.

Her grandma released a sob and covered her mouth. She slid out of her chair and stood next to Tildy.

Tildy couldn't hold back either. She let the sobbing begin. And it seemed to want to go on and on. She wrapped an arm around her grandma's waist and hung on tight.

It felt huge. This admission from her grandma was a big deal. She didn't lie to Tildy, even though it seemed obvious she was worried what it would mean for Tildy to know about her dad. And Jesus's words were proving true. But the flood of tears thinned to a trickle when Tildy wondered how much more she could ask. Was it too much to take the next step? Too much for Grandma?

"I'm, uh, glad you told me. It feels so good." Tildy was looking up at her grandma, who had leaned back a little. "Can I talk to him, maybe? Or maybe even see him?"

Grandma's arms slid free from Tildy. "I don't know. Maybe. I'll have to talk to ... my lawyer." She stepped back. "There was a disagreement before. And I didn't trust ... I didn't know what he would do. Your dad. But he's been so good about sending those checks even though I never asked him to. He didn't have to do it." She shook her head as she studied the dishes still on the kitchen table.

The way her grandmother's words shadowed what Jesus had said warmed Tildy immensely. But she still battled an urge to shout, "Why didn't you tell me all this?" Actually she knew why. Her grandma had just said it. She didn't want Tildy caught in the middle. How could Tildy *not* be in the middle when this thing was about her dad, her relationship with her dad?

"What about Mom?" Tildy hadn't planned that question any more than the others. She wasn't even sure what she meant. But if Tildy was in the middle of the issue of her father, then surely her mother was too.

"What are you asking?" Grandma was frowning again, but it was more the questioning sort of frown than the worried-about-a-sick-kid frown.

That reminded Tildy of school. Teachers would respond to a student with "good question." But rarely did Tildy ask one of those. She never seemed to know which one was a good question.

The crease between her grandma's eyes wasn't so long or deep now. "Your mother always trusted your father more than I did."

Tildy blinked at that for a few seconds. Here was the first bit of information that Jesus had not included in his revelations. But it wasn't really surprising, just interesting to hear Grandma say it.

"So, she probably wouldn't mind if I talked to him?"

"I need to talk to the lawyer first just in case." Grandma glanced at the window again. It was late and the window was a black mirror. She probably wasn't seeing the cold, snowy yard behind the house. Was she looking at the reflection?

"He's not dangerous, is he?"

"Oh, no. I don't think so, Tildy. He was just upset about your mother's ... problems. He was worried about her taking care of you. It made him a little ... desperate, I think. And he and I didn't really get along. So maybe we didn't understand each other."

"But him sending money makes you think you understand him better."

"He didn't have to do it, and he's kept it up for years. And he hasn't caused any problems about ..." She looked at Tildy and then glanced away. "I think your mother was a little ashamed of taking his money, for whatever reason."

"Huh." Tildy felt that trapped sensation her grandma must have been struggling to avoid. There might be parts of this Tildy didn't want to know. Just like she didn't even know exactly what drug her mother was using. They had assemblies at school where the kids were told all about various kinds of illegal substances including cigarettes and alcohol, which were illegal for kids. It all felt like too much information. "TMI." A.J. liked that phrase. Annabelle, that was.

Tildy wanted to keep her place in the discussion even if she didn't want all the gory details. "Thanks for looking into it, Grandma. I won't bug you about it. I know it will take a while."

Grandma grinned. It was a freer smile than Tildy had seen on her old face in a long time. "Thanks, Tildy." She shook her head a little. "You're getting so grown up."

That reminded Tildy about an earlier thought. Maybe part of her *was* getting older. Or maybe part of her was starting to listen to Jesus.

Chapter Nine
Try Offering Her a Little Tenderness

Tildy knew she could do it for a while, but how long is a while? She could wait for her grandma to call the lawyer, probably to get advice on how to keep Tildy safe in case her dad still wanted to take her away. Or maybe it was about something else. She knew Grandma wasn't telling her everything.

After that talk with her grandma, Tildy lay awake in bed until nearly midnight. Mostly she was constructing an imagined life with her dad. Of course the dad in her imagination was blurry and distorted. Maybe more what she wanted him to be like than who he really was. After all, he couldn't be perfect. Only Jesus was perfect.

"One thing you know about him is he loved your mother."

That was just a thought, not an actual voice. But it was a thought so unexpected to Tildy, even deep into a sleepless night, that it had to come from a different imagination than hers. What did he say? Loving her mother? Well, she did guess that her dad had loved her mother. At least in the beginning. When they made a baby girl and named her Matilda. Tildy knew that much about babies and parents—and about her particular parents.

She had one very deep memory of her dad tickling her mom until she cried for mercy lest she wet her pants. The wetting her pants part stuck with little Tildy, maybe four years old at the time. But the memory also included a clear and smiling mother. Not a blurry facsimile. Something real about her mom lived on in that memory. Something free from the anger and hurt that clouded her mother's face so much of the time.

It was something in her mom's purest, happiest face that stopped Tildy from fantasizing about going away with her dad.

But it was probably too much to try imagining all of them together and happy.

Less clear, but still powerful, were fragments of shouted accusations. Maybe five or six years old, Tildy had known something was wrong. Something was breaking. And it was something she could not possibly put back together.

Her alarm woke her. She had a sore stomach and sticky, itchy eyes. That was the not-enough-sleep feeling she knew too well. But she did wake up, which meant she *did* sleep. At least for something like six hours. She breathed hard, trying to feed her brain enough oxygen to fuel a rise from bed. The alarm had gone off and was on snooze. She wasn't a hundred percent sure about that, but that's what it felt like. She'd probably hit snooze.

Gym again today.

"How am I gonna face Darla today?"

"Try a little tenderness."

Apparently Tildy had spoken her question aloud, and Jesus felt free to answer in kind. His voice was even lower than hers. Not scratchier, but quieter. And saying something way nuttier.

"Tenderness? Are you kidding?" She nearly squeaked and then lowered her voice at the end.

"Them young girls, they do get wearied."

"Wait." She whispered now. "Are you quoting song lyrics to me? Is that a song?"

"She has her grief and care." Jesus appeared out of the closet. He nodded.

"It *is* a song. And it sounds familiar."

"Your mom and dad like that song. And it's a fitting answer to your question."

"Which part?"

"What I quoted. Darla needs tenderness because of her grief and weariness."

"Wha—?"

"Tildy? Who are you talking to?" Her grandma was standing in the doorway.

74

Jesus had disappeared, maybe hiding in the closet again. Why did he do that? Why did he do any of the things he was doing these days?

"Uh, well, maybe I was sort of praying."

"Oh. You were?" The wiry lift of her grandma's voice implied a large portion of skepticism.

Tildy didn't blame her. They didn't talk much about praying, apart from suppertime. Grandma hadn't gone to her prayer group since Christmas as far as Tildy could recall. And Tildy wasn't really a big pray-er.

Shrugging in response to her grandma's doubtful tone, Tildy slowed over whether she was being dishonest about praying. Talking to Jesus, who is in fact God, seemed like praying. Sort of. She wasn't a great scholar of prayer any more than a practitioner.

Neither of them said any more about it, but Tildy did catch her grandma staring at her during breakfast. She didn't ask why. She had certainly given Grandma plenty of reasons to wonder, if not worry. And the most worrying things in Tildy's life she hadn't mentioned to Grandma ... yet.

"Hey Grandma, Jesus came out of my closet." No. She couldn't imagine saying that. And she had a good imagination.

What about Annabelle? Her family went to church practically every week. They were Catholics. But would she believe the Jesus-in-the-closet story? Would anyone from *any* kind of church?

Waiting for the bus and for Annabelle, Tildy turned to wondering what Jesus meant about a little tenderness for Darla. She was, what? Tired? Something like that. Darla seemed mean. But maybe that was about being weary. Weary of things that make you act mean. Maybe Tildy should try that tenderness.

Annabelle came around the corner just in time to interrupt Tildy juggling how she could possibly offer Darla tenderness. "Hey."

"Hey."

"You look tired."

"Was up too late."

"Texting with Justin Timberlake?"

"Ha. I wish. I just found out that my dad has been sending money to take care of me, and I might get to see him."

"What? I thought no one knew where he was."

"I don't know what my grandma knows, but maybe there's a return address on the checks he sends or whatever."

"Yeah. That makes sense."

Peter and James were approaching the bus stop now.

Tildy looked down the block. Sure enough, the bus was in sight at the same time as the boys. For some reason, that reminded her that she would ride the activity bus tonight. "I'm staying for stage crew tonight."

"Wednesday. I know. But what about your dad? You might get to see him?"

"Well, I don't really know." Tildy lowered her voice and huddled close to Annabelle. It was almost up to freezing this morning. A bit of an improvement. But the air seemed wet, like when it was about to snow. "My grandma's gonna look into it." She didn't want to drag out those gory details.

"Got it." Annabelle looked at the boys. They seemed to be waiting for the girls to get on the bus first. That was new.

The order of entry put Peter right behind Tildy, James doing the women-and-children-first approach today. Big eighth grader.

"Your arm all better?" Peter spoke to her as soon as she glanced even near him.

Tildy flexed her arm. "I actually forgot about it. I guess that's good."

"Yeah. Hey, are you painting scenes tonight?"

"Yeah."

"I'm gonna help with some of the building. Got recruited out of shop class."

"You one of the hot shop-class recruits?" Tildy was thinking basketball, but why not shop stars?

"Ha. Yeah. Varsity hammer-and-saw guy. It should be fun though. I hear Mrs. Lohan is pretty cool."

"She lets us be loud and rowdy as long as no one gets hurt. Unless they're actually practicing the play. Then we have to keep it down."

"Oh. Sure." At a push from his brother, Pete slipped past the seat selected by Annabelle. He looked like he wanted to say more, but nothing materialized.

Annabelle gave him a lingering stare, like someone keeping track of the wasp in the room. Not mad, but wary. Wary of his attention to Tildy? Maybe Annabelle was interested in Peter.

Tildy didn't know if *she* was interested. He was cute in a shy and skinny way. No glasses. Braces. Almost always wearing a hat, so she couldn't say much about his brown hair. Tildy let Peter go, turning her attention to Annabelle. "I got the draft of my story typed up."

"Me too. My mom helped. She said she missed typing. She used to work for a religious newspaper before she got pregnant." Annabelle described a pregnant belly with her two hands looped away from her torso.

"Pregnant with you?"

"Yeah. I was the one that ruined everything for her."

"What?"

"It's just a joke."

"Why would you joke about that?" Tildy didn't say it forcefully, but it didn't seem right that someone would tell Annabelle she had ruined anything by being born. But maybe there was something less nasty behind it than what Tildy was thinking. She had stayed up way too late and probably wasn't her sharpest.

Annabelle shrugged. "I just heard my mom say something to my dad, but she was just kidding. I mean, it wasn't about me, it was about her getting pregnant." Annabelle stared out the window at the endless whiteness of January in Illinois.

Hearing about Annabelle's parents talking privately felt like sneaking into her grandma's office to look at her mail. "Well, I could see Benny and Keith ruining all kinds of things, like that American Beauty doll with the haircut." Tildy clumsily tried to lighten things up.

"Oh, dang. Don't remind me of that. I don't wanna go to prison for murder. I have my whole life ahead of me." Annabelle craned her neck to look at someone behind them as the bus pulled onto the long, wide arterial road on which their middle school resided.

"Who you looking at?"

"No one." Annabelle snorted. "Except Peter. You think he likes you. He keeps talking to you about his arm. I mean *your* arm."

Tildy shook her head. "Maybe he just wants to be a doctor someday."

"Or a nurse." Annabelle quirked a side grin.

"Or maybe he just wants to arm wrestle me."

"Or— Uh, no. Forget that."

Tildy could guess what Annabelle had almost said. That was probably more A.J. than Annabelle. Annabelle was reforming. Restraining the feist of A.J.

That brought Tildy back to wondering what she would say to Darla.

As it turned out, she didn't see Darla until she was walking out of the locker room for gym. They nearly rubbed shoulders going in opposite directions.

"Hi, Darla." She said it in the most normal way she could, not overfriendly. That would be fake and maybe the start of more fighting. Her tone wasn't angry either. Though probably not tender.

Darla just looked at Tildy, a slight flicker of confusion on her face. Then the encounter was over.

On the court, Tildy discovered her elbow wasn't fully recovered. She dribbled with her right hand a few times and that made her especially glad about being left-handed. She was thinking she could go out for the school team in seventh grade if she practiced. Her first shot was an air ball, reminding her she needed two hands for shooting.

As she retrieved the ball, settling near the baseline, she tried to recall what Jesus had said about Darla.

"You could just ask me again. I'm happy to repeat myself."

Now she was really distracted. Someone yelled at her where she stood holding an orange basketball. She passed it to that shouting boy without even registering who it was.

Tildy tried talking to Jesus in her mind. *"This is kinda distracting. Is it gonna make things worse?"*

"Like basketball, this will take some practice. Talking to me without moving your lips is like dribbling with your off hand, your right hand."

"Off hand" was a phrase her basketball coach had used with her once he discovered she was left-handed. "It can be an advantage when defenders are used to covering right-handers." Did Jesus know her old basketball coach? Crazy question.

"There are some funny questions, but no crazy ones."

Tildy realized that she was still standing near the wall, staring. A ball bouncing off the wood floor and just missing her face reminded her.

"Hey space cadet, can you throw me that ball?"

Reentering the world outside her head, Tildy grabbed the ball and one-arm push-passed it to Shiv, who had spoken to her for the first time she could remember. He had called her a space cadet, but it was a start.

Then Darla jogged onto the court, followed by Bethany.

In that moment, Tildy remembered that Bethany had been at the after-school program at the church on Burchard Road. That was the church where Tildy's grandma had a prayer group. A random connection, probably.

"Ask Darla how her dad is, and tell her you're sorry it's so hard on her."

This was the tenderness thing?

But the flow of the class, the pairing off for drills, and the separate half-court games they played offered Tildy no chance to talk to Darla. She wasn't avoiding it, though maybe Mr. Enriquez was avoiding them running into each other. He had learned his lesson.

"Tell Darla when Mr. Enriquez asks you to help gather the basketballs."

Tildy was puffing hard at the end of the half-court game and thinking of the closest drinking fountain.

Then Mr. Enriquez interrupted her multiple layers of distraction. "Tildy, please help me gather the basketballs."

Fortunately her feet obeyed him automatically, even though she caught herself with her mouth hanging open and had to remember to start breathing again. She stumbled once, but turned that into a jog. That put her next to where Darla was kneeling on the floor untying one of her shoes.

Without looking up at her, Darla said, "This sock was messed up the whole time. It was driving me batty." Then she looked up, clearly surprised to see Tildy.

"Yeah, that can be a bummer." Tildy sympathized automatically and sincerely.

Darla pulled that shoe off and stood up, still wearing her other shoe. She used her shod foot to kick a ball closer to Tildy.

Tildy bent to pick up the second basketball. "Uh, how's … how's your dad doing these days?" Her throat felt gummy. She really needed the drinking fountain soon.

"My dad?"

"I don't know the details, but I'm real sorry it's … uh, hurting you so much." She had forgotten exactly what Jesus had said. Now she feared she would get in another fight for saying the wrong thing.

"Oh. I ... Thanks. Thanks, Tildy." Darla stood there with a shoe dangling from her hand. "Uh, and sorry for what I said about your mom. I don't really know about her either."

Tildy snuffed a laugh through her nose. "What do we really know about our parents, ever?"

Darla nodded and started to limp toward the locker room next to Tildy.

Tildy diverted to where she could kick another ball toward the rack at center court.

"Right. And the stuff they do can totally mess with us. But do they think of that?" Darla rolled her eyes.

It was generic, but it was a uniting bond. Parents. Mostly clueless, most of the time.

The sound of someone clearing his throat drew Tildy's attention. She glanced around. Mr. Enriquez was on the other sideline, simultaneously dribbling two basketballs toward the rack. Showing off.

Then who was the guy who cleared his throat?

"Tell her you'll pray for her and her dad."

Maybe Tildy was intoxicated with having Jesus in her head. "Hey, Darla. I'll pray for you and your dad."

Darla was a couple yards ahead as Tildy diverted toward the ball racks. Her jaw hinged wide, and her eyes popped, Darla hesitated. "Oh. Wow. That would be great. Bethany says her mom is praying for us. I guess it all helps."

"I hope so. I think so." Tildy stumbled a bit with her feet as she did with her words, but it was a happy little trip. The surprising responses from Darla were mind blowing.

To think ... all it took was a little tenderness.

81

Chapter Ten
Am I Gonna Get in Trouble?

On the activity bus, Tildy rode alone after working on the scenery in the auditorium until four fifteen. At first she was alone. Then she felt a person sitting next to her. Her spine tingled at the sensation. Someone was there, but invisible.

"Can you guess who?" Jesus laughed inside her head.

"Holy sh—" She just stopped herself from saying that and jumping out of the seat. To escape though, she would have to scramble over Jesus, who was apparently on the aisle.

"I know. I'm totally rocking your world, Tildy. But you needed a bit of a boost, remember?"

It had only been Monday when she was thinking of cutting herself. Another bunch of those spine tingles hit her at the thought. "Yeah." Then she remembered to talk inside her head. *"I did need something. It's hard to believe that was just two days ago."*

"Time flies when you're having fun."

"Fun?" She was about to argue inside her head. That wouldn't have been so unusual. She did it a lot. But generally she was arguing with herself and not an invisible Jesus sitting with her on the activity bus. She reconsidered. *"I think you're right. It was fun to see Darla change like that. All it took was a little tenderness."* She wondered if she could get a copy of that song onto her MP3 player.

That was when she realized her MP3 player was still in her backpack. It had to stay in there during school, of course, but the ride home was prime time for listening. She still didn't have that Avril Lavigne music from Annabelle.

"Are you gonna pay for those songs?"

82

"Avril Lavigne?" She knew which songs he was talking about. She had only paid for about a quarter of the songs she had on discs and on her player. That's how all the kids did it.

"Of course other kids don't pay for all their music." He replied to her unspoken thoughts.

"Right. It's just the way things go."

"And other kids would never tell Darla they would pray for her and her dad."

Clearly this was unfair. With parents, Tildy could tell only the stuff she wanted them to know. Jesus being in her head was really unfair.

He chuckled. Inside her head.

She resisted swearing out loud. Her mother used to swear a lot. Tildy took a big breath and tried to climb past what Jesus was saying about the music. *"You think I will actually remember to pray for Darla?"*

"You can do it every time you see her."

"Really? Like, won't that be awkward?"

"Thoughts can be awkward, but you have them. Why not turn your thoughts into prayers?"

"Like how?"

"Like, instead of 'Oh, there's Darla, I hate her and hope she doesn't talk to me,' you could say, 'There's Darla. Jesus loves her, and I hope he blesses her and her family today.'"

The internal conversation was weird, but kind of exciting. Communication with this man in her head was so immediate. Right here. Right now. And right on target. But it was still weird.

"Wait. Does that count as a prayer? What you said?"

"It does. Prayer is talking to God. Talking inside your head is something you know how to do. Talking to someone that's always with you inside your head should be the easiest thing."

"I don't know. I'm kinda worried that all this is gonna make me ... crazy. I'm gonna do something that gets me in trouble or something."

"Crazy is as crazy does."

83

"Are you quoting Forrest Gump *to me?"*

"Sort of." He laughed again.

Jesus laughing inside her head was the weirdest thing. Weird because she heard a man inside her head, but really weird because she felt his ... humor. His pleasure, maybe even.

"What's up with Darla's dad?" She asked even though she expected Jesus to say it wasn't really any of her business.

"He was suspended from his job while being investigated for a crime."

"Oh." That felt very heavy. Too much for an eleven-year-old to deal with.

"Yes. Darla is still only eleven, like you. It is hard for her to deal with."

Of course Tildy had been thinking about herself and the burden of getting involved with Darla and her dad's crimes, but now she felt guilty for just thinking about herself.

"That guilt won't help. You're not supposed to take responsibility for Darla's dad and his problems. That's why you pray. The same way you should pray for your grandma and your mom and your dad. You can't carry any of them, but you can care. So you can just bring them to me."

"Do I really care about Darla and her dad?"

"I can help you with that too. In fact, I already have. Now you think of her not just as the mean girl. You think of her as a girl who has problems and fears and needs help. She needs prayer. She needs a sympathetic friend."

"Bethany is her friend."

"That's true. And Bethany's mom really does pray for Darla's family."

"I guess more prayer is better."

"I know you haven't thought much about it, but you have a good imagination. Imagination is about directing your thoughts beyond what you see and feel immediately around you. If you can imagine a story about an old man's ghost coming out of your closet, you can also direct your thoughts to

pray for Darla and her family. You will also have to imagine how best to pray for them, but you're good at that kind of thing."

Having Jesus say she was good at something was like a happy high five from a superstar.

"Like Michael Jordan?"

"Ha. You think you're as big a superstar as Michael Jordan?"

"Well ..."

Now Tildy was laughing and fighting back the laughter in the real world outside her head. As the bus slowed to her stop, she was grateful she had not laughed right past the corner. It was getting dark, and she didn't want a long walk. She glanced around to see if anyone had noticed her laughing. The seats were mostly empty. She was near the end of the line on the way home. The few kids still on the bus had earbuds in, probably.

That took her back to what Jesus had said about paying for music. How weird would it be for her to insist on only listening to music she had paid for?

She snorted as she descended from the bus. *"I'll try to pray for Darla, but I don't know about the music. It's expensive. I don't get allowance."*

"Ms. Sullivan needs someone to help her in her studio once a week. You could earn some money that way."

"Really? She can do that?"

"Just a few hours. It's legal."

"You're a lawyer now?"

"I know things, Tildy."

"Ha." She was on the sidewalk near her house. She could laugh out loud at Jesus. Though maybe he wasn't exactly joking.

"Should I ask Ms. Sullivan about a job?"

"Ask your grandma first. Then see what Ms. Sullivan says."

"Do you really have to call her 'Ms. Sullivan'?"

"You mean, can I call her by her first name?" He was fully visible now as she turned to walk up toward the house. At least visible to her. He had laughter on his face as well as in his voice.

"Okay. Whatever." She looked at him as she fished for her key. "And thanks."

"You're welcome, Tildy." And he faded away.

At dinner that night, she ran the idea past her grandma. "There's a new art teacher at school, and I was thinking it would be cool to see what she does, like, with her art outside school. I was thinking I could offer to help her in her studio and maybe even earn some money."

"Money for music discs and MP3s?"

Her grandmother's bullseye stopped Tildy's chewing. The spicy Mexican pasta skillet filled her nose and reminded her to swallow. She reached for her water glass. "Uh, yeah. I think I should try to pay for my music more. Most of the kids just pirate the music most of the time."

"Who's this new art teacher?"

"Ms. Sullivan."

"Did she say she needed help?"

"No, but I have class with her tomorrow, and I was gonna ask her. Thought I should talk to you about it first." Tildy was worried she was getting herself in trouble. She wasn't telling her grandmother everything. Was that dishonest?

"That sounds wise. Thanks for asking me first. Let's see what she says before we make any final decisions."

"Yeah. I was thinking maybe Saturdays, since I'm not playing any sports this year."

"Maybe. Not Sunday. We might go back to church sometime."

"Right." Tildy tried not to sound skeptical on that last point. She had been thinking more about going to church lately, for obvious reasons. Though those reasons wouldn't be obvious to her grandma.

Apparently it was necessary for Tildy to consult her grandma before offering to work for Ms. Sullivan, but not to consult her about Jesus coming to talk to her. Maybe *consult* was the wrong word. More like a revelation. Or something.

The test for all this would be tomorrow in class. If Ms. Sullivan looked like she had never even considered hiring a kid or maybe didn't even have a studio, that would make Jesus look bad. Or maybe it was Tildy who would look bad. Crazy, really.

On Thursday, when she cranked up her courage and dragged Annabelle to the front of the classroom with her, Tildy got her answer.

"Tildy! That would be wonderful. Are your parents okay with you working? We would need their permission." Ms. Sullivan's eyes were wide and her grin expanding.

"I, uh, live with my grandma. She said I could ask you and see if you needed help. I guess she would need to know, like, where you live and all. She works most days. She's a realtor."

"Sure. Maybe you could come over for a few hours on Saturdays? I have a studio in Warrenville."

"That's where I live." Tildy tried not to squeak.

"Very nice. Well, that should work out, then." Ms. Sullivan put one finger to her chin. "But how did you know I was thinking of hiring someone?"

"Well, I didn't know for sure. It was just a ... hope, really."

Annabelle watched the conversation with stars in her eyes and a lopsided grin. It was priceless to have a witness.

On their way to their lockers, Annabelle stopped puckering, finally. "Something is different with you these days." She gave Tildy a conspiratorial squint.

Tildy looked at Annabelle and then bumped into a large eighth grade girl, who muttered some insult. "Uh, well, maybe it's because my best friend is now Annabelle and not A.J. anymore."

"Like an upgrade?"

"Definitely." But that playful affirmation came out at only half strength. At some point, Tildy would probably have to tell someone the real reason for the upgrade.

Chapter Eleven
Still Looking for Someone to Tell

On Friday, Tildy called the phone number Ms. Sullivan had given her. Grandma was in the kitchen with her. Part of the question was whether Ms. Sullivan could be flexible about the hours so Grandma could drop off and pick up Tildy around the schedule for her house showings.

"Yes, that's no problem. Most Saturdays, I work all day in my studio. Any hours you could put in would help. I hope you don't mind doing some sweeping up and sorting things."

"Oh, I don't mind. I'd just like to see how you work. And I could use the money."

"Okay. How does six dollars an hour suit you?"

"That would be awesome." Tildy knew she wasn't using good negotiating tactics, but this was all working out too well for her to play it coy.

Clearly Grandma had heard enough of the conversation to be satisfied. She gave a tight-lipped smile and nodded when Tildy was ready to hang up. "I'm amazed at how this all came together for you, Tildy. Kind of miraculous." Grandma shook her head loosely.

A wash of warmth ran up Tildy's neck and over her head. She was surely blushing. But it wasn't about modesty or embarrassment. It was guilt. But hadn't Jesus told her not to feel guilty? Or was that just about Darla? She took a deep breath. "I know it *is* pretty miraculous. I feel like … like the whole thing was … Jesus's … was God's idea, sort of."

"God? Really? How's that?"

Oh no. A direct question. "Well, do you ever get this feeling that God is right beside you? Like, so close you can almost touch him? Or even, like, inside your head? And there are these thoughts that are just too good to come only from yourself?" Tildy felt like she might need to go back and clean up the pile of words she had just made.

But then her grandma surprised her. "Huh. I guess I know what you mean. Sometimes God sort of shows me that I'm not really alone." Grandma snorted a small laugh. "I guess you're giving me one of those feelings right now." She shivered briefly. "It feels like a reminder. Or maybe it's even a new thing, but a thing I sort of knew all along." She snickered, shaking her head. "I don't know what I'm even saying."

"It makes sense to me. I've been feeling like it's really hard to put into words what's been happening—with Jesus feeling really close to me."

"Well, that does sound good." Grandma took a pensive tone. "I wonder what started it."

Oh no. That wasn't a direct question, but it was pretty close. "I, uh, was feeling really bad about someone at school saying something mean about Mom. And I think Jesus, like, wanted to save me from those bad feelings." Tildy swallowed hard. She stood from the kitchen table and opened the spices cupboard before remembering the drinking glasses were on the other side of the sink.

Instead of tracking down what Tildy was saying, her grandma remained silent, as if backing away from that delicate edge her granddaughter had led them both to. Maybe it was as scary to Grandma as it was to Tildy. They weren't just talking about God, which was unusual enough, they were talking about God being close.

Tildy ran water in the sink for a few seconds to clear the pipes like Grandma had taught her. And she rubbed against some other really uncomfortable things she wasn't saying. That was another habit her grandma had taught her. But Tildy had said some of what she'd longed to share. That was important. Maybe they could come back to the harder topics later.

On Saturday, the trip to Ms. Sullivan's studio was like the first day of a vacation. Not that Tildy had taken a lot of vacations. She and Grandma and Mom had gone up to Wisconsin the previous summer to stay in a cabin along a lake not far north of the border. It was owned by one of her grandma's clients—a favor to Grandma on a weekend when her client would be summering somewhere more exotic than southeastern Wisconsin.

That lake was exotic to Tildy. She had breathed relatively fresh air at her grandma's house that summer, her first summer living in the western suburbs, but this was a destination even wilder than the green spaces of the 'burbs. The cabin by the lake with tall cattails growing along the edges had an old wobbly boat dock. There, Tildy found a canoe knocking gently on the unpainted planks.

The algae smell over water the color of tea was like the atmosphere of another planet. Tildy had sort of visited that planet once before that. The aroma recalled a school field trip for fourth-grade science, a trip to one of the forest preserves of Cook County. But this time was more like a gift she could savor—no crowd of rowdy kids bumping shoulders, no worksheets to fill out.

Maybe that was the connection—Tildy would have Ms. Sullivan to herself, no classroom full of miscreants to interrupt them.

Ms. Sullivan's studio was in a newish part of town among various single-story office buildings and small industrial plants.

"You think this is it? It's not what I pictured." Grandma had turned the car off. Now she leaned forward and scowled at the buildings through the windshield.

"This is the address." Tildy opened her car door and stepped out. There was a puddle right where she stepped, but not deep enough to soak her socks. She was wearing clogs, just tall enough to keep her above the new melt. A sunny day above thirty degrees was a welcome break.

Out of the car and up the sidewalk, Grandma followed close behind.

Ms. Sullivan greeted them in the little lobby of the building, squinting in the sunlight that angled through floor-to-ceiling windows. "Hello, I'm Jade Sullivan."

"Carolyn Hawkins."

Tildy watched the two women revealing their alter egos. She wasn't ever going to call either of them by those names. It felt somehow wrong that she had even heard them spoken. But that was just nerves. The feeling of first day of vacation had traded places with the first day of school. Tildy had never had a job before. Maybe her nerves were typical for the first day of work.

"You wanna come in and see my studio?" Ms. Sullivan was still talking to Grandma. She led the way down a short hall past dark brown doors with little name plates on them or next to them. "I'm the only artist in this building—unless you count the brewers on the other side." She gestured beyond the little hallway they were entering. "Mostly small offices like lawyers and accountants."

Tildy didn't expect Grandma's lawyer was in an office like this. But then, everything about that attorney was essentially invisible to her.

Speaking of invisible, what about Jesus?

As soon as she thought that question, she felt that warmth she had noticed on the bus when an invisible Jesus pressed up next to her. She fought a shiver. The two women were engaged with each other and might not have noticed Tildy stiffening her back against that shudder.

"How long have you been here?" Grandma was looking around at the clean and bright studio. Those full-length windows in the lobby ran around this part of the building. Would an accountant need big windows like that?

"I'm still moving in. I was teaching out in Rockford before. I just moved to the area. Real estate is a bit more expensive around here, but it seems there's an abundance of small industrial space." Ms. Sullivan was talking to Grandma like the realtor she was.

That seemed like a good approach to Tildy. In the familiar frame where she waited for the grown-ups to get done doing what they needed to do, Tildy let her feet keep moving. The easels and canvases, the paint tubes and sketch pencils were all there. But there was more. The objects on some of the surfaces reminded Tildy of her found-art collection. They were piled in a jumble that begged for arranging.

Ms. Sullivan had mentioned paintings and collages. Clearly her collages had a strong three dimensionality to them. Some of what Ms. Sullivan had plastered to those canvases would be junk to most people—an old sprocket, a work glove with a torn finger, a rusty protractor like they must have used in school before plastic.

The women were talking. Tildy was ignoring them. Until they fell silent. She turned to find them both staring at her. She had not touched anything, but she was reaching toward one of the piles of hardware tangled on a new wooden shelf. She closed her mouth, catching herself gaping again. Then she smiled at the looks on those two faces.

Ms. Sullivan was grinning with a sparkly glisten in her eyes.

Her grandma was smiling, wide-eyed.

Tildy stretched a grin back at them. Caught. But she felt like she was catching them right back. What were those looks on their faces? Was Ms. Sullivan seeing herself in Tildy? Of course Tildy fantasized something like that. Was Grandma seeing something in her granddaughter for the first time?

"I love it." Tildy's voice was thin as paper. She turned toward the rugged surface of one of the collages. "Where do you get all that stuff?"

Ms. Sullivan chuckled warmly. "Here and there. Anywhere I can find it. I do visit the dump when I can, but that's hard these days. Lots of rules about that." She shrugged and tilted her head briefly. "Construction sites are good. Usually I don't get in trouble for picking up bits and pieces around new construction."

"Usually?" Grandma's voice rose more dramatically than Tildy's would have, but Tildy had the same question.

"Don't worry, I'll stay out of jail as long as Tildy's working for me." Her grin was elfish. Puckish. Tildy had learned that word in the fall when the high school did *A Midsummer's Night Dream*.

"Oh." Grandma's response sank as low as her previous one had arched high. Maybe she realized the teacher was joking. Tildy expected there was no serious prospect of Ms. Sullivan being thrown in jail in pursuit of her art.

Tildy allowed herself to wander away from that collage. She could see some canvases stored in vertical shelves, tall wooden slots.

"A friend helped me make the shelving. I need to store things vertically a lot of the time." Ms. Sullivan gestured toward the golden wood in front of Tildy.

Tildy could smell the sweet pungency of the new lumber along with the art-supply odors.

Grandma's voice was warm and amused. "Well, I see I've brought Tildy to the right place." She chuckled. "I expect I can pick her up around five. Is that all right?"

"That would be fine. You have my number in case you need to adjust?"

"Yes." Grandma patted her purse. Tildy knew her cell phone was in there.

Glancing around the room, Tildy could see no landline phone. Ms. Sullivan must have a cell phone. She tried to imagine herself having one someday. Another fantasy.

But the idea of Tildy spending the entire afternoon with Ms. Sullivan was a fantasy realized. Just the two of them. And she was surrounded with real art. Tildy shook her head in little fits several times that afternoon between listening to instructions for cleaning and sorting. Part of the sorting was getting stuff out of those piles, and some packing boxes into more permanent storage locations. Sorting those myriad items was something of an art itself.

"So, here I want the heavy objects. Metal and wood in this big drawer here. And here you can put the lightest materials like these feathers and those dried flowers. And in between, you can put the in-between things." Ms. Sullivan grinned her teachery grin. She was excellent at giving instructions, of course.

"Did these shelves cost a lot?" Tildy had no idea what would constitute *a lot*.

"I sold a collage to a collector in Oak Park. That paid for the wood and the plans. My friend is an expert carpenter, and he put it all together with a little assistance from me."

Immediately, Tildy was curious about this unnamed friend. A guy. She would have to hold that thought for later when she could linger over speculations about the man who might be Jade Sullivan's boyfriend. A large sigh escaped Tildy.

Ms. Sullivan might have misinterpreted that sigh. "Are you hoping to be an artist someday? You definitely have talent."

Tildy had recognized her own talent around the time her first art teacher singled her out. That teacher beamed the same sort of smile Ms. Sullivan wore when Tildy handed in her first sketch of the new semester. Still, the renewed affirmation of her talent was a lift, her toes just skimming the floor as she floated on it. But there was a question hanging there for Tildy to answer.

"Yeah. I think that's what I'll be. I mean it's what I'll do. Art of some kind. Sometimes I think I mostly like collecting stuff and just appreciating it, but I like making art too."

"Interesting. Then you could work in a museum in what they call 'acquisitions.' And you could still do your own art on the side." Ms. Sullivan was mixing some kind of paste, sifting her hands through the goo.

Tildy couldn't pry her eyes from that mixing process. "On the side like you?" She dropped an old doorknob into the heavy-items drawer. "Teaching at the same time you're still making your own art?"

"Yes. It is possible to love your day job *and* your night job both." She bumped an elbow against some cardboard boxes as she transferred the bucket of paste to the table where she was working on a big canvas.

"I'll move those. Do you want me to stack them to save or something?" Tildy tried to guess if the empty boxes would nest together. Lots of them seemed to be the same size. Office paper boxes.

"That would be great. Maybe fit as many as you can into the biggest one and then break the others down for recycling. There's a big bin at the back of the building. I can show you where, and how not to lock yourself out."

"Oh, that sounds important."

"Yes. It is important that you not freeze to death on your first day of work."

Tildy pushed a box of odd items away from the edge of the counter. Compacting the empty cardboard boxes seemed more urgent. She wondered if Ms. Sullivan had started her with the found-art items because she thought it would be more interesting. Tildy *was* interested, but she was fascinated by everything about Jade Sullivan. And she was here to work. She didn't mind getting her hands dirty. The flecks of paint at the edges of her nails from painting scenery at school were testimony to that. Maybe when she got older she would care more about paint on her nails, but she hoped not.

"So, I'm not sure you told me how you knew I would be hiring someone to assist me here. I mean, you're perfect for this, and the timing was absolutely ideal. It was all pretty miraculous."

Wincing at another direct question as well as the word *miraculous* delayed Tildy's answer. Finally she cleared her throat. "Do you really believe in miracles?" She pushed that out at half volume.

"Hmm. Literal miracles? Maybe. I guess most of us use that word pretty loosely."

"Yeah, I know what you mean. But I'm starting to believe more in real miracles."

From the corner of her eye, Tildy could see Ms. Sullivan nodding her head slowly. It felt like she had given her teacher something to think about. She suspected Jesus would approve.

Chapter Twelve
Meeting with a Very Important Person

When Grandma hit the button to end a call on her cell phone in the middle of Sunday afternoon, she seemed to be intentionally avoiding looking at Tildy. But maybe she was just thinking and not looking anywhere in particular.

"Was that the lawyer?" Tildy could ask dangerously direct questions too.

Grandma looked at Tildy and seemed to be testing her teeth with her tongue.

Tildy didn't think she had a piece of candy in her mouth, though that would have explained the set of her jaw.

"It *was* the lawyer. He said we should start by meeting your dad in a public place with me present. He doesn't think we need to write up a legal document unless we can't agree between us."

"Between you and my dad?"

"Right. I thought that was interesting. Mr. Sparger is a very respected lawyer. He could have insisted I meet with him just to collect the fees from such a meeting." Her eyes drifted over Tildy's head. Then she seemed to come back down. "But of course you don't need to worry about any of that."

Tildy nodded. Once again she was waiting for the adults. Trying not to worry about any of it.

"So, want me to call your dad to ask when we can meet him?"

Tildy just nodded. Her grandma didn't say "*if* we can meet him." She said *when*. That settled right where Tildy needed it. And when it did, she felt an extra affirmation, like a word blossoming inside her. The word was *yes*. She assumed the speaker was Jesus. She wanted to laugh. And she wanted to tell her grandma about Jesus speaking to her. But the very thought took her breath away. It was almost like she was worried Grandma would somehow stop Jesus from talking with her. But how would she do that?

She was drifting. Tildy knew it. She was sailing on open water. But maybe that wasn't the best image. The one time she had sailed on Lake Michigan, she got sick to her stomach. Her stomach was fluttering a little now. She had enough to worry about regarding meeting her dad. She had no extra room to think about telling Grandma about Jesus.

"That's okay." Jesus gave Tildy permission to be shy, apparently.

That evening, Tildy didn't mean to listen to half the conversation when her grandma called her dad. But she stood frozen in the hallway outside her grandma's office when she realized who she was talking to.

"No, Derek, you don't have to scramble around to see us tonight. We can see you tomorrow. I don't have any showings scheduled, and Matilda has a school holiday. We can be flexible." She listened some. Then, "No, Monday is fine. Right, just this first time. And that's not so far from you, is it?"

Again the nervous silence, though it was probably more Tildy's nerves than her grandma's. She did detect a higher tone in Grandma's voice. And Grandma called her Matilda. Tildy's dad wasn't going to insist on calling her Matilda, was he? He didn't used to. As far as she could recall, he had been the one to dub her Tildy in the first place.

"It was her idea," her grandmother answered. "Yes. She asked about you. She wanted to know if she could talk to you."

Tildy held her breath.

"It's fine. She doesn't know everything, but it's fine."

Tildy wondered if she should sneak away now, but she couldn't get her joints unlocked.

"Of course. Yes. I've really appreciated you sending them so regularly."

What was he saying? It sounded like they hadn't spoken for a long time.

"I have, and you'll see that she's quite well. You've helped with that."

Her grandmother was on the other side of a door, so Tildy could hear none of her dad's end of the conversation. She tried to remember his voice. Derek. His name was Derek. Had she forgotten that?

"Good. Then we'll see you tomorrow." A short pause. "Of course. Good night." And her grandmother ended by exhaling loudly enough for Tildy to hear through the door.

Tildy turned and snuck into her room, her knee cracking slightly as she passed through the doorway. She hissed a wince. Then she closed the door very quietly, only to open it much more loudly. The latch clicked and the handle sprung with a metallic ring. She cleared her throat. Was that too obvious? She stood in the hallway again, but decided to head for the family room. They usually watched TV on Sunday nights.

Her grandma finally opened her office door. Maybe she had called from in there because it was on the other side of the bathroom and the hall closet. It was a bit farther from Tildy's room than Grandma's bedroom was. Grandma would think of things like that.

Turning around to see her grandma, Tildy didn't even dare to ask.

"Tildy. I just spoke with your father. He's ... He can meet with us tomorrow night."

99

"Where?" Tildy's voice wavered.

"The big bookstore down on 59. They have a nice coffee shop now. And I thought maybe I could peruse books while you talk with him one-on-one." Grandma was a great planner and plotter. It was wonderful to have her making a plan for Tildy to be alone with her dad.

Suppressing a giggle, Tildy settled for a big smile. "Thanks, Grandma."

"You're welcome, of course. I should have set it up sooner. I just wasn't sure if you were ready." She stepped into hugging range, and Tildy obliged.

Tildy wondered why Grandma would think she might not be ready. Not ready to talk to her dad? Or was it something else? Had he changed? Was Grandma protecting her from discovering that? But Grandma had clearly not talked to him for a while. How would she know how he had changed?

"On Highway 59? Where does he live?"

"He's in Downers Grove, I think. Not far from Naperville and that bookstore." She looked distracted, like she was trying to think of something. Maybe she was trying to remember the address on the checks or envelopes.

"Huh." Tildy didn't know much about Downers Grove. She had been to Naperville, to some of the big-box stores along Highway 59 and the intersecting main roads. Obviously people also lived there, didn't just shop there. Tildy's braids were done by a lady in Naperville at a shop not far off Highway 59.

"Did Dad pay for my braids?" That just hopped out.

They had stepped out of their hug. Her grandma raised her head and snorted, then looked like she wanted to say something else, but that didn't make it over her lips. She laughed uncomfortably. "He did. I did use some of the money he sent for that."

Tildy fondled a few of the braids dangling onto her left shoulder. "Cool." Those intricate braids suddenly became even more valuable. And hadn't Jesus told her about Dad paying for them?

Grandma just nodded and laughed in a self-conscious way.

Tildy didn't know what that was about. She knew her grandma pretty well, but that didn't mean she always understood her.

"Wanna watch TV, then?" That was Grandma on any given Sunday evening. It was reassuring to see a normal Sunday evening unfolding even if Monday would be monumental.

School would have been impossible to focus on the next day. Staying home for the Martin Luther King holiday was maybe worse. Part of the problem was another dream the night before. At least Tildy was mostly certain it had been a dream. Jesus had been in her closet and was calling her from in there, but she was so busy worrying about seeing her dad that she kept ignoring those pleas. It seemed to go on and on all night. At least that's how it felt by morning.

"You think he'll bring you presents?" Annabelle came over for a few hours in the early afternoon. She was lying on Tildy's bed.

"Presents?"

"I'll bet he does. It's what parents do when they haven't seen you for a while."

"How would you know that?" Tildy was leaning against the headboard, idly pulling on her lower lip.

"My cousins. Their dad was in the army. And I've seen it on movies too. On TV you see it. When the dad finally gets to visit the kids, he brings a bunch of presents."

"My dad isn't in the army." Tildy knew that was a lame answer, but she didn't want to hang her heart on her dad giving her presents. Getting together with him was way bigger than that.

Annabelle could surely tell how wigged out Tildy was. "It'll be good. You'll get to see him and get to know him, and he'll get to know what you're like now. How many years has it been?"

"Like, five. Or almost."

"Wow. That's a long time. I bet you've changed plenty."

"I wonder if he's changed."

"He must have changed if your grandma wants you to meet him now. She didn't want you to before, right?"

When Annabelle left late that afternoon, Tildy couldn't even eat a token snack. More of those knotted fists in her stomach. Maybe the fists were gripping rocks now. She plopped onto her bed in the same indentation she had occupied most of the afternoon, the mark of Annabelle's smaller body next to her.

"I will be with you, Tildy." Jesus pushed the door to the closet open.

Tildy did a sort of delayed startle. She didn't jump until he said her name. That felt like its own level of crazy.

"Not crazy, just nervous. But you have nothing to fear. Your father loves you. He's excited to see you too." Jesus rested an elbow atop the dresser much like the mysterious man she dreamt about those many days ago.

"I kinda don't get why this is happening now." Tildy pulled her braids free of her collar. Those braids tugging back as she tried to turn her head toward Jesus seemed tied to her approaching insanity.

"It's happening because you asked the right question at the right time."

"The right time for me, or for my grandma?"

"Both. Plus, remember your dad."

"He wasn't ready before this?"

"Ready? Well, let's just say all the parts and players are together on the same page now."

"Like in play practice?" She sat up a bit straighter, repositioning her pillow behind her back. She thought about one play rehearsal she had overheard. Being on the same page literally made sense as the kids walked through their parts with scripts in hand.

"Exactly like that." Jesus pushed her found-art box away from the edge of her dresser with his elbow. "Rest in the knowledge that Grandma and Dad are both ready. You can just go along with the plan. Because you're ready too."

"I am? Really? Then why am I so freaked out?"

"This is even bigger than the first day at a new school. Remember how nervous you were on the first day?"

Tildy could remember that day. Not just the first day of school, the first day at a *new* school. She had hung on at her old school as long as possible and past when it was convenient. She and her mom had lived with Grandma months before the end of the last school year. In lots of ways, Tildy's life had been crumbling bit by bit. Big bits. Her dad already gone, her mother falling apart, and Grandma staying with them for a few weeks at a time. Then short recoveries for Mom just to fall apart again. Enrolling in the new school confirmed that there would be no complete recovery for a long time.

Stepping toward her bedroom door, Jesus reached for the handle.

Tildy, of course, scooted herself to the end of her bed and followed him. What was she supposed to do, let Jesus roam around the house unsupervised?

Having him lead the way directly to the kitchen as if he was used to having a snack with her was like seeing a video of herself that she didn't know had been recorded. Only it wasn't totally weird now. Not really. Because Jesus wasn't just acting. He wasn't pretending to be something. He *was* something. And it was more like Tildy was just seeing what he was for the first time.

Jesus chuckled as he stopped and leaned casually against the kitchen counter. "Part of you being ready has to do with how flexible your imagination is. You've been hoping for things that weren't easy to hope for. You've had to imagine things working out in ways that were impossible for others to conceive." He stood with his arms crossed.

Something occurred to Tildy. "What would happen if Grandma came through the door right now?"

"She would be, what? Surprised?" He flexed his eyebrows up and down, then shrugged one shoulder. "I can be visible or invisible. For most people, invisible is normal most of the time."

"Yeah. I was thinking no one could ever see your face. Isn't that in the Bible?"

"That's true about my Father in heaven."

"We can't see your Father?" Tildy let that bobble up against her feelings about not seeing her own father for so long. "You're not like your Father, then?"

"I am his Son. We are very much alike. If you see me, you see him."

"But I can't see God or my eyes will, like, explode?" She might have mixed in a scene from a movie or two.

Jesus laughed from his chest. "Maybe the real question is how much it matters since you can see me, and since I am just like my Dad."

"Your Dad? You actually call him that?"

"Look up the word *Abba* in the Bible sometime."

"Abba? Like, google it?"

He laughed again. "Sure. Though there are also some old-fashioned ways to search the Bible."

"I should probably read it more." She wanted to get ahead of what would surely come next.

"That would be good. I suggest starting with the Gospel of John. I think you and he would get along quite well."

"Me and him? John? Like, the disciple?"

"Right. One of the 'Sons of Thunder.'"

"What?"

"Sounds like a rock band, doesn't it?" His laugh started low this time and swelled to nearly booming. "The look on your face is precious, Tildy."

Now he was sounding more like a dad and less like a son.

"Dads are sons, and some sons become dads. Some things we never grow out of." He nodded toward the fridge. "All the grown-ups you know are still carrying parts of themselves from childhood. It affects their behavior sometimes."

"Are you talking about my dad?" She watched him step to the refrigerator.

"All grown-ups." Jesus opened the fridge and pulled out the milk carton.

She nodded at him, sensing that she didn't have to comprehend everything he was saying. Understanding God in heaven was too big. What lay ahead for her relationship with her dad was huge.

In this moment, just for today, it would probably be enough for her to just have milk and granola bars with Jesus. Maybe more than enough.

Chapter Thirteen

Dad Looks **Sorta** Like Someone Famous

When Grandma came home, her chattery talk and constantly moving hands probably proved she was nervous too. Tildy thought of what Jesus had said about all grown-ups still having parts of their childhood with them. She tried to remember what she had heard about her grandma's relationship with *her* father.

That side of the family was pretty conservative and pretty religious. They didn't do many divorces. And they didn't have kids with boyfriends or girlfriends. Maybe that was because it was so long ago. Maybe they would have done all those things if they lived in 2003. Tildy didn't know.

She didn't know much about her great grandpa. Grandma rarely mentioned him. But Tildy did recall one thing Grandma had said. She played on the girls' softball team in high school. Her dad rarely came to her games, but she told Tildy the story of him coming to the district tournament when Grandma was a senior. Her dad didn't see girls' softball as important, but apparently a district tournament with his daughter batting leadoff was just important enough to get him there. He even left his job at the car plant early to attend. That seemed like a big deal—taking off work—the way Grandma said it.

"He sat on the third-base side even though our fans were mostly on the first-base side. He did that because I played third base. My dad was like that, breaking the mold for what he thought was important." That sounded inspiring. Why did Grandma have so little else to say about her dad?

Tildy was too nervous to ask about that on Monday. She had also been too nervous to concentrate on her science reading. It was a clever and contemporary science textbook, but she wasn't that interested in it on the best day. She didn't want to know how much time she'd spent staring at the page with the aquatic iguana on it. By the time her grandma called her for supper, Tildy had decided the iguana was ugly after gazing at it too long.

Fish sticks were something she'd loved when she was little. Maybe that was what Grandma had been thinking. Tildy had taken a minute to look up John the disciple in her study Bible when she was supposed to be reading science. John was a fisherman, but Tildy figured he wouldn't have liked fish sticks when he grew up even if he had craved them when he was a little guy.

Absurd thoughts seemed to abound in those oxygen-deprived hours before the trip to the bookstore. A few thoughts even bloomed into shaky words. "I hope I don't totally freak out and cry when I see my dad." Tildy hadn't been thinking about that until she said it.

Her grandma stared at her, half a fish stick skewered on her fork and her eyes scary wide.

Tildy skipped ahead to reassure Grandma. "I don't think I will. It was just a thought that popped into my head."

Grandma chewed that bite of battered fish and blinked. Was she reconsidering the wisdom of having Tildy meet her dad in a public place?

When she started to worry that she had broken something in her grandma, Tildy felt a warm touch on her back. The weirdest thing about that touch was that it didn't make her jump, just like when Jesus stepped out of the closet. How did he do that?

"I'm sorry this is so stressful, Tildy. I suppose it will just get easier the second time." Grandma's sympathetic smile was lopsided, emphasized by raising one eyebrow. Tildy probably did a version of that half-surprised face sometimes.

Right now she was feeling that warmth fill her entire body. And it probably wasn't just from Jesus touching her. The idea that there would be a second meeting with her dad was like discovering money in the pocket of her jeans. Something extra. Tildy took a deep breath and let it out. She took another stab at finishing her green beans at least. Her rice was all gone, but the fish sticks were still lying there trying to spell something. Something simple and a bit dull.

Finally they left for the bookstore. Tildy changed her shirt three times before puffing at herself for being so predictable. She asked Grandma for some makeup, but Grandma talked her out of it.

"He knows you as his little girl. I think makeup might be a shock."

After that, Tildy had to swallow hard to keep from bawling in the bathroom. She remembered her mom putting makeup on her when Dad was still around. "My little princess," her dad had said when Mom presented her in the living room.

But Tildy agreed with Grandma this time and wasn't sorry when she later looked in the little mirror under the car sun visor and saw just plain skin and eyes and lips. Maybe a little lip gloss would have been nice. She shook that off and caught something out of the corner of her left eye. She snorted on second look. Jesus was sitting in the back seat of the car behind Grandma. Tildy stared at Grandma and wondered if she could see Jesus in the rearview mirror.

Jesus shook his head slowly, and Tildy knew that was his answer to her unspoken question.

Tildy warmed to the idea of Jesus riding in Grandma's car to go meet Dad for the first time in years. As fun as that idea was, however, she was getting tired of resisting looking at him back there. Having him in her peripheral vision was more than distracting.

"It's okay, dear. It will be fine." Her grandma reached over and patted Tildy's leg. She must have seen her granddaughter looking and trying not to look in the back seat. That probably made Tildy's nervousness look pretty frantic.

Jesus waved and then disappeared. Or did he just go invisible?

"Mm-hmm." It was almost a voice. Could he speak so close to her ear that Grandma couldn't hear? It wasn't a whisper, really. Just a low, calm assurance.

Tildy looked at her grandma, who was concentrating on the traffic on Highway 59 as they pulled out of the housing development. She showed no sign of hearing that little hum from Jesus. That set Tildy to wondering how all this worked. Were there rules? Just when she thought she knew the principles governing Jesus's visit, he did something different. *Governing principles.* Was that from her science reading, or something else?

Spinning questions around her head like a basketball on her fingertip made the trip up Highway 59 zip past, though the ride was quite a bit longer than the brief seconds she could actually spin a basketball on her finger. She was still working on that skill.

The air was medium cold when they got out of the car at about seven that night. The big-box stores and the highway created their own daylight, the sky a sort of glowing tan against some clouds. The clammy air felt like it might snow, but Tildy hadn't paid attention to the forecast.

She shivered as she walked with her hands in the pockets of her downy coat. She had mittens in her pockets but hadn't bothered to put them on. She forced herself to keep up with Grandma on the walk to the giant bookstore. It glowed golden, offering cozy corners and thousands of books and hopefully hot chocolate. Tildy wondered who would pay for the hot chocolate.

Like her visit from Jesus, a visit to her estranged dad seemed outside the rule book. Or at least it was from the part of the book she hadn't read yet. Her feet were heavy, so stepping at her grandma's pace was hard work.

Pushing through the tall glass doors, they breathed air filled with aromas of coffee, cinnamon, and sugar. The coffee shop mostly disguised the new book smell.

The coffee shop was to the right as they entered. And there, Tildy saw a familiar man. At first, she felt like he was someone famous. She recognized that face. And he was someone important. He was famous to her. He was her dad.

Tildy barked a little sound that was part greeting, part discovery, and part sob. She clapped her hand over her mouth. It wasn't that she had to be library-quiet in the bookstore, especially in the coffee shop. She just needed to hold in whatever was jumping out of her. Maybe that was what people meant when they said "jumping out of your skin."

"Tildy!" Her dad stepped easily between empty tables with his arms spread wide enough for her to fit right in.

She didn't hesitate. Her whole self leapt at him and grabbed him right back.

"*Oof.*" He probably exaggerated the impact of her rush into his arms. And he chuckled. Hearing him chuckle with her ear to his chest reminded her of the way Jesus sometimes laughed.

"Oh, Dad, I'm so glad to see you." She loosened her ardent grip and released a fluttery laugh. For an instant, she wondered if she was allowed to say things like that.

"I'm extremely glad to see you too, my girl." He was grinning big.

Tildy knew that grin. His lower lip formed another smiley curve at the bottom of his big smile. That's how she had sometimes thought of it at night when she couldn't sleep. And here it was, in real life.

"Hello, Carolyn. How have you been?" He reached a hand to shake instead of offering Grandma a hug.

Grandma seemed to hesitate. Maybe she was wondering whether a handshake was enough. Or maybe too much. She grabbed that hand as she must have done every day with sellers and buyers as well as lawyers and agents. This time it was her almost-son-in-law. And this was a momentous meeting. At least it was for Tildy.

"I was thinking you would want time alone with Tildy. I need to find a new book, so I have plenty to do." She waved a hand toward the book displays and chuckled in a way Tildy had never heard before. It was like when Annabelle got caught red-handed at something that wasn't really so bad. Then Grandma stopped mid-turn. She reached for her navy-blue Coach purse and started rummaging. "Let me pay for the hot chocolate, at least."

"Oh, no. You don't have to do that." Something seemed to catch in her dad's throat. "Go ahead and find a good book. And feel free to join us when you're done." His voice rose just slightly as if to force it past some small obstacle. Tildy couldn't tell if that was just nerves or if Grandma had offended him somehow. Maybe it was about the money. Grown-ups usually got weird about money.

That familiar invisible hand patted Tildy warmly on the back again. It reminded her to relax and let the adults work out the details.

Grandma gave up pretty easily on the money dispute as if she wasn't sure she should have even offered. Her surrender was unusual, but then, everything this evening was unusual.

"See you in a bit." Her dad gave Grandma a little wave.

And Grandma practically staggered out of the coffee shop, just missing the railing that guarded the front counter.

Tildy let her eyes land on that counter and the two people behind it. The menu was posted above and behind them.

"Hot chocolate, is it?" Her dad raised a hand toward the awaiting baristas. "You're not into coffee or tea yet?"

"No. Hot chocolate is the thing." Her words staggered just like Grandma did on her way to the books. Tildy cleared her throat. "I still like hot chocolate."

Without thinking about it, Tildy took his hand as they walked to the counter.

He glanced down, but held on tight.

She didn't look squarely at her dad, but she thought his near eye looked a little damp. Tildy didn't try to figure out what he was thinking. She was having enough trouble keeping herself standing. Maybe that was why she took his hand. Or maybe it was an old habit she had completely forgotten about.

They got their drinks. Her dad ordered a latte. And they got pastries. He had a fig croissant, which was not tempting to Tildy. Figs? She got a chocolate scone.

"I guess there can never be too much chocolate," her dad teased her.

She smiled up at him. It felt more like core truth than a tease to Tildy.

At their table, her dad maneuvered a chair into position for her. "I don't know how much your grandma told you about what I'm doing these days."

"Uh, I didn't know you talked to her except that once." She settled her cup on the table next to the scone, which was wrapped in brown paper.

He nodded slowly as if discovering the starting point for the conversation. "We spoke a few times last year. When your mother had to get help." He sat down and seemed to lose what he was saying. "I'm glad your mom is getting help. I'm sorry it's been so hard on you."

How much did he know about how hard it had been on Tildy? Or was he just guessing the obvious? She didn't know what to say in response, so she just sipped her hot chocolate and recoiled as her tongue got scalded.

"Too hot?"

She nodded.

Her dad stood and strode to the counter. He said something and then stood waiting.

The barista handed him a small paper cup.

Dad returned to the table. "Some milk to cool it off."

Something about that was like a magic trick. Of course you could cool off hot chocolate with cold milk. Why hadn't Tildy thought of that? "Thanks. Good idea." She let him set the small cup on the table as she removed the lid from her steaming cup. She dribbled in the milk prudently, not wanting to dilute the chocolatiness too much.

"Leaving the lid off will help too." He held his hand up and seemed to stop himself from saying something else.

Tildy watched that hand. He wore a maroon knit sweater that seemed to make his brown skin richer, deeper. His hand didn't look old to her. How old was he? There were only the usual lines around the knuckles, his harsher than hers. Her hand rested on the table near her cup. She was a predictable blend of her mother's paleness and her father's darkness. Her caramel brown ran right down the middle. But she knew no one would hesitate at the picture of her with her dad. That contrasted sharply with the unavoidable looks she got when she was with her pale mom or grandma.

They settled into talking about school, about his work at a computer store near the city, and about basketball.

"You still playing?"

"Only in gym." Tildy resisted an urge to reach for her elbow to check its progress. "But I'm thinkin' of going out for the team next year. It's a new school."

"Yeah. Sorry about that. I know that must have been hard."

"It's a good school though." She lifted her hot chocolate, about half gone now. "Mostly White kids, but they don't give me trouble, really."

"That's good. There's supposed to be total tolerance in schools these days, no room for people picking on you 'cause o' your skin."

"It's good. It's cool."

The look in his deep brown eyes was something like admiration. Or maybe his hatchling smile was about satisfaction. Whatever it was felt good to Tildy.

"You ever think about getting back together with Mom when she gets outta rehab?" That was probably the third time in their meeting Tildy had let loose a question she hadn't paused to weigh first.

Her dad grimaced with the right side of his face. Only briefly. And his answer escaped as quickly as Tildy's question. "I don't think so." He looked toward the front counter. "She's a good person, Tildy. I don't blame her for her problems. But I ... I have a ... a new girlfriend now."

She didn't say anything for a few seconds. Her whole heart sank under the pressure of a very heavy "Oh." It sank and sank. Her breathing had been cut in half. Her hand shook a little as she started to lift her cup. She changed her mind and let it settle back to the golden-varnished wood of the square tabletop.

"I can still help your mom. And I will always be friends with her." He puckered thoughtfully. "You and I are inseparable, and that makes her part of my life from now on."

"I know." Tildy had to answer. She wasn't happy with how that answer came out. She forced a smile to soften her stark words, to expand her response to more than mere acknowledgment.

He did another partial wince with one side of his face and shook his head so briefly that it only looked like a small turn to the right that he stopped midway. "Life isn't supposed to be so hard for kids, but lots of kids have it real tough."

"Yeah. I know a girl at school whose dad is being indicted for something he did at work. She's been real mean since that happened." Tildy didn't actually know whether Darla had always been mean. She was filling in some backstory Jesus hadn't provided.

Where was Jesus now, by the way? Tildy's stomach was less fists and stones and more like churning water. Half her hot chocolate and half the scone remained, but she was done.

Her dad turned his head, and Tildy followed to see her grandma approaching, a plastic shopping bag dangling from one hand, her purse slung over her opposite shoulder. She was wearing her dark red coat, almost the same color as her dad's sweater. Tildy noted all this in a sort of bubble. Things she would see but could not control were going to happen outside that bubble. The grown-ups would do what the grown-ups would do. She took a deep breath.

Grandma grinned tightly, her mouth a straight line. Her hair was falling over one eye as if she had survived a struggle to acquire the books she sought. "How's the hot chocolate?" She was looking at the table, not particularly at Tildy.

"It's good. Cooled off now." Talking inside her bubble seemed to make Tildy's voice small. She didn't check the eyes of either adult for signs that she wasn't responding the way they hoped. A weariness about meeting the expectations of adults was resting on her shoulders, though she couldn't recall when she had put it on.

"Don't worry, Tildy. This is just the beginning. It will get better." Jesus answered her question about where he had gone and answered some bigger questions too.

Grandma sat across from Dad. Tildy barely noticed the words passing between the grown-ups. It was generic mostly, but they talked about her, and they talked about the future.

She forced herself back into that moment, back into that coffee shop. "So, I can see you again?" Tildy tried not to look or sound like she was begging. But controlling how she looked and sounded seemed beyond reach. She might figure out how to do that later. Maybe she could become regal and unflappable like Ms. Sullivan. Jade Sullivan would surely say exactly what she wanted to in that bookstore coffee shop.

"Of course. We just agreed to that much. Let's talk about when. Do you have a cell phone?" Dad pulled a phone out of his pocket. He flipped it open.

Tildy just shook her head. It didn't seem right for her to answer that aloud. Her disappointment was multiplying. She was even disappointed that she was disappointed. But she tried to rally, pressing a small smile and looking at Grandma.

"I don't think we're ready for that, but I'll give Tildy your cell phone number. And you have the home number and my cell. Tildy keeps track of messages on the machine at home." Grandma didn't sound upset, really. Still nervous, probably, but her voice was softer than the business tone she used on her calls with clients or agents.

"Sure. I guess it's not common for kids yet."

"Yet? You really think kids with cell phones will become common?"

"Our store has cell phones as well as computers. We're seeing families come in to get phones for the kids. It's kind of a safety thing, especially for people who live in the city." Her dad almost sounded like a sales guy for a second there, though he worked in technical support.

A half an hour before closing time, the three of them left the bookstore.

"Maybe we can go see a basketball game together." It didn't sound like her dad was just making that up as they stepped into the cold. It felt more like something he had been saving and had almost forgotten.

"The Bulls?"

"Ha. No. Those are still pretty expensive tickets." He grinned a little less fervently than at the beginning of the night, but maybe that was mostly about disappointing his little girl. "College basketball is good around here. Maybe DePaul."

"Okay. That would be fun." Tildy perked her voice as much as she could with those bags of weariness weighing her down.

They hugged and said goodbyes. This time Grandma hugged Dad briefly too. And Tildy watched him walk to his car, where he turned and gave her another wave. He looked far away and lonely in that big parking lot, flakes of snow beginning to fill the air between them.

Tildy sighed and followed Grandma to the car.

Chapter Fourteen
How to Deal with a Disappointment

"Maybe when your mom gets back and he sees her all fixed up, he'll dump this new girlfriend." Annabelle seemed to be putting some effort into lifting her voice toward optimism.

Tildy loved the effort. She joggled her head left and right, a stream of vapor curling from her nose. The snow the night before had passed and left bitter cold in its wake. Not as bad as the previous week at least. The bus was only freezing, not deadly. "I was just fantasizing, I guess. Like, making up this fiction story."

"A romantic comedy, right?"

"Right. Where you know who's gonna be together at the end of the movie no matter what stupid things they do in the middle of it."

"Yeah. It sounds bad the way you say it, but that *is* why we watch movies like that. I mean, how mad would I be to see Jennifer Lopez *not* get the guy in the end?"

"My mom's not gonna win guys like Jennifer Lopez does."

"Who knows? Maybe they can do miracles in that rehab center."

The mention of miracles awakened Tildy to a sort of whisper in her other ear, the one away from Annabelle. She turned to make sure Peter wasn't trying to get her attention. He was playing some electronic game two rows back, his head bowed and his shoulders shifting and dodging toward victory or maybe just survival.

"I can do miracles, Tildy. I can heal people." It was one of those whisper thoughts. A voice so low it might not have even

been a voice. Tildy's imagination never had a voice before Jesus walked out of her closet.

"You believe in miracles?" Tildy leaned her head on the back of the seat.

"Well ..." Annabelle tipped toward the window and looked at Tildy out of the corner of her eyes. "I go to church, of course. And they're always talking about different kinds of miracles from the Bible and from the saints."

It wasn't an answer. Not a real commitment. But Tildy didn't feel like pinning Annabelle down. Her friend surely wouldn't be easy to literally pin. Annabelle, when she was A.J., had tried out for a wrestling team. But it got too "squirmy," as she said, so it had ended before Tildy met her.

"I wonder if hoping for a miracle means you *do* believe. Or is it just like a sort of desperate thing people don't really believe but just say?" Tildy's church talked about miracles. But they didn't have stories of saints and places where miracles happened like Annabelle's church did. There were some church ladies who talked about a miracle of found money or an open parking place, but Tildy always wondered if that was just about someone forgetting something and then remembering it later, or simple coincidence. That wasn't so miraculous for her.

"Art today." Annabelle poked in her backpack.

"Yep." Tildy smiled automatically.

"So, you didn't tell me much about Ms. Sullivan. How was it working for her? Was it like a real job?"

"I don't know. I've never had a real job before. It wasn't like working in an office like on TV. Not like McDonalds, I guess."

"But, I mean, did she really make you work and not just pay you out of niceness?"

"She is nice, but she's serious too. And she's real serious about her art. Artists have to be serious or it's not worth the trouble at all." Something in Annabelle's questions was fueling a more vigorous defense than Tildy had intended. Maybe it was her friend's lack of reverence for Ms. Sullivan. Tildy wasn't ready to hear any criticism of her favorite teacher.

"So, you cleaned up and stuff. Did you clean her brushes?"

"I actually did clean one brush. She was using it to lay on this glue stuff she used to stick things on this canvas. I mean it was like a real canvas, like a piece you would use to cover stuff in your garage. She said the glue sticks to that better than to a smoother canvas you get at the art store."

"I've never been to an art store."

"She said she would take me with her to help her carry stuff sometime."

"Awesome. Shopping with the coolest teacher. That's awesome."

Tildy snickered and looked down her nose at Annabelle before lifting her head off the back of the seat. She hadn't slept so well last night. The meeting with her dad had the feeling of an unfinished story. And she kept wondering if Jesus was trying to talk to her in her sleep. Two or three times she had woken with a start and made some noise, like "Wha—" in response to something he might have said to her.

That brought her back to what Jesus, or a voice very much like his, had said about doing miracles. She didn't want to get into it with Annabelle again, so she just asked a question inside her head. *"What kind of miracles can you do for my mom?"*

The voice in her head didn't hesitate. *"Healing. She needs healing. I can give her that."*

"Really? Why don't you do that for her in the rehab place?" Tildy had a very sketchy concept of the rehab facility. She tried picturing a sort of fountain in the middle where her mom would drink and be cured of her drug addiction. That would be a stellar miracle. She almost said that part aloud, but was glad she didn't.

Then Jesus said something even stranger. She was more certain it was from him by how odd it was. *"I can heal her with your help when she gets out."*

It would have been nice if everyone on the bus had earphones on like Randy Voss and Kevin Stinger sitting in a pair of seats in front of them. Tildy wanted to talk this out with Jesus. It was getting confusing to do it all inside her thoughts. *"Can we talk about this later?"* She stopped herself from scowling.

"Of course we can. I'm always available. And you might find it easier at home."

Before she realized it, she was nodding her head.

"You don't even have your music on. What are you nodding your head to?" Annabelle had a laugh in her voice. She was good at laughing gently when she laughed at Tildy.

Tildy grinned sideways. "I have my own tune in my own head, girl. Don't you?"

Annabelle did her freaky eyes along with a tight pucker. *"Oookaaaayyy."* She slid a bit farther away from Tildy, then laughed.

Throughout the morning, Tildy struggled to concentrate. Part of the time, her mind was hurrying to get to art class, but then she worried that it would be weird in there. Ms. Sullivan had mentioned something about not letting the other kids know Tildy was working for her. The teacher had slipped it into a bigger conversation about school, but she hadn't insisted on some kind of promise from Tildy. Still, Tildy wasn't inclined to brag. And she wanted to keep what she had with her favorite teacher a private treasure.

Finally it was time to shuffle from the hallway into the big art room, big enough for thirty kids to be spread out at tables for two. The tables were large enough to lie on and still have room to roll one way or the other. Not that Tildy had ever tried that.

She was grinning at some silly thing Annabelle had said, when Ms. Sullivan entered from what might have been an office. The other door was definitely the storage room, from which she had distributed the sketch pads. Tildy reached for her backpack when she recalled her pad. She wondered if they would have to show what they had drawn over the long weekend.

Tildy had finished her second drawing this morning, one started last night when she couldn't sleep. She had done a sketch of an old porcelain teapot in the kitchen on Monday, but the one she really wanted to show Ms. Sullivan was a pair of hands. Her father's hands.

Doing his dark hands in soft pencil was captivating. Digging into the creases and lines from dark to darker had kept Tildy pasted to the task this morning. The night before had just been about trying to capture a rough sketch of what she recalled of those hands.

Hands were hard to draw. Tildy had learned that early. That made it a challenge she chased. A real artist could draw hands. She would prove herself by mastering hands. She wanted to show that mastery to Ms. Sullivan. She also wanted to show her how dark her father's hands were. Was the teacher from mixed-race parents? Was *her* father Black? Her mother White? Or was that just Tildy's fantasy?

Tildy had noticed Ms. Sullivan's hands while working for her. She had watched her teacher mold an old glove onto that canvas with heavy glue. Tildy had been mesmerized even as Ms. Sullivan was asking her about her name.

"Do you know where your parents got the name Matilda?"

"It was my great grandmother's name. My dad liked it even though it came from my mother's family." In that moment, Tildy had wanted to explain everything about her parents. That they weren't married. That they weren't together. That her father was Black and her mother White. She wanted Ms. Sullivan to know all that. But it was too much to fit comfortably into that working conversation.

As she waited for class to start that Tuesday morning, she was still saving all those revelations. Maybe the drawing of her father's hands would be the beginning.

121

Apart from a single wink from the teacher while everyone was focused on drawing a stuffed armadillo on the front table, Tildy didn't really connect with Ms. Sullivan that day. But that was reassuring in a way. They could be a normal teacher and student. Nothing was changed as far as that was concerned. Just one small wink.

Tildy did get to turn in her drawing of her father's hands. Writing that title on the back of it, she dropped it onto a stack of sketches the teacher was going to evaluate after class. So the conversation would have its start. Perhaps it would continue next Saturday.

The other thing Tildy had looked forward to that day happened after she ate a banana and drank some milk at Grandma's kitchen table. She always felt like she could breathe better at her grandma's house. That was probably about letting loose the muscles that tensed against the punches and kicks of the school day. Usually those were just figurative punches and kicks.

"How much do you remember of the stories about me healing people?" Jesus stood in the kitchen with her. He had greeted her at the front door as if he were waiting for her to come home, but the cheesy grin on his face reminder her that it was a trick. Like he was checking to see if she was paying attention to the things he said. Things such as that he was with her all the time.

"How much do I remember? Well, there are some famous ones about loaves and fishes and about walking on water. And there was the water you turned into wine."

"Ah, yes. My food and water miracles."

"Uh, right. But you said something about healing?"

"Blind men. Lepers. A woman with a bleeding problem. A boy who had seizures. Any of that sound familiar?"

"I guess. Don't ask me to tell you about any of those though."

He laughed and took a seat at the table.

She scooted a chair out and dropped the banana peel in the garbage.

"I'm not testing you, Tildy. Just trying to make you a little hungry."

Tildy thought about the banana she had just eaten, but figured he didn't mean literally hungry. "You want me to want to know more about those stories?"

"Yes. Very good. And I want you to get hungry to see things like that happen in your own life."

Her mind drifted to whether she knew any lepers. She did know some older girls who had bleeding problems. At least she had heard stories. Her mind tended to drift after school. That made homework a challenge.

"But you see people all the time who have illnesses. You should look up the times the gospels say I healed everyone in a crowd. That included all kinds of illnesses and oppressions."

"Oppressions?"

"That's how people talk about emotional and spiritual problems that need healing."

"I don't think I've ever heard of that."

"No. It's not something they talk to kids about in Sunday school."

"Yeah. I think some parents would be pis— upset if they did."

"Right. But you're old enough to think about things that hinder people and things that need my healing."

"Okay. Like what?"

"Like fear, for example."

"You could heal someone of fear?"

"A lot of fears come from past experiences. If one of your parents leaves you, and you fear being all alone, you might receive an emotional wound from that fear. And it might look like those dreams you have about being surrounded by bears."

Tildy nearly dropped her milk glass. It was almost empty, fortunately. "Wait." She scrolled into the shadowy images evoked by his summary of one of her dreams. "Yeah ... those bears. Huh."

"Not the football team."

She snickered. "No. I think, in the dream, someone usually says something about how these bears are different. And they're different from other real bears too, not just different from the football team."

"It feels vulnerable. Like you're lost."

"It does. Yeah. Did I have the same dream more than once?"

"Yes. Several times with small variations. It's always dark. There are always some kind of exotic bears blocking your way. Sometimes in a forest. Sometimes in a city. And you are always alone."

"*You're* telling *me* what's in my dreams. That's freaky."

"There's a story in the Old Testament about Daniel doing that."

"So, you can do miraculous things like in the Bible, still? I mean, today?" This was a piece he had set between them several times, of course, but she hadn't picked it up to look at it carefully.

"I can. And I can use you to do some of them."

"But not for lepers. More like for modern problems."

"For problems you see around you and problems you experience yourself."

That brought her back to those dreams. "Are you saying I'm afraid because I'm having those dreams?"

"No. You're having those dreams because you are afraid."

"Afraid of bears?" She couldn't resist joking with Jesus.

He laughed deep in his throat. His smile was always pure and genuine. Maybe that was why she couldn't resist joking with him. He would never roll his eyes at her or make fun of her. But maybe all that was because he existed only in her imagination.

"If you're keeping track, you should know that your imagination has been pretty accurate about some things." Again, he answered unspoken thoughts.

"Like asking to see my dad at just the right time? I never would have asked to see him if you hadn't said something." She could feel her heart racing a little. "And saying those things to Darla and having her be so blown away by it? And Ms. Sullivan having a job for me?" She inflected those like questions, but she knew the answers. She knew those were all things beyond her imagination's normal powers. But she didn't know what this all meant. "Am I, like, a saint or something? Since I can see and hear you like this?"

"Yes. And no." He paced the words for added drama. Then, of course, he grinned at her. "Folks have different ideas about what makes a saint. Strictly speaking, it means the ones who are set apart. Everyone who chooses to follow me is set apart from those who haven't yet accepted."

She shook her head the way she did after a bath. "Wait. So, you mean everyone who is a Christian is a saint? But isn't that just a thing people say? Not literal?"

"You're recalling that visiting pastor. He addressed the congregation as saints." This was not a question from Jesus, just clarification for Tildy. He surely didn't need any kind of clarification.

"Okay, but when Annabelle says saints, she means, like, those kids who saw Mary in a cave or something. Or someone who was fed to the lions."

Jesus pressed a thin grin like one Tildy often saw from Grandma. "I am willing to open the category much wider. I would like more people to include themselves among the saints. And not just as a cute thing for a pastor to say." He lasered his eyes into hers. "Everyone who is with me is set apart. Some just need to be reminded who they are."

Tildy allowed a long pause. "You're saying I am actually a saint, and not because I can see you or can heal people? I just *am* one?"

"Exactly. It's like being a member of the family. The odd thing is the way some don't come inside when the kids are called to supper. You're in the family. You belong. You just have to act like it."

Something in what he was saying seemed even bigger than getting her head around a Jesus that shows up at your house and makes jokes. Even bigger than Jesus teaching her Bible lessons. At least it felt bigger to her. Maybe just because it was so strange. New. Not strange in a bad way.

"I don't want your head to explode, so I'll leave you with that much. Remember you have to finish those rewrites on your short story tonight."

Tildy started to chuckle in her throat, and it went on for longer than she expected. Maybe she was a little crazy. Crazy was fun, it turned out. Unless you stopped to worry about it. She did that, and the chuckles stopped. She took a deep breath.

Jesus was advising her on her homework. Why not? Some people did call him *Teacher*. She snorted another laugh. She liked telling herself jokes too.

As she told herself that one, Jesus disappeared from sight, but his laughter lingered in the kitchen.

Chapter Fifteen

Alone After School in the Auditorium

Tildy liked being behind the stage to work on sets for the school play. She also liked walking down the aisle between rows and rows of empty seats. Having such a large and elaborate space all to herself felt like great riches. Her auditorium. Her stage.

At least until some seventh grader walked through the doors and started testing for echoes. "Hey! Hi. Ho!" There wasn't much reverb, but that didn't stop kids from trying.

Part of what made the place special for her was knowing so many of its secrets. Tildy actually knew how to open and close the huge black curtains. She knew what those curtains smelled like. Not that she really wanted to know that part. It was something she had learned when some eighth graders decided to trap her inside the heavy velvety fabric. She knew how that fabric felt against her cheek.

She wasn't about to say any of this to anyone. Not even Annabelle.

"What about me? Do you trust me?"

Tildy was at the front of the auditorium now. There was no one near her. No one she could see, anyway. "Do I trust you?" She started aloud but tapered her volume. Two of the nerdy guys who were part of tech crew were stomping down the aisle in their too-big shoes on their too-big feet. Eighth graders.

She turned away from those guys, as if that would help, and tried talking to Jesus internally. *"Is that why I don't tell anyone about seeing and hearing you? I don't trust them?"*

"You know the answer to that, of course." His voice seemed to come from all around her and inside her at the same time. She

shuddered at the sensation. It was like feeling someone's breath as they whispered in your ear. Sound paired with a skin sensation.

Two girls Tildy worked with on scenery came out from behind the curtain. "We're gonna work over there." Missy Rico pointed to her right as she faced Tildy.

"Oh, okay. Are we doing those flowers today? The vines and stuff?" Tildy had been looking forward to the three-dimensional project involving black electrical wire and fake leaves intended to look like vines in a forest.

"Yeah. Ms. Sullivan is gonna help us with it."

Tildy's heart leapt and she just suppressed a giggle. "Oh. Cool." Her voice quavered slightly. She hoped no one was close enough to hear it. The old theater was built for quiet except voices coming from onstage. Tildy had no idea how they did that, but she was pretty sure those two eighth grade boys staring at her now could explain it. She escaped the grip of their eyes and climbed the stairs to the stage, arrowing for the opening in the curtain at stage right.

The girls, four of them now, pulled supplies out of boxes where they had sorted and stored them a week ago. Though it had been simple manual labor, Tildy enjoyed it for the project it anticipated. She had no idea it would be a project led by Ms. Sullivan. Nor did she, at the time, know how much that work would be like her work in Ms. Sullivan's studio.

Jade. Tildy kept that name hidden inside. The point of even thinking it was probably that she had it to hide. She had something private with Ms. Sullivan that the other girls wouldn't have. Knowing she would not say any of this to the other girls made it even more valuable, more precious. Like the silence in the theater before others arrived.

"Hello, Tildy. I didn't know you were working on scenery." Ms. Sullivan swept into the offstage enclave in her long black sweater. She wore a teal satiny blouse under it that glowed against her golden-brown skin.

Tildy stared at her a bit longer than she would have liked. Then she tried for a quick recovery. "Oh. Yeah. Always looking for ways to use my art." Where did that corny answer come from? Had Tildy ever said that to anyone before? Had she ever even thought it? She noted that this sort of mouth leak was happening a lot lately.

Ms. Sullivan grinned, maybe amused. Hopefully she wasn't laughing *at* Tildy. That didn't seem likely. "Well, I'm counting on all of you to do the hands-on work. I'm not dressed for sitting on the floor." She raised her hands, presenting her black slacks and sweater as evidence of what she was saying.

"Are we gonna do the papier-mâché part today?" Courtney Greene scrunched her nose as she asked. Maybe she was thinking of the sour smell of the paste.

"Not today. I still need to get the frames for several more of these." Ms. Sullivan reached a long arm and tapped twice on a papier-mâché stump. "Just the vines today. We can do the rest of the stumps and logs later when the carpenters get finished."

Tildy thought of Ms. Sullivan's friend who helped her with the shelves in her studio. She also thought of Peter, the shop class recruit. He was more likely to be one of the carpenters they were waiting for, more likely than Ms. Sullivan's man friend.

"Not all of these leaves are green." Missy was riffling through the box of fabric leaves, like ones you can buy at a craft store. There were thousands in the huge wooden box.

"We should intersperse the various colors to highlight the vines. Not too many green in a row. Then it will actually look more natural even if it looks strange up close."

"Did you study this in art school?" Tildy watched Ms. Sullivan sift her hands through those cloth leaves but still listened to what she was saying.

Ms. Sullivan turned toward Tildy and laughed. "No. Not in art school. In high school, doing staging for plays. And I even did a cousin's wedding in their backyard when I was eighteen."

Picturing Ms. Sullivan as an eighteen-year-old hypnotized Tildy. She found herself blinking uncontrollably. She raised her hand toward her eyes to make it look like she was cleaning some dust out of one. She didn't know exactly what started that blinking, but she didn't want everyone wondering.

"You look shocked at the idea I was once a high school girl." Ms. Sullivan set her hands on her hips in mock horror.

"Oh, you're not that old." Courtney fanned a hand at Ms. Sullivan to shoo away such nonsense.

They all laughed. But Tildy guessed they weren't all laughing about the same thing. She didn't know what *she* was laughing at. Just nerves. Probably.

Fortunately they had real work to do, and it was fun and interesting, so they could all get past that awkward start.

Tildy unspooled a long black wire. She suspected the manufacturer of that wire didn't have vines in an enchanted forest in mind, but that was part of the fun of stage crew. Creativity on numerous levels. And Ms. Sullivan's work outside of school with found items surely equipped her especially well for this project.

As Tildy threaded green, brown, golden, and russet leaves onto the wire, wads of scrunched dark green crepe paper in between, she sat pretzel style on the wooden floor. For whatever reason, the shiny wood floor extended far behind the part of the stage visible from the theater seats.

Ms. Sullivan squatted next to Tildy, helping her arrange the wire so the finished part didn't twist back into what Tildy was working on. "You, of course, have a knack for this. Did you tell me you had some found-art items at home?"

Tildy had mentioned her box of treasures that Grandma called junk, though she hadn't said that about her grandma. "Yep. I guess no one could find a green vine in the dump or a construction site." Tildy grabbed another stack of leaves and unspooled more crepe paper. She noticed her hands were greenish blue from the scrunching of the crepe.

"Oh, some things are fun to find, others are fun to make. You're doing a great job." Ms. Sullivan patted Tildy on the back before standing up.

As she finished her first vine, Tildy noted that the teacher offered the other girls as much attention and encouragement as her. But that was what she expected. That was the right way for a teacher to act. So why was it bothering Tildy? She snorted at herself for the obvious jealousy. And, for whatever reason, she started missing her mom.

Of course she had been missing her mom for weeks and weeks. She and Grandma only saw her for a few hours on Christmas Day. Otherwise, Tildy was an orphan. Or she had been until she drank hot chocolate with her father.

Living with her grandma didn't really feel like being an orphan, but Tildy missed her mother. She even missed the weepy and cursing mother she had sometimes found when she came home from elementary school. She missed the mother who made excuses for being fired from another job, excuses Tildy knew she didn't have to believe.

And the scissors Tildy was using to cut the crepe paper reminded her of wanting to cut herself. Why remember that now? Why miss her mother now? Or, at least, why start sweating and itching at the realization that she was missing her mother?

The part that bugged her most was how stupid it was to miss her mother's messes. And sometimes her mother just seemed like one mess piled on top of another. How could Tildy miss picking up those messes? Some were literal, others were just the weepy mess that was her mother. Tildy hadn't gotten big enough to physically pick up her mom when she was crashed on the floor sleeping something off. Was it downers? That's what Tildy found online when she searched for what illegal drugs would make you sleep on the floor.

She was breathing like on the basketball court, and she realized she was stuffing the leaves on that wire with more force, as if annoyed at every little resistance. Then she stopped.

Someone put a hand on her shoulder. But Ms. Sullivan had left to get more supplies. Still, Tildy felt that hand on her shoulder. And she allowed warmth to ease over her like poured honey.

She was shaking. Not violently. But shivering, sort of. What happened? What started all this?

"Jealousy."

She stopped her hands when her brain stalled over that word. She felt cold all of a sudden. And the voice wasn't the same. Was it the word itself that made the difference? Did Jesus have to say a word like *jealousy* differently?

"That's not me. That's your accuser."

By now Tildy was on her feet. She couldn't remember standing, but there she was, looking down on her second vine.

"Tildy?"

She was standing with her arms spread slightly, her feet planted like she was defending on the basketball court. Or like she was being pulled in two directions. She turned to look at Ms. Sullivan and stood up straighter. "Huh?"

"Are you going somewhere? Did something happen?"

Something *had* happened. Tildy didn't really know what it was. But something had happened inside her. Something had popped like a soda can she once left in the freezer too long. For a moment, more than one foreign voice was humming in her head. What was that?

"Oh. No. I think this one is almost done." Tildy nodded to the vine at her feet. "Uh, is there a certain way you want it finished?"

Nodding for a few seconds, Ms. Sullivan was still looking at Tildy, not at the homemade vine. "Well, that's a good question. Let's look at the other one you did. We need to leave some wire at one end at least—maybe both ends—to attach it. Maybe you can slide the leaves away from the other end so there's wire free on both of them." She sounded almost mechanical in her answer, like the configuration of the vine wasn't what she really wanted to talk about. Or maybe that was just Tildy's imagination.

They made eye contact for a couple seconds, then Tildy refocused on the job at hand. Maybe her next job was figuring out how to act normal when she didn't feel normal. "Okay, I'll adjust it."

"Then maybe you could look at what the other girls are doing and give them a hand. We want them all to look pretty much like the ones you made."

It was a compliment. A vote of confidence. And maybe it was a way out of whatever bog Tildy had gotten mired in.

"Tonight. We can talk about it."

That was a familiar voice. The voice of reason, really. The voice of someone she was becoming more and more aware of. And someone she was needing more. At least feeling that need more.

Chapter Sixteen
Tell Me about This Jealousy Thing

Tildy stood in the bathroom, her bare toes curled against the chilly tiles. The eyes in the mirror had arrested her. Her own eyes, of course. They seemed mad. What was she mad about? Maybe it was worry. Worry about people. Her protection from going crazy and doing things like cutting herself was mostly other people. How reliable were any of them? Could she rely on any of them to tell her the truth?

The feeling that her grandma had held back big parts of the truth about her dad was sort of strapped down inside Tildy. Under some big Band-Aids maybe. That Tildy had learned early not to trust her mother was a fact just waiting for a good scream. Something about seeing Ms. Sullivan being friendly to the other girls had stirred that same kind of distrust. What if Ms. Sullivan went away?

Back in her bedroom past bedtime, Tildy said good night to her grandma at the door before slipping under her covers. She rubbed her feet back and forth to warm them against the sheets. Just then, in the hallway, Grandma had seemed to look right past Tildy, pulling out an old good night from some past day when she was paying better attention. Grandma seemed to worry a lot. Maybe she worried about some of the same things Tildy did. Weren't they both worried about Tildy?

"She has worries you don't yet know about. She's having heart palpitations, for one thing." Jesus spoke gently from where he stood next to her dresser. But even his muted tone might have been loud enough for Grandma to hear.

Tildy looked toward the door.

"Your grandma is distracted, so she might not notice low voices in here, but I'm using a voice only you can hear."

"Huh."

"You can just whisper. I can hear you when you whisper no matter how far away I seem to be."

Tildy adjusted her covering for her braids and settled her head on her pillow, blinking rapidly as if each bat of her eyelids tabulated one of the numerous oddities in what Jesus was saying. She found one thing she couldn't simply bat away. "What's a heart ... pal ... pap ... uh, what you said?" She squeezed her voice down from low to a whisper.

"It's a missed beat or two. Sometimes a fast beat. She feels it as a fluttering. It's not serious at this point, but the doctor is debating putting her on medication. Not a pacemaker yet."

Tildy was blinking again. "Wait. Why are you telling me this? Should you be telling me something my grandma hasn't told me?"

He released a long breath through his nose and nodded slowly. "I'm glad you're thinking of that, Tildy. Confidentiality is important in lots of things. And, when I tell you about what's going on with someone's health or emotions, it would be good for you to keep it between you and me. Of course you can talk to the person—to your grandma in this case—about what I tell you."

"So, like, I should go to her and say, 'Hey, Grandma, Jesus told me you have heart problems?'"

He chuckled, keeping his voice low. "Actually, that might be something you should do in some cases, but first you have to decide whether you want to tell your grandma about how we've been communicating lately."

Obviously that hurdle had not been moved out of the way yet.

Jesus pushed on after a brief pause. "She's basically healthy. You don't have to do or say anything right now. But think about whether you're willing to be used to heal her."

"Think about it? How?"

He smiled broadly. "That's a profound question. Figuring out how to think about all these things is important. I'm in no hurry. I'm not going anywhere."

How many times had he emphasized that he wasn't going anywhere? It seemed an important point to him. It was probably an important point for Tildy.

"What was that thing that happened to me in the auditorium? With the jealousy?"

Jesus showed no sign of surprise at the change of topic. He answered without hesitation. "You heard my voice. But you also heard the voice of the accuser."

"The accuser?"

"Satan. His name means 'the accuser.'"

"Satan was talking to me?"

"Not himself. He has minions that do his bidding."

Tildy couldn't help smirking at what sounded like something out of a superhero cartoon. "He has minions?"

Smiling briefly, Jesus nodded and spoke seriously again. "One of them was accusing you of being jealous."

"Wasn't I? Wasn't I being jealous?"

"You were, weren't you?"

"Yeah. So why does Satan bother telling me about it?"

"Sometimes speaking the truth can be an accusation. Like someone pointing out a flaw, and not doing it in a way that helps you. Satan accuses in order to make you feel condemned. Like a failure. But of course you're not a failure even if you feel some jealousy once in a while."

A deep breath helped her sort some of that. Not all of it. "Aren't I, like, jealous all the time though?"

"I don't think so. You don't obsess about it every moment of every day. But you do see some lives around you that seem enviable. You should, however, remember what you discovered about Darla. You envied her assertive confidence before you found out about her father's troubles. No one is set up perfectly in this world, my dear."

"So I shouldn't be jealous of anyone?"

Jesus had walked to the side of her bed. He easily slipped down to sit on the floor next to her, leaning back on the little dresser that served as her nightstand.

The move stunned Tildy into sustained silence.

"You don't mind, do you?" He looked up at her with questioning eyes, but no sign of anxiety.

"Uh, no."

He returned to his teaching voice. "A bit of envy at someone else's apparent situation is hard to prevent. Not impossible, but hard. It's important not to condemn yourself if you feel a little jealous. It's important to get help if you're obsessing over it."

"Where would I get help?"

"I'm never far away." He raised his left hand like he was in school.

"So, you can, like, heal me of jealousy?"

"You're a bit skeptical about that, but the answer is actually yes."

She breathed out of her nose and tried to imagine how he could do that. Then she snorted a laugh. She was stuck here trying to imagine such a thing when she could just ask. "So, how do you do that?" Her whisper had a little laugh in it this time.

His chuckle bounced his chest but remained so quiet that she hardly heard it. "I'm so glad you asked," he whispered back. Then he seemed to corral his humor. "Contentment is a lifelong project—learning to be content in all circumstances. You can read what my friend Paul wrote about that." He paused as if waiting for her to figure out who Paul was. "And I know you don't want to hear about a lifelong project at age eleven. That's worse than the social studies assignment." He rolled his eyes and ended with a grin. "But you can take comfort in the fact that you have a whole life to work on it. I'm helping you start by reminding you what you found out about Darla. Don't forget to pray for her, by the way."

Tildy had not even thought of praying for Darla since they talked last. "Sure. I should do that."

He raised his eyebrows. What was that look supposed to mean?

"You mean I could do it right now?"

"Right. Tell me what you want."

"What I want for Darla? I hardly know." She shook her head slightly at her lack of detailed understanding. "Maybe I could just pray that you take care of her and her family and sort of leave it to you. Like saying, 'Your will be done.'"

"Excellent. I'm already working on it. Thanks for asking."

She rocked the bed with her chuckles. It was still hard for her to tell when he was joking. Part of it was how much fun he seemed to have with serious stuff. He didn't seem worried. But here he was, sitting next to her bed to help her with the stuff that worried *her*. Tildy's eyes stung with the thought.

"I love you, Tildy. That's what it's all about. That's what everything is all about."

That didn't help stop her from crying. The bed rocked harder with her barely-contained sobs. What would she tell her grandma if she came in to check?

Jesus reached up and patted Tildy's hand where she was gripping her pillow. Then he reached above his head and found a tissue without even looking. He handed it to her.

She laughed aloud, then covered her mouth with the tissue. Holding all that in literally hurt. Her chest ached. And that reminded her about Grandma. "You sure she's gonna be okay?" Again, she didn't stop to introduce the change of topic.

He nodded in long sweeps. "It bothers her, and she's worried. She's worried the treatment may be worse than the condition. Right now it's not going to kill her or even put her in the hospital."

In a way, his assurances sobered Tildy more. That's what was at stake? Her grandma's life? Or at least a stay in the hospital?

Jesus patted her hand again.

When he dropped his hand, she followed it downward, her eyes closing in the process. That was a mistake. Getting them back open was hard work.

"Don't worry. Get some sleep. It will be good for you to rest and recover. I bless you with sweet rest, Tildy, and complete recovery from the stresses of this day."

She had never had such an elaborate good night before. Or maybe what he said was more than just good night. A blessing? Was that what Jesus was doing? Blessing her sleep?

She could feel her breathing deepen, and still she could hear Jesus breathing right next to her. She pried her eyes open for half a second. Then she tried again. The second time, she managed a smile before her lids shut and sleep took her away.

Chapter Seventeen

Sorry about the Basketball Game, Tildy

Her dad called her on Thursday. Grandma had already agreed that Tildy could go with him to the DePaul women's basketball game on Friday night, so why would he call on Thursday?

"Tildy, he wants to talk to you." The sad resignation in Grandma's voice answered the why questions.

"Tildy, how are you?" There was a lot of background noise, though none of it sharp or loud. Her dad didn't sound like he was shouting.

"I'm okay. Where are you?"

"I'm in the server room of a business client. They had a drive system crash on their main file server and then a crash on their backup system server." He seemed to sigh, but it was hard to tell amidst the rushing noise behind his voice. "It's a big crisis, and I'll be on it right through the weekend." He paused. "I'm sorry. I'll check for the next game that's in town. It might be the men's team. I hope you don't mind."

Out of the huge disappointment at hearing her dad cancel their basketball game, she extracted a small packet of assurance that he was sincerely trying to reschedule. He wasn't just blowing her off. "It's a major disaster?" She didn't want to just say okay and goodbye.

"It's one of those things where the solution to fix one problem fails and needs a solution of its own. I'll be on tech support calls all night and will try to get some sleep on the floor in between."

"You can't go home at all?"

140

"I need to be here when files finish copying or if the copy fails. That way I can restart, or I can advance to the next part of the recovery. People really rely on the data on their computer networks these days. It's a big deal to the company. Someone told me they would lose twenty-five thousand dollars a day until this is fixed."

"Are they blaming you?"

"No. Fortunately, I wasn't the one who set all this up. And even the guys that built it aren't to blame for the hardware failures. A string of unrelated breakdowns. Really a perfect storm of disasters."

Tildy knew that phrase, "Perfect storm," though her grandma hadn't let her see the movie when she rented it on tape. "Okay. Well, don't drown in that storm."

Her dad laughed. "Don't worry. I won't. I'll lose some sleep, but that's all. The good thing is, I get paid for all these extra hours."

"Oh, that's good. Maybe you'll get enough to pay for Bulls tickets."

"Ha. No. I don't think so." He sounded a little distracted.

Recalling something her grandma said about her dad not being rich, Tildy thought of how to apologize. "Anyway, I'm glad we can go later."

He laughed uncomfortably as voices in the background seemed to accelerate his tone. "Okay. I've been on hold. I need to talk to these people now." He paused. "I love you, Tildy. We'll get together as soon as possible."

"Okay. Love you too."

She couldn't remember saying she loved him when they met at the coffee shop. Nor during the one short phone conversation to set up the basketball game. But maybe he said it now to make up for letting her down.

Grandma was looking at her. Tildy didn't like that pitying look. She averted her eyes and carried the cordless phone to its cradle. Her dad would take her out to a basketball game. Tildy didn't need anyone to feel sorry for her, not about anything.

"That's too bad, kiddo. We'll get another date set up."

Tildy nodded, still avoiding that look on Grandma's face. But avoiding Grandma felt angry. And Tildy didn't want to be angry with Grandma. Her grandma had real things to worry about, bigger than Tildy's hurt feelings. She raised her eyes and checked for some sign that her grandma was ill.

She still looked young to be a grandma. She had colored her hair recently, so there was none of that gray trail that showed along her parting every few weeks. Would Tildy go gray some day and need to color her hair to keep looking as young as she felt? Grandma might not have spent much time feeling young with her daughter in drug rehab and her heart palpa ... papal ... whatever that was.

Grandma got a call on her cell phone. She answered as she walked toward the hall, probably headed for her office. She wasn't likely to be going to the bathroom. She had a rule about talking on the cell phone while using the bathroom. Tildy knew that from trying to call her when she missed the bus home once. Grandma didn't answer that time because she was "indisposed." Tildy wasn't sure she would ever want a cell phone.

As Grandma drifted away, Tildy drifted back toward her dad's excuse for canceling their date. If he was faking it, he was *really* faking it. The sound of the computers whirring away and that voice that interrupted their call. He had all the sound effects together for a convincing story. But he wouldn't make it up, would he?

Just how much she needed to go back and rewrite her past with what she had recently learned about her dad was still unattainable. A big project. Hopefully not lifelong. And that reminded her to get back to her research paper for social studies.

As she clicked on the shortcut for the online encyclopedia allowed as a source for school papers, the house phone rang. Grandma seemed to be on another call on her cell, so Tildy stood from the computer desk and grabbed the handset. "Hello, this is Tildy."

"Tildy, Annabelle."

"Hey."

"What ya doin'?" Annabelle had a lying-down sound to her voice. She had a phone extension in her bedroom. A privilege she could have until she "abused" it. Whatever that meant.

"I'm working on that research paper for social studies."

"I wonder why *we* don't have to do that. Or maybe it's just later."

"I'm pretty sure you have to do it. It's part of that integrated learning thing they're advertising."

"Mm-hmm. Are you excited about the basketball game with your dad?"

"Uh, we're gonna have to reschedule."

"Oh no. What happened?"

"Work. He had an emergency with a client and has to work nights and weekends until it's all fixed." As her own words threatened to sink her into murky depths, Tildy sensed a sort of glow. Like a beam of sunlight penetrating those depths. She turned and jumped, just stopping herself from screaming.

Jesus was sitting at the computer scrolling on the encyclopedia site.

She really wanted to say, "What are you doing?" but she didn't want to hang up on Annabelle right away.

"You think he really has work?" Annabelle made half a sound at the end that implied she wanted to say more.

"I don't think he's lying to me. If there's anyone I should suspect of lying around here ..." She lowered her voice. "It's my grandma. And probably my mom."

"Any word from her?"

"Grandma said she called asking for some insurance information today while we were in school."

"You think she calls while you're not around because she's, like, hiding?"

Annabelle seemed to want there to be trouble between Tildy and her parents. The trend was annoying Tildy. "She has a schedule. There are rules about when she can do things like outside calls. She probably needed the info right away to pay for something or other." She sniffed hard. "And I don't think my dad's lying. He just has an important job and there was this perfect storm kinda crisis."

"Perfect storm? Like the movie?" Annabelle did get to see movies like that. She was her dad's movie buddy. Her mom only liked romantic movies, and her brothers were too young, so Annabelle got to watch action movies with her dad.

"It's what he said. I think he was sort of joking." Tildy was looking at Jesus, who seemed to have found what he was looking for on the computer.

He turned and smiled at her like he was waiting.

Waiting for what? To use the phone?

He laughed aloud when that thought rattled through Tildy's brain like a gumball on the way out of a machine.

She grinned at him as she listened to something Annabelle was saying about that movie with George Clooney in it. Then it seemed that Annabelle was done, and Tildy had missed what she said. "Well, I gotta get back to work. I wanna get all my resources ... uh, documented tonight."

"I don't like how that sounds. I hope we don't have to do that project."

Tildy was pretty sure Annabelle's class would do it too, but she was in no mood to spoil even a slim glimmer of hope. "See ya."

"Yeah. See ya at the bus tomorrow."

When she hit the button to hang up the phone, Tildy looked down the hallway. She heard a bump like a drawer closing in grandma's bedroom. Then she looked at Jesus and forced herself to talk inside her head. *"What are you doing?"* Maybe it would have been better to whisper that. A harsh, suspicious whisper seemed in order. It was like Jesus was misbehaving.

He stood from the chair and gestured his relinquishment with one hand. "All yours."

Again, Tildy looked down the hall.

"She can't hear me. I'm talking so only you can hear. *Or would you rather I just talk inside your head like this?*"

The transition from an audible voice to one inside her head made her stagger on the way back to the chair. Tildy shook that off as she sat down. *"Are you really asking what I would like, or do you know which I'd rather have already?"* Though she kept her reply internal, she realized she made a little grunting noise as if for emphasis, which was a weird thing to do.

"You're a smart girl. Of course when I ask you a question, it's not because I don't know the answer. I ask you so you can answer for yourself. And to show you that you have choices." He sat in the swivel rocker not far from the computer desk. He spun it away from the TV toward Tildy.

That raised another question. *"If my grandma came out of her office, would she see you moving that chair?"*

He grinned and looked down the hall.

Just then, her grandma opened the door to whichever room she had been in. She was wearing her slippers, which made a shushing slap with each step.

Tildy's heart did something that might've been one of those palpa things her grandma had. Was Grandma going to see Jesus? The prospect frightened Tildy, but maybe it wasn't really fright. Maybe she was excited. Having Grandma see Jesus would change everything. But Tildy wasn't sure she wanted everything to change.

Just as Grandma got to the end of the hall where she could see Tildy clearly, Jesus disappeared. Tildy assumed he was just invisible. She studied the chair for a second to see if it was moving at all. It seemed to rock just slightly—in her imagination at least.

"You expecting a guest? Or are you hoping I'll help you with your research paper?" Grandma looked at that empty chair. She cast a glance toward the kitchen. That probably implied she was not planning to help write a sixth-grade research paper this evening.

"Uh. Ha. No. You take it easy. I think I have what I need." That was when Tildy realized the encyclopedia article currently opened on the computer was exactly what she had been looking for. As she scrolled through, she also found links to other good articles. "Huh." She said that louder than she'd intended. And she was looking at that chair again when Grandma asked about it.

"What's that?"

"Oh." Tildy turned quickly back to the computer. "I just realized I found the perfect article." But that sounded dishonest. "I suppose Jesus helped me, really. I must have been praying for help without even knowing it."

"Huh. Well, good, then." Grandma sounded less convinced by the goodness of Tildy's story than the words implied. She gazed at Tildy a bit longer before turning toward the kitchen.

Tildy was glad to be rid of Grandma's eyes crawling up her neck. She pulled her yellow hoodie closer against a shiver. Then she looked at the chair. She still felt like someone was watching her.

Jesus came into view for a second and then faded out again. The chair joggled just a little after he did that.

"What's wrong with the chair?" Grandma crunched a cracker as she poked her head out of the kitchen.

"Oh. I wasn't ... I mean, it's not the chair. I was just looking that direction. I was thinking about ... some stuff."

"Ah. 'Staring into space' is what it's called. But you have to get older before you can get away with that, dear."

Tildy snickered, though she didn't know exactly what her grandma was talking about. It was more nervous laughter at being caught staring at someone who had just gone invisible. Jesus really was messing around. At least messing with Tildy.

She felt a gentle pat on the back and shook her head, returning to the computer screen and hoping her grandma hadn't seen that head shake. Tildy was running out of gas. It was getting close to bedtime. She wondered if Jesus would sit by her bed and talk to her as she fell asleep. That sent a warm wave up her spine. She copied the links to the articles and printed everything in about ten minutes. Then she gathered her pages and logged out of the computer.

Though she couldn't see him, she felt Jesus accompanying her. That feeling was so strong that she changed into her pajamas in the bathroom. She didn't even say it internally, but she hoped Jesus would get the hint and not follow her in there.

She met Grandma on the way out of the bathroom. They hugged and said good night.

When Tildy got back to her room, Jesus was already seated next to her bed. She had to climb up from the bottom to get past him comfortably.

"You realize your restrictions for me being with you are the same ones your grandma has for cell phone usage." His head was cocked a little and his eyebrows raised. He was joking. That much Tildy figured out. But it took her a second to catch what the joke was.

"Oh. The bathroom. Yeah." She hissed a laugh.

She settled under her blankets and looked at him. This time no crisis topic came to mind even after her dad had canceled on her. She could see peace in Jesus's eyes. There was nothing to worry about with her dad. She did tell Jesus she wanted him to help her dad get his work done and to be healthy even if he didn't get a good night's sleep.

And eventually they said good night. Just like that. A normal good night between Tildy and Jesus.

Chapter Eighteen
What's the Beauty of Being Tildy?

Watching Ms. Sullivan scrub rust off the spokes of an old bicycle wheel, Tildy tasted a metallic tang from two feet away.

"You see, it won't all come off. But that's fine. We want it to look natural. We just don't want flakes of rust falling off and messing up the other items in the collage."

Tildy wondered about the word *we* in that explanation, as if they were partners in this enterprise. Yes. She agreed. They both wanted the collage to be free of rust flakes. And they agreed the old bicycle wheel should look natural and not pretty and shiny.

"Maybe that's what attracts me to this kind of art." Ms. Sullivan set the wheel down and handed Tildy the steel wool. Tildy took it in her gloved hand.

"What?"

"Imperfections as beauty. I think that makes me feel more confident. It makes me feel like I could be beautiful even with my dings and dents." Ms. Sullivan had never said anything so deeply personal in their hours together. But this was just the second Saturday of Tildy working for her. Maybe that was how it would be from now on. Two girls sharing their hearts.

"But, you mean you don't think you're beautiful?" Tildy pushed against a feeling that Ms. Sullivan should realize how lovely she was. And yet she pulled back from being a mindless admirer, like a groupie or something.

Ms. Sullivan slipped her gloves from her slender hands and snorted a laugh. "Thanks, Tildy. But beauty is something you have to feel in here." She rested a few fingers on her chest just above the *V* where her lavender plaid flannel shirt showed a black T-shirt. "Compliments from people are nice, but until you feel it in here, you're deaf to what's said out there." She waved a hand toward the tall windows.

The day was bright and cold. Snow that had been on the ground for weeks still sparkled in the yard outside the studio. Tildy knew Ms. Sullivan wasn't talking about hearing compliments from the yard. She knew what *out there* meant. She had been preoccupied lately with listening outside compared to listening inside.

The conversation lagged as Tildy contemplated what made something beautiful. She turned to scouring the spokes of a second bicycle wheel.

Ms. Sullivan would be working on another project entirely, one that included paint and brushes. But the teacher didn't go far away. Her easel was near the windows, full sunlight falling over her shoulder. "Those were your father's hands you drew for class?" Ms. Sullivan was focused on the photo she was painting from.

It took Tildy a second to transition back to school. In her mind, they were working in a space entirely disconnected from school—or anything else for that matter. "Oh. Yeah. That was my dad."

"Ah, nice. He' s dark, then?"

"He is. And my mother's White."

"Oh … Just like me." It was the girliest thing Ms. Sullivan had ever said in front of Tildy. Then again, this was just their second day working in the studio.

"Really? I wondered. You never can tell."

"No. No use assuming."

Tildy stalled again. This time she wondered if Jesus had fed her the hope, if not the assumption, that Ms. Sullivan might have mixed-race parents like her.

"I saw those hands so well rendered in that heavy pencil, and it made me wonder if you had a mother of a paler shade." The teacher smiled benignly, still looking at the photo and at her canvas. She held a medium-weight brush tipped in yellow acrylic paint.

"Maybe that's part of what I question about myself being beautiful." Tildy stayed focused on her own hands as she said that.

"Oh, yes. The history of race in America greatly complicates one's ability to feel acceptable and even beautiful."

"It was a little strange seeing my dad. I mean, I live with my White grandmother, and I live around here where almost everyone is White. So, seeing him was like seeing a stranger. I guess that was for lots of reasons."

"You hadn't seen him for a while?"

Tildy realized she had jumped right past introductions and explanations. She blamed Jesus for that. He was always blurring the line between what she was saying and what she was thinking. Blaming him in that way made her smile as she turned the rusty chrome wheel to get a good angle on more spokes. "I haven't seen him in the last few years. There was a big break up with my mom, and he tried to take me away from my grandma, apparently. I missed it when it was going on. I was, like, six. Anyway, I get to see him now. My grandma trusts him more now."

"Where's your mom?"

Tildy inhaled long and slow, measuring how much she was willing to reveal. "My mom is ... in drug rehab. She should be getting out in a week or two. Depending on how she's doing."

"Oh, Tildy. I'm sorry to hear that." Ms. Sullivan settled her brush on her pallet. "I guess it's good she's getting help though." She took a deep breath and looked more squarely at Tildy. "I had a cousin who really turned his life around after going to a day program for a month. So it is possible to overcome an addiction." Her smile had a question woven into the attempted reassurance. Maybe she didn't know how much Tildy needed to hear that hopeful story.

"My dad was gonna take me to a basketball game last night, but he canceled because of work." Was that a complaint?

"Huh. What's his job?"

"He's some kind of computer repair guy. He works for a store closer to the city that has contracts to help companies with their networks and stuff." That Tildy couldn't explain it precisely didn't worry her. She doubted Ms. Sullivan needed the technical details.

"Sounds like a good job."

"Yeah. I don't think he had such a good job when he left my mom. I think that's one reason why my grandma didn't trust him so much before."

"But she trusts him now?"

"He's been sending money to help us out even though they never said he had to do that."

"Oh, that's good. There are men that have a court order to send support that don't do it. So that's good for him. And for you."

"Yeah. I guess I got used to not trusting him 'cause my grandma only said bad things about him before if she said anything. Lately it was like he didn't even exist."

"You know, it's hard to feel good about yourself if you don't feel good about your parents. So that can be hard on you." Ms. Sullivan held a smaller brush with darker paint on it now.

Her words sounded a lot like what Jesus said earlier. He said that about her cutting herself. Tildy wondered if she could tell Ms. Sullivan about the temptation to cut. She wasn't ready to even consider telling her about Jesus.

But Tildy stuck to firm footing. "Someone else was telling me about that. I guess I thought my dad was out of the picture, like, not impacting me. But maybe there's no way to really not be impacted by our parents."

Ms. Sullivan let out a long sigh. "My father was a good man. He worked hard for the family. But he didn't take good care of himself. He had high blood pressure all the time I knew him, and he died of a heart attack a few years ago. I really miss him. We weren't always really close, but having him gone is a big loss."

Tildy knew she was supposed to say something. Grown-ups did that. But the things they usually said didn't come to mind. What came to mind was that those usual responses never sounded real to her. "I guess there are lots of ways to lose our parents."

"Yes. And a few ways to keep from losing them entirely. Or to keep from losing what they give us."

"Really? How do you do that?"

"My dad worked his way up in a sanitation company. From riding a truck in the old days, to supervising workers, to managing the operation for a whole town in Ohio, where I grew up." She nodded toward the pile of found objects on the table in front of Tildy. "I often think of him when I find a treasure buried in garbage. He taught me that a lot of treasures are like that." Her voice fell to nearly a whisper.

Tildy glanced at Ms. Sullivan to see if she was crying. It was hard to tell with the light from the window so bright behind the teacher. And Tildy allowed silence to enter the room, silence only interrupted by the *shush shush* of her steel wool on the spokes.

That night at home, Tildy and Grandma watched a video together. Hugh Grant was funny and charming, and there was a kid in the story who wanted him to be his dad. Tildy avoided eye contact with Grandma as she sorted through feelings the movie stirred. One of those feelings was suspicion about the way Grandma shifted so often in her seat and ate popcorn so quickly. She and Grandma rarely finished a whole bowl between them.

No way was Tildy going to say anything. She was still sorting how she felt about Grandma keeping her dad away all those years. Talking to Ms. Sullivan had stirred an ants' nest that afternoon, and Tildy was pretty sure Grandma didn't want to talk about any of it.

They said a muted good night after the movie, and Tildy did her bedtime routine in distracted silence. She went to the bathroom to brush her teeth a second time before finding her toothbrush wet and remembering she had done that already.

She let out a long sigh when she landed in bed, adjusted her hair covering, and scrunched her pillow into just the right thickness.

"How are you doing, Tildy?" Jesus was there by the closet door.

She shook her head at him even as she lay on her side. "You know, you don't have to hide in the closet anymore." Her voice scratched in her throat. She only remembered to lower her volume at the end.

He smiled and stepped toward her bed, squatting easily into that spot in front of her nightstand. "I know, but I thought it was sort of funny. Me hiding in your closet."

"I guess the joke got old."

"Ah, yes. Jokes age even faster than girls do." He winked at her and rested the back of his head against the little nightstand.

She liked the way he settled in wherever they were. Annabelle wasn't even that comfortable with Tildy yet.

"You and I are much older friends than you and Annabelle." He turned his head so she could clearly see both of his eyes. Friendly eyes. Knowing eyes.

"I think what gets me the most is the way you look at me like you know all about me, and you're not mad about any of it." She kept her voice low, just above a whisper.

Jesus replied at the same volume. "It's what you were designed for—an open and trusting relationship without any little parts reserved for doubt and fear."

"Reserved?"

"It's easy to get used to people not meaning what they say all the time. Words lose their strength because people so often withhold a true investment in what they're saying. Withholding your trust becomes a habit and then it becomes an expectation."

"So I don't trust one person just because other people aren't worth trusting?"

"What you live with is generally *partial* trust. Trust with a *but* at the end." He quirked a little grin.

Tildy didn't know if that was a butt joke, but she smiled at it anyway. "Like the way I worry that my dad really doesn't want to see me even though he says he does."

"That doubt is also the work of your enemy. He takes something that's true and applies it in a way that's *not* true." Jesus seemed to check with her and then continued. "It's true that you hadn't seen your dad for a long time, and it's true that people haven't always been trustworthy, but that doesn't make it true that your father is lying to you about wanting to be with you. He is true in his love for you. Trust me on that, Tildy. And trust him. He's not perfect, of course, but you can trust him. What you can't fully trust is all the circumstances of the world working in favor of your relationship with him."

"But can't you take care of that? Can't you make things work out so we can be together?"

"I could, but that would break the rules. If people are going to be free to choose good or evil, then it's not fair for me to force them to always do good." He leaned his head away and squared his face toward her. "The world you live in has been controlled and manipulated by your enemy for thousands of years. That means bad things are going to happen. That's how much influence the devil has around here."

"Around here?"

"Earth. We threw him out of heaven. Good for heaven, but we threw him down to the earth where he has been messing things up for millennia."

"A thousand years?"

"Many thousands of years."

"So why do people blame God when things are messed up?"

154

"Exactly. Why do they? The devil is in the disaster business. My Father is in the redemption and reconciliation business. And he's not done with his work yet."

At that moment, Tildy wished she had a recording of what Jesus was saying. How could she understand all this now? But later ... Maybe it would be important for her to know this stuff when she grew up.

"Read the Bible, Tildy. It's all in there. Read it with me in mind. And don't let anyone read it for you in a way that doesn't fit with my part of that story."

She raised her weary eyebrows at the commercial for Bible reading. But she knew it was true, of course.

"And you can always consult me directly. I'm not going anywhere. You just have to remember to consult me even when there are lots of distractions."

"So you're gonna always be like this for me? Sitting next to my bed at night?"

He smiled, maybe a bit sadly. "This is unusual, as you know. But I'm right next to everyone who follows me whether they sleep or work or play. You just have to trust what you can't see most of the time. Just like you have to trust your father's love for you when he's working a long weekend."

"Are you helping him now?"

"You want me to?"

"Yes. Of course. Help him with his work. Help him get sleep and stuff." She took a deep breath. "And help him think of me."

"He's already thinking of you."

"Then help him know ... help him know I love him."

"He knows, Tildy. He already knows."

Chapter Nineteen
Fixing That Thing with Grandma's Heart

On Monday morning when Grandma said she would be home late because of a doctor's appointment, Tildy remembered what Jesus said about the problem with Grandma's heart. Tildy even took a moment to pray for her grandma while she was waiting for her toast to brown. When she stopped praying, she kept worrying. And she wondered how to turn her worries into prayers. All that accompanied right up to time for the bus.

"Goodbye, Tildy. See you tonight." Grandma was wearing her robe, her hair wet from her shower.

Tildy waved as she slipped out the front door and offered a muffled echo of that farewell. She had wrapped her scarf around her face to defend against the early morning freeze. Her breath billowed around her head as she prayed silently. *"Please protect Grandma's heart. And keep her from worrying."*

"I will do that. I will protect her. She gets to choose whether to worry or not."

Though still invisible, Jesus was answering her. She couldn't tell if the words had come from his invisible mouth into the cold air or right into her ears under her hat and scarf. A patch of ice distracted her from that question, forcing her to shuffle for several steps.

Tildy laughed when she saw Annabelle ahead of her, skidding a few feet on another patch of ice closer to the bus stop. She was glad she was far enough away that Annabelle didn't hear her.

Instead of laughing at her friend, she wanted to be huddled together against the cold. And she paused to envy Peter and James their perfect timing. She didn't wear a watch, so she didn't know how long the wait would be. And she envied those kids whose parents thought it too cruel to make their offspring wait in the freezing cold, giving them a ride in a heated family car instead.

Those were not warming thoughts, but Annabelle's bright eyes above her white scarf had a comforting warmth to them. "Good morning, fellow arctic explorer." Her shorter friend was hunching even lower, though there really wasn't much wind this morning.

Tildy looked around at the snow. "You think we could find the north pole if we explored around out here?"

"Yes. We don't have to take a sled to the north pole. The north pole has come to us."

Tildy chuckled. Annabelle could be particularly funny when she complained about things.

In stark contrast to the bus stop, the school building was extremely warm that day—some malfunction with the thermostat. No one complained much. It was better than the furnace breaking down. Though on a day like this one, they would get to go home if the boiler broke.

In gym, Tildy nearly ran into Darla, who was wiping something off her face where she stood by one of the drinking fountains.

"Oops. Sorry. Didn't see ... Are you okay, Darla?" Tildy almost didn't recognize her own voice. Her throat was suddenly squeezed. And it was weird hearing herself sounding concerned about Darla.

A hard sniff, and Darla shook her dark hair out of her face. She didn't look directly at Tildy. "I'm okay. Thanks for asking." Then she turned and faced Tildy. Her eyes and mouth shifted in a way that worried Tildy. "My mom is coming to get me after this class. Something happened with my dad's case. They want me at home." Her lowered head and hooded eyes seemed to dare Tildy. Dare her to do what? To make fun of Darla or her dad?

"Oh no. That doesn't sound good. Well, I'll keep praying for you." Tildy hitched a little on that last line, worried that she hadn't actually remembered to pray for Darla as she had intended. But she *had* prayed that time Jesus reminded her.

Darla looked toward the red brick wall and sniffled again. Then she faced Tildy. "What happens if he has to go to prison?"

"Oh man. Is it really that bad?" Tildy's back and neck prickled.

"I don't know. They called me to the principal's office. My mom wouldn't tell me anything. But it can't be good if they're pulling me out." Her face was red, her dark blue eyes flashing.

"Parents are hard to deal with." Tildy shook her head and avoided staring at Darla. Other kids were shuffling past, a couple bumping Tildy where she blocked the way onto the court.

"You got that right." Darla's eyes softened even as she pressed herself against the wall. She was looking intently at Tildy. "Thanks for talking, Tildy. We should get together some time and hang out."

Tildy smiled slightly. The gentle tone in Darla's voice was enchanting, but Tildy had to force that smile to stay in place when she realized she didn't really want to hang out with Darla.

"I guess we'd better get to class." Tildy led the way onto the court, Darla dragging along behind.

Tildy didn't envy Darla having to go through a whole gym class wondering what her mother was going to tell her. She shook off another shiver at the thought.

Her elbow recovered, Tildy played well during the half-court scrimmage. She scored twice and stole the ball once.

Todd Barnes gave her a high five when the game ended. He was one of the cool jock guys. He was probably happy because she'd passed him the ball several times, leading to two or three baskets.

Tildy saw Darla leaving the locker room without changing out of her gym uniform, but she didn't get to say anything more to her. Tildy wondered if she would find out about more sad dramas by Jesus telling her the problems of other bullies.

The fact that Tildy wasn't planning to become best friends with Darla made her feel half relieved and half guilty. She was still thinking about it when she got home that afternoon. With Grandma going to the doctor, Tildy was tempted to invite Annabelle in, but she suspected Jesus would get her for breaking the rule on after-school activities. And then there was Annabelle's mom or dad—whichever one was at home today. Her dad was a firefighter and worked odd hours sometimes.

"G'bye." Tildy's voice was less muffled this afternoon. The temperature was less deadly. She and Annabelle exchange farewells from faces free of swaddling scarves.

"See ya tomorrow." Annabelle shuffled toward home.

A note on the kitchen table about what to warm up for supper focused Tildy's anxiety on her grandma's health. That worry would probably keep Tildy from eating an early supper. Her stomach didn't usually have room for both worry and real food. A small yogurt was all she ate before homework. Then she sat down at the computer to dig into the social studies articles Jesus had helped her find.

He took his spot in the swiveling rocker. "You need some help?" He said it with such bright innocence that she only recognized the joke when she sat down and looked him square in the face.

"Hmm. I guess I never thanked you for finding that article for me last week."

"Right. There were other things going on that day."

Tildy scooped another dollop of yogurt and ignored the urge to remember exactly what had been happening that other night. She was stretched between wanting to get done with the social studies research—at least the part she could do on the computer—and her worries about her grandma.

"Instead of worrying about Grandma, why don't you heal her instead?" Jesus had said some crazy things over the last two weeks. Sometimes he was joking. This didn't seem like a very good joke.

"You mean, like, praying for her to get better?"

"You could do that. Sometimes that's enough for certain ailments. But sometimes you have to reach out and touch someone."

That sounded like a TV commercial Tildy had heard someone making fun of, but it was an old ad and an old joke. On the other hand, Jesus *was* pretty old. She turned toward the computer and shook her head. Scraping the last of the yogurt out of the cup, she licked the spoon. "I have no idea what you're talking about."

"Really? Are you sure?"

That stopped Tildy. She set the yogurt cup down and put the spoon inside, careful not to tip the cup over with the weight of the metal spoon. Maybe she did kind of know what Jesus was talking about. He had said something about it before. But she still didn't see how it applied to her and Grandma. She glanced at Jesus. "So, you can heal her, but you need me to reach out and touch her?"

He nodded in a way that rocked the whole chair. Clearly he was trying to teach her something, but his patient smile and relaxed eyes implied he wasn't nervous about her getting it.

"You act like you're used to people not understanding what you're telling them." She clicked the shortcut for the encyclopedia. Then she spun toward him a little. She was in an old kitchen chair, so she had to provide all the swivel herself.

He chuckled. "You're very intuitive, Tildy. You can tell what I'm thinking."

"Maybe 'cause you're really just inside my head." She focused on the computer again.

"It's okay. Go ahead and get your homework done. When your grandma gets home, she'll be tired. When she sits down on the couch and asks if you don't mind cooking supper, you'll know it's time to heal her."

Tildy's head dropped forward one notch, and she turned toward Jesus like a rusty robot. "What? Are you, like, predicting the future?"

"I am. And if it happens as I say, then you'll know I'm not just a guy who lives inside your head. And you'll also know it's time to offer your grandma healing."

She snorted at him and shook her head. "Okay. If you say so."

Her confusion over what Jesus was saying made the social studies homework seem more attractive, if not really interesting. She told herself she would figure it out when Grandma got home. Hopefully she would be done with homework by then.

But it proved difficult to concentrate, and the research probably took her twice as long as it should have. She did manage to document her sources, summarize her conclusions, and explain what other sources she would seek out at the library. They were going to the school library during class sometime this week as far as she could remember.

Tildy was starting to recognize how hungry she was when Grandma came in the door. She entered through the kitchen with a puff of cold air and a heavy sigh.

"You okay?" Tildy hadn't planned what she would say to her grandma about the doctor's visit. She was used to not knowing any of the details about Grandma's health. But her worry squirted that question right out of her. And she recalled what Jesus said about being able to sense what other people were thinking. All that nearly obscured Grandma's answer in Tildy's ears.

"Oh, nothing to worry about. I just have to make a decision ..." It could have been a complete thought, but Grandma said it more like a sentence fragment. Though Tildy still wasn't exactly clear on what constituted a sentence fragment.

"A decision about what?"

Grandma was taking off her coat. She paused and faced Tildy from outside the doorway to the kitchen. "The doctor wants to

put a pacemaker in my chest to keep my heart in rhythm ..."
Again, she seemed to cut off rather than complete her answer.
She stepped to the closet and started to hang up her coat.

"Pacemaker? That sounds serious."

"Well ... that's part of what I'm deciding about. The cure may
be worse than the disease. They're not even sure I *need* a
pacemaker. He just wants to be safe. Doctors are often just
trying to cover their ... tails."

Tildy didn't know what Grandma meant by that "tails"
comment, but she was interrupted from trying to figure it out
when Grandma started doing things that felt to Tildy like a part
in a play.

Shuffling into the family room, Grandma plunked down on
the couch. "Would you be willing to warm up the supper? I'm
exhausted."

Tildy paused to see if she knew what would happen next in
this rehearsed scene. Jesus had predicted this, hadn't he? Even
the basic news about Grandma's heart should have surprised
Tildy, except Jesus had told her about it before. So she was only
acting surprised. Maybe the rest of the scene was still unwritten.
Was Tildy supposed to write it? To do something?

"Now would be the time, Tildy."

"I know." She said it half complaining and half laughing. She
stopped abruptly when she realized she had responded to Jesus
aloud.

"You know? You know I'm tired?" That deep line between
Grandma's eyebrows showed like a knife cut.

"Uh, yeah. I mean ..." Tildy didn't want to be dishonest,
especially not now, with Jesus and pacemakers and her
Grandma's heart all in play. "I have this ... I have an idea that ...
that Jesus wants to heal your heart. I, uh, actually knew you had
... palpitations before you told me." That was the first time Tildy
had successfully pronounced the *p* word.

Grandma tweaked her head a bit to one side. "But I didn't tell
you that part. I didn't say anything about palpitations."

"That *is* what you have, though, isn't it?"

Grandma had relaxed a little. She sat up a bit straighter. "But what are you saying about Jesus?"

"He wants to heal you."

"You say that like he told you directly or something."

A very strange giggle escaped Tildy's throat. Though, compared to the truth about Jesus hanging around with her, that goofy giggle wasn't the strangest thing happening to Tildy.

Grandma, on the other hand, was staring wide-eyed.

Tildy straightened her face out. She wanted to do one of those Three Stooges face wipes that Annabelle used to do when she was A.J., but she had to get serious here. "I don't know if you will believe me ... I mean, I wouldn't believe me if I hadn't ... but I have. I mean, I really feel like Jesus is communicating with me these days. He even told me you would ask me to cook dinner, and you would sit on the couch, and then I would know it was time to offer to heal your heart. Or maybe for *him* to offer to do it." She stumbled back into the part she couldn't understand. It was like giving a class presentation and having some smart kid ask a good question she should have known the answer to.

Jesus came to bail her out. At least that's what it felt like. He appeared next to her and smiled. He nodded but didn't say anything, like he was waiting for her to put a quarter in and ask him a question. That was a weird thought, like he was one of those fortune-teller booths at the fair.

"What are you looking at?" Grandma's voice cracked.

"Well, for me, it really seems like Jesus is standing right there between us." She stood from the computer chair. She almost asked whether Grandma could see him, but it was pretty obvious she couldn't. Grandma probably would have screamed like she did when that chipmunk found its way into the house last year.

"He is? I mean, you do?" Grandma was rattled. That was concerning. Grandma rarely got rattled.

"Let's heal her now, Tildy." Jesus turned to look at Grandma.

"He wants to heal you now." Tildy flipped her gaze from Jesus to Grandma.

"She can wait to believe you if her palpitations stop. She's having one right now, by the way."

"He says you can believe if you're healed, and that you're having a palpitation right now." Tildy's eyebrows were raised so high that it started to ache. "I mean, it can't hurt to try, right?" Her voice cracked too.

Grandma didn't look convinced on that last point, but Tildy followed Jesus when he stepped over to the couch.

Monitoring Tildy with those haunted eyes, Grandma finally said something. "How did you know I was having a palpitation right then?"

"Jesus told me."

"If this is a game, Tildy, it's such a strange game." Grandma's face seemed unable to settle on a recognizable expression, her mouth and eyes in constant motion, almost twitching.

"But if you're healed, then maybe you'll believe me." That seemed like a good solution to Tildy. She was even more certain that she was really seeing Jesus now. Grandma had just confirmed it yet again by admitting that Jesus was right about the current heart palpitation. She could tell her grandma wasn't convinced, but she couldn't imagine a better way to persuade her than having those palpitations go away.

Grandma was breathing hard through her nose. Was that part of the palpitation?

"You would be able to tell when they went away, right?" Tildy paused next to the couch.

"I don't have them all the time." Grandma had raised her eyes toward Tildy, but she sneaked a peek to where Jesus was standing.

Tildy knew Grandma was just reacting to her, not seeing Jesus for herself. And there were some pieces of this that needed to be cleaned up, but Tildy was anxious to get past the awkward part.

Jesus seemed willing, if not anxious.

"You should sit down and put a hand on her shoulder. Then say what I tell you to say." Jesus gestured toward the couch cushion next to Grandma. He sat down on the opposite side.

When Tildy looked past her grandma to Jesus, she could sense the couch vibrating. That was not normally a feature of this couch. More likely, Grandma's leg was doing the nervous bounce thing Tildy had seen kids at school do. Her mom did that sometimes too, but she had never seen Grandma do it before.

"Just ask for permission and then follow my lead."

"Ask for—" Tildy cut herself off and turned from Jesus to Grandma. "Sorry. Is it okay if I put a hand on your shoulder and ... pray for you to get better?"

For a moment, Grandma stared straight ahead, which was weird. When she looked at Tildy again, her eyes were still haunted. She stuttered, "I—I ... f-feel this strange s-sensation right ... here." She raised her wavering hand to her chest.

Tildy recoiled involuntarily, but then proceeded to place her hand on Grandma's near shoulder. Jesus had already done that on the opposite side. That was when Tildy decided the vibrating wasn't the same as those nervous leg bounces. It was something more. She looked at Jesus.

He was smiling, as usual. But he was smiling at Grandma. That was new.

Tildy just stared at his smile for a few seconds.

He woke her from that stunned study by nodding toward Grandma.

Grandma was smiling. That was much more unusual.

Though there was no angel choir singing an a cappella chord, Tildy suddenly had a revelation. Grandma was smiling because she was being healed. That was a wild leap, of course. Grandma was smiling because something nice or something happy was going on. That didn't necessarily mean she was actually being healed. Right?

"Ask her." Jesus was still there. He hadn't wandered off, even if Tildy's mind had.

"Grandma?"

"I feel good. I feel very good." She stopped smiling at the opposite wall and turned. Now Grandma was smiling at Tildy. Just like Jesus.

Chapter Twenty
Including Grandma in Her Big Secret

Tildy couldn't have easily described everything that happened that evening. She felt a bit like she had left the room several times, missing some critical events.

And Grandma seemed suspended between shocked and doubtful. That added to Tildy's lost feeling.

After supper, Tildy wandered around the house. She got on the computer, but forgot why she did that. She turned on the TV, but didn't find anything appropriate. She talked to Grandma, but spoke about everything besides what had happened on the couch with Jesus.

Maybe Grandma was still thinking of it as what happened on the couch with her crazy granddaughter. Though she should probably say something about counseling or meds if that's still what she was thinking.

Finally, when Tildy arrived in the kitchen for a bedtime snack, Grandma came in right after her. She was wearing her long pink robe, her hair squashed forward as if she had been reading in bed already.

Grandma looked at Tildy for a few seconds as if she didn't recognize her. Then she smiled with her eyebrows slightly cocked. "I'm feeling very good, Tildy. No palpitations since ... since you prayed for me." She reached up and adjusted Tildy's purple satiny covering for her braids.

Tildy didn't remember exactly praying for her grandma. The sitting on the couch and the hand on the shoulder, she could remember. Grandma vibrating was unforgettable. Jesus smiling like he was excited about what was coming—that was clear. But what had she prayed? It might be useful to remember that part.

It seemed to work. It might be useful for healing something else in the future.

"I'm glad you're feeling better. I was a little worried about you."

"When I told you about the pacemaker?"

Tildy let her head bend to one side, her braid cap brushing her shoulder. "Well ... actually it started when Jesus told me you were having those ... pal-pit-ations." She grinned. "I was having a hard time saying it before."

"Before?" Grandma reminded Tildy of a cartoon where someone's eyes are spinning around. It was almost that bad.

"When he told me about it." She let a little whine sneak into her voice for a couple syllables. Grandma wasn't getting it. And it seemed like she was trying *not* to understand what Tildy was saying.

Grandma leaned back against the counter and crossed her arms, a thoughtful pause on her face, her lips puckered just slightly. "So ... you can tell what Jesus is thinking?"

Nodding, Tildy leaned her hip on the kitchen table, but she didn't cross her arms. "He pointed out once that I was doing well at figuring out what he was thinking. Maybe I'm just getting to know him better."

"Well, that's a good thing, I would think."

Tildy couldn't figure out what kind of response that was. She also pondered how strange it felt to know something her grandma didn't know. And this was even more important than knowing the capital of South Carolina.

"I think he started coming to me because I was having trouble. Kids at school were saying mean things about Mom and me. And me not knowing anything about Dad. And Jesus came to talk to me in my room."

"You mean it was just like he was actually there?" Grandma's voiced slipped toward a more childlike tone.

"It was. And it wasn't creepy like I think it would be to have a man come into my room."

Grandma's head rocked back. "It was or it wasn't like having a man in your room?"

The creeped-out look on Grandma's face warned Tildy to be careful what she said next. As she thought about it though, she almost laughed. What was Grandma going to do, send Jesus to his room? Force him to stay in his closet? She corralled the smile starting to stretch her face and cleared her throat. "Not like having some stranger in my room. That's what I was saying. It was Jesus. And he knows me. And I know him. I asked him into my heart, remember? So it's like he's always been close to me."

"Oh. Sure." The wrinkles on Grandma's forehead intensified. "But how did you figure out you could pray for me to be healed? I mean, you just knew I needed it, and you seemed confident it would happen."

"I was only confident because Jesus told me it would happen." Tildy hesitated. "Actually, he didn't really promise anything in particular would happen. He just told me it was time for me to … to offer to … pray for you." Tildy wasn't sure she was getting that exactly right. It was hard to stride past Grandma's confused eyes when Tildy wasn't totally sure where all this was headed.

Grandma nodded and stood up away from the counter. She kept nodding and just walked out of the kitchen. Had she come in here to get a snack? If so, she had forgotten.

Tildy had to pause for a few moments to recall what it was *she* had wanted. She was distracted by Grandma's unhinged staring. Her mute confusion made Tildy more uncomfortable than having a man appear out of her closet.

That thought seemed to strike Jesus as funny. She could feel him laughing like he was right next to her, his warm breath against her cheek, laughing and hugging her. But when she paused in the middle of the kitchen to try and focus on that feeling, it went away.

She was pretty sure Jesus didn't entirely go away. She was starting to actually believe he was there when she couldn't see or hear him. And maybe she should have believed it all along. That was probably part of what bugged her about the way Grandma was acting. She seemed surprised about Tildy speaking to Jesus and him speaking back to her. How could you invite someone to be in your heart and never know he was there, never know what he was thinking?

Well, Tildy had lived like that herself, of course. Before the closet incident. *B.C.*—before the closet. She laughed at her own silliness and pulled a box of whole wheat crackers out of the cupboard, still chuckling.

A dog barked across the back fence. She turned toward the kitchen window. The corners of that black mirror were decorated with a fractal pattern of frost from the very cold day. The reflection was of Tildy looking out and another set of eyes next to hers. She glanced over and saw no one there. Was that Jesus? If it was, then he was doing something different. "Was that you?" She said it aloud, hoping Grandma was too far away to hear.

"Tildy." Jesus said her name, and the feeling was entirely different from when she saw those strange eyes.

The feeling from that reflection reminded her of the voice that said "jealousy" in the school auditorium. The shiver this started was not exciting or fun. Her voice low, she spoke to Jesus. "No. Those eyes weren't yours. It ... felt different."

"Right. You can tell the difference if you take a moment to pay attention."

That made paying attention a bigger deal suddenly. In school, of course, teachers were always talking—sometimes even shouting—about paying attention. That was usually related to hearing instructions. But Jesus was sort of saying she had to pay attention even when there were no instructions.

"That's true. You're getting it."

The affirmation swirled a sort of giddiness into her head. Tildy realized she had a cracker in her mouth and wasn't chewing it. She restarted that part of her brain. But as she chewed, she still focused on what Jesus was talking about. There was a kind of paying attention that didn't come from a teacher scolding. It came from being aware of something that was always there but often ignored. Jesus was there. At least she was starting to feel like he was there. "But why those other eyes?" She shivered that creeped-out shiver again.

Something like a sigh preceded his answer. "Spirit. God is spirit. And you are seeing and hearing me by the Spirit that lives in you. The Holy Spirit of God." He let that resonate in the air— or in her heart, if he wasn't speaking aloud. "And there are unholy spirits that want your attention too. They will threaten and distract. They're hoping for fear and worry. That's their food."

Tildy finished chewing that cracker and sipped her apple juice. She hesitated to pop another cracker in, as if it might be rude to eat while having such a holy conversation. But then, Jesus had started this encounter when she already had a cracker in her mouth.

"Don't worry about those kinds of rules, Tildy. They're superstition. To think that God can only talk to you when you do or don't do something leads to magical superstition."

Those were bad things, she knew. Magic and superstition. Things Christians didn't need. But she wasn't sure why they were bad or what his warning meant to her. She got the feeling Jesus was throwing her small amounts of truth. Not big, two-handed scoops. Only what she could fit in a closed fist.

"I will only give you as much as you should be able to receive. And it will be up to you to try to receive it. But don't get distracted by figuring all of that out right now. Just know that I will never leave you. Even if enemies threaten you, I will be there. I *have* you." A pause. "And you have me."

She was leaning against the counter with the heel of one hand on the cool surface, another bite of cracker in her mouth. Not chewing. When she realized it again, she rebooted her brain. "I have you." She said it aloud. But not like a declaration. And not a question.

171

With Grandma nowhere in sight, Tildy slipped the last few crackers back into the waxy paper inside the box. Eating may not have been sacrilegious right then, but it was interrupting her comprehension of what Jesus was saying.

She swallowed the last of her apple juice and set the glass in the sink. She turned off the kitchen light at the switch next to the fridge and wobbled to her room.

"I have you." When the words sifted through her mind again, she couldn't tell if she was saying it or Jesus was. But, according to him, it was true either way.

That realization captured her imagination. What a fantastic thing! This *having* went both ways. Jesus in her and her in him. The second part of that was the hardest to plug into her imagination, but she tried. She tried as she got dressed for bed. She tried as she lay under the covers. And she was still imagining being *in* Jesus the last moment she was awake and aware.

Which probably explained the dream.

She was in the woods. They seemed familiar, like a place she had played when she was little. But that bothered her. She never played in any woods when she was little, so why was this place so familiar? Maybe it was a familiar dream place. The notion of a dream place seemed liberating. It seemed to explain a lot. But then, she wasn't sure exactly what it explained. And she couldn't tell if it was right.

The arrival of three bears interrupted this exploration. She was walking in those woods, and the path ahead of her was blocked by three bears. Not the fairy tale three bears. These were a more intimidating gang of carnivorous beasts. She was familiar with these beasts, though something about them was different this time.

In the dream, Tildy realized she was surrounded. But not by the bears. It was like being engulfed by the big dark curtains on the school auditorium stage, but less dusty and musty. She was warm. She was enclosed. But she could still see the way ahead.

What she could see was those bears backing away like three large trucks. They should have had that beep-beep-beep sound warning folks they were backing up. That's how big they were. Tildy noticed what a silly thought that was. And she realized she was free to have a silly thought because she was surrounded. She was in a shelter even though she was walking.

Then she knew she was in Jesus. Maybe just like she was inside his coat. Something about him was with her. Surrounding her. And those bears had to back away.

She had nothing to fear.

That discovery made her laugh.

She woke herself from the dream. Laughing.

Chapter Twenty-One
Finally Getting to See That Game

Tildy's dad came to the house to pick her up on Friday night. They were going to a home game for the DePaul women. He was certainly focused on that team for Tildy's sake. And because they played not too far away. It was even closer to where her dad lived, apparently.

"Hello, Carolyn." He smiled at Grandma, who was still dressed for work. Maybe she kept her sharp real-estate-lady blazer and skirt on in anticipation of his visit. Tildy only noticed it when her dad greeted Grandma so politely.

"Hello, Derek. How are you? How are things at work?" Those weren't really friendly questions in themselves, but Grandma's tone was friendlier than when she was talking business over the phone.

Of course this wasn't just business for Tildy. This was her dad. This was her first time going somewhere with her dad since he'd tried to take her away from her mom at age six. Tildy didn't really remember that event as such, but she had been reconstructing it in her imagination as she anticipated seeing him. She wasn't really worried he would try it again. In her head, it only made sense as the desperate act of a much younger man. He was different now. Her new dad, the new man he had become—at least in her imagination—wasn't desperate. He just wanted to spend time with his girl.

Tildy stood grinning through those thoughts when she realized someone was talking to her. Grandma was. "What?"

"I asked if you had everything you need. Gloves or mittens?"

Patting her coat pockets and trying to remember if those lumps were gloves or mittens, Tildy tried to recover her dignity.

Or at least her focus. "Yeah. I have 'em here. She put her hands in her pockets and was relieved to find knit mittens, saving her from having lied to Grandma.

"Okay, kid." Her dad reached a hand toward her. "Let's get going. The game starts in less than an hour." He said it with a grin, as if he knew he was playing a part. The part of the responsible adult.

Tildy nodded. She gave Grandma a side hug and said goodbye.

Her dad drove a four-door sedan that seemed pretty generic. Tildy wasn't a car expert, so she didn't recognize the logo on the steering wheel. The car was nice enough. The heater worked very well. That was crucial. Her dad ran the defroster on high for a while to keep the windshield clear.

"What's your favorite subject in school these days?"

She couldn't recall if he had asked her that when they met before. She hoped not. She hoped he didn't ask questions like that and then just forget the answer.

"Art. There's a new art teacher. I like her a lot. But I liked art the best even before she came this year."

"Oh, yeah. You told me you were working on painting scenery for the school play."

She nodded, tallying one point for Dad at least remembering *something* she had said to him before. She turned to watch him as he drove, the lights of approaching cars sparkling in his eyes and off his teeth. He seemed to default to a slightly open-mouthed smile. His resting face.

"Did you and Mom go to church at all?" Tildy somehow molded that question out of seeing his peaceful smile.

He glanced at her and shook his head. "Hardly ever. Maybe a couple weddings. Christmas once. She seemed sort of afraid of it."

"Why afraid?"

"I'm not sure. You'd have to ask her." Glancing her way again, his face lost that smile. "I wonder if it was because she felt

175

bad about the drugs. The folks at your grandma's church—either one of your grandmas—didn't have much room for drug addicts. They probably didn't say enough about forgiveness and such."

"I haven't seen my other grandma in a long time." Tildy hadn't even thought of her much until lately.

Her dad's lips tightened, and he tilted his head away. "I can talk to her." His voice was low and slow. "I ... she had some problems with your mom. She ... they didn't get along real well. But that's not about you. I bet she'd love to see you."

The way he blinked when he looked at her again made her wonder if he was just recognizing the favorable odds for that bet. Tildy wasn't inclined to push. She was content to take this one step, to do this one night. Maybe it was something like their second or third step together.

The basketball game was fun. Her dad was a fan of the sport, though she was right about him not knowing anything about the teams they were watching. DePaul won easily, which was exciting at first. Total domination is fun when it's the home team, but Tildy got bored after a while, and her dad seemed to know it right away.

"How about we take off and beat the crowd? Maybe stop somewhere and get some pie or something." There were still ten minutes left on the game clock.

Pausing to appreciate the feeling of her father paying enough attention to her to know she was bored, Tildy nodded and smiled. "Pie sounds good." She was thinking something sweet would help her recover from the hot dog and the nachos. Maybe *recover* wasn't the right word.

She almost laughed as they shuffled down the row to the nearest aisle. There was a kind of joy about both the normalness and the specialness of this time with her dad. Even dropping her box and cup in the trash barrel on the way out was normal in a very hopeful way. She did laugh then. Laughing at herself.

"What's funny?" He kept an eye on her as he led the way through a crisscross crowd of people coming and going from concession stands and restrooms.

Tildy wondered if he wanted to hold her hand, but she wasn't sure if it was up to her to initiate it. "Oh, I'm just having a good time, is all." Her smile felt silly, but she wasn't ashamed of it. She just wanted to laugh some more.

Then she did take his hand when he slowed to reflect her silly smile back at her. He laughed too. A very free and easy laugh. Not as silly as Tildy's, probably.

They found a diner that was mostly empty when they pushed through the heavy glass door into the warm lights. Her dad let go of the door once she was clear, then leading the way toward a waitress who motioned for them to find a seat.

The waitress was White and older, but she looked at them as if this was all good. The ease with which that stranger looked at Tildy reminded her of how awkward it sometimes felt to go to new places with her mom or grandma.

Her dad was darker than her, but she assumed White people would just see them as the same. Two Black people. Probably father and daughter. And the simplicity of those labels felt good, even though part of her knew it was annoying that it mattered so much.

Ordering pie and milk while her dad settled for coffee, she paused to stare at him across the shiny black table. She took snapshots in her head. She would look at him for a second—not more—and note what she saw. Paying attention. She paid lots more attention to her snapshots of her dad than to the other people and scenes in that diner.

"Why did you ask about church before? Are you going with your grandma?"

Tildy scrunched the corner of her mouth. "Not very often. She goes to a prayer group, and I used to go to an after-school program at another church before I started doing stage crew at school." She felt like her response was getting clouded by something.

Then she noticed a nudge on her side. She made a twitch toward turning to see who was there, but stopped herself in time to not look too weird. Hopefully.

Her dad squinted toward the parking lot, stray snowflakes starting to fall. "I grew up with church. I went all the time when I was your age. Learned about the apostles and about Jesus and such. I guess I miss it."

"Maybe you and me could go to church sometime when Grandma isn't going." Only as she said that did Tildy feel like the person who had nudged her had inspired the idea. That assumption evaporated the top layer of regret for blurting it.

Her dad puckered and nodded. "Sure. I should get back. Though I'm not sure what church I would go to these days. I can look it up. Maybe something between my place and your grandma's. I'll see." He sounded like he was working it out as he answered, and he kept doing that little nod with his lips pursed.

It wasn't overwhelming and she didn't even get a chill, but Tildy felt a warm pleasure coming from the invisible person sitting next to her. When he nudged her, it had felt like he was slipping into the seat, but now it felt more like he was inside her.

Inside me. Inside you.

"I had a dream the other night that I was, like, riding inside Jesus's coat. He was protecting me from these ferocious bears." Tildy just resisted a wince when she heard herself say all that.

The waitress approached with their order just then, slowing her dad's response.

"Do you often dream about Jesus?"

Tildy snorted even as she appreciated the super tall slice of chocolate cream pie. "I dream about bears more often than about Jesus, apparently." Of course she had only realized how often she dreamt about bears when Jesus pointed it out to her. But she wasn't going to say all that.

Her dad chuckled as he pulled the little bowl of creamer cups toward him. He chuckled more when Tildy tried her first bite of pie and got whipped cream on her upper lip.

She fumbled to unfold the paper napkin next to her plate and wiped off the sweet mustache. She raised her eyebrows at him. "Well, did I get it?"

He pointed to part of his own lip where he had a real mustache, thin and well-trimmed.

She mirrored his location and expanded her efforts to make sure she got all of it.

He nodded and just grinned at her. The light in his eyes seemed real. And it felt great to have it aimed at her.

At home, in bed late, Tildy took a last big breath that seemed required for letting go of the day. She nestled her head into her pillow. As usual, she lay on her side facing her nightstand. And as was becoming usual, Jesus appeared there, fading into view. He made no pretense of coming out of her closet this time. And his sci-fi materialization by her bed didn't startle her because she felt him there already. Maybe she had even asked him to show up.

"Did you nudge me to get me to ask my dad about church?"

Jesus nodded, smiling but not laughing. "You can call it a nudge. Mostly I just wanted it, and you sensed that I wanted it. But you also sensed that *you* wanted to know. So, you could say I just reminded you of what you already wanted."

"Isn't that all kinda confusing?" Maybe her question was whether this was too complicated to talk about so late on a Friday night after a hotdog, nachos, and chocolate pie, not to mention the car rides and the exciting basketball game.

Jesus smiled some more. His restful eyes gave the impression that he too was tired at the end of a long day. Tired and satisfied. She read a contentment on his face, and she accepted some part in it. Maybe not responsibility for it, but she felt she had at least cooperated with Jesus getting what he wanted.

"Exactly. You cooperated." He smiled up at her. "It feels good, doesn't it?"

She nodded. "You sound like you felt it too."

"Oh, I did. We cooperated, you and I. And you felt it, and I felt it. It's one of the most satisfying feelings we can share. You were designed to cooperate with me just the way I was designed to cooperate with my Father."

"Your Father ..." She wasn't asking who he meant. It wasn't really a question at all. Just a wondering. And a connecting. She had been with *her* father that evening. Something new for her. A good feeling of its own.

His nod and smile assured her they were understanding each other.

She was glad because she didn't have any energy for working hard at anything just now.

"Good night, Tildy. Sleep well."

And Tildy accepted his wishes, his blessings. That was the last conscious idea in her head.

Chapter Twenty-Two
Sharing A Jesus Sighting with Annabelle

Ms. Sullivan wasn't ready for Tildy to work for her that Saturday. She had things to do that would keep her out of her studio most of the day. She apologized over the phone, but she didn't really sound stressed about it.

After the first wave of disappointment, Tildy's lament faded like ripples in the bathtub. Excitement about seeing Ms. Sullivan that day leaked onto the floor but would leave no permanent damage. Her teacher did sound regretful. And everything she said seemed sincere as Tildy read her voice and measured her words.

Maybe Tildy was feeling better equipped to discern if someone was telling her the truth. Jesus seemed impressed with her ability to read people. Tildy flexed those intuitive muscles, hoping she could develop them some more.

News of Ms. Sullivan's cancellation provoked a grimace from Grandma that passed quickly.

"I can stay home alone. No problem." Tildy was alone almost every day—for a while at least. She had been doing it since her mom went to rehab.

"What about A.J.? Maybe you could go to her house. I'm gonna be gone most of the afternoon."

Tildy called Annabelle without reminding Grandma of the name change.

"That would be cool. The boys are driving me nuts. You could come over and listen to music in my room. That way it won't feel so much like I'm hiding in here."

Not having siblings, this was all mysterious to Tildy. And boys were thoroughly strange. What would it be like to have to live with two boys, even little ones that hardly even counted as people yet? She didn't say any of that to Annabelle on the phone or when she walked to her house after lunch.

"We coulda fed ya, Tildy." Annabelle's mom welcomed her at the front door.

Tildy could see Annabelle peeking out of the kitchen. The house itself felt similar to Grandma's, but it had an upstairs. And two little boys. Tildy could hear one of them barking like a dog. She assumed it was part of a game. Probably.

"Come keep me company. You can have a homemade chocolate chip cookie." Annabelle was probably recalling that Tildy's grandma was not a baking grandma.

"Great. Thanks." Tildy set her backpack against the wall just outside the kitchen. No one said she shouldn't. People in Annabelle's house rarely told Tildy she shouldn't do something like that. The Jamison's house wasn't as neat as Grandma's house. Tildy blamed that on the boys too. May as well.

The chewy, chocolatey cookie Tildy ate while Annabelle finished her peanut butter and mayonnaise sandwich nearly made her eyes roll back in her head. "Oh my gosh, that's good!"

"See, Mom? You gotta get these out to the world. Mrs. Fields will be jealous."

"Oh, yeah. These are way better than Mrs. Fields. And I *love* Mrs. Fields." Tildy did another fainting eye roll.

Annabelle's mom chuckled evenly like she had heard it all before. She grinned the very same grin Annabelle did, wide and full of dimples.

As they tromped up to Annabelle's bedroom, Tildy dragged her backpack behind her, bumping it against half the stairs.

"So am I gonna get paid for, like, babysitting you today?" Annabelle didn't even look over her shoulder for that tease.

"What do you charge?"

"I think the going rate is, like, five dollars an hour per kid. Though I'll have to check with my accountant on that."

"Okay. Get back to me when you have those numbers." Tildy could hear her grandma's voice when she said that part. "Hey, I brought that CD my dad gave me. Mariah Carey. I was hoping we could rip it on your computer so I can put the songs on my MP3 player."

"*That's* what he wants you to listen to?"

"Well, he doesn't really know what I like. I mean, I like some of it. It's not all that sleepy stuff."

"Mostly it is, I think." She glanced at Tildy. "Though I haven't heard the whole thing."

"I wanna listen to it though. For him."

"Sure. I understand. So, you're going legit? Just using music you have on CD?"

"Saves me getting sued by some giant music company."

"Yeah. I wonder how far down their list I am." Annabelle flared her eyes in mock fright.

"I'm not telling them anything." Tildy gave a reassuring nod. "Unless they torture me."

"What, by making you listen to gangster rap?"

"I wonder if my dad listens to Mariah Carey or if he just thinks it's what *I* should listen to."

"Yeah. No matter how cool your parents are, they probably still wouldn't choose the right music for you."

"You think I should tell him what I like in case he's gonna get me more CDs?"

"Get him to take you to the store, and you can show him what's good."

"Is that your expert advice?"

"It's my fantasy. 'Go ahead, dear. Just buy anything in the store.'" She did a generic dad voice.

"Hmm. Your dad doesn't take you to music stores?"

"He did once, and he let me get this Christina Aguilera CD. Then my mom saw some of the lyrics. Banned!" Annabelle pantomimed pounding a gavel.

"Let's get dirty?"

Annabelle cackled. "You don't sound very dirty, girl."

"*Eeuuwww.*" Tildy hit maximum cringe.

"They caught me watching a Britney Spears video on the family computer downstairs. That's one reason I don't have the internet up here." Annabelle had the old family computer in her room. It had a CD player and just enough memory for writing papers and ripping music from CDs. Not much more.

"Hey, what did you get on your story in English? You never told me." Tildy unzipped her backpack.

"C plus." It was Annabelle's turn to cringe. "I suppose you got an A."

"A minus. Some typos. I didn't proofread it enough times, I guess."

"My mom usually helps me with that, but she didn't have time to help with typing the last draft on this one." Annabelle spoke mournfully.

"What did Mrs. Fredericks say about the romance?"

"She didn't. She just dinged me for bad grammar and bad punctuation errors, etc., etc. I guess it wasn't that good a story. Did she like your story?"

"I think she wrote something like 'Interesting' at the bottom." Actually, Tildy knew Mrs. Fredericks had written "Intriguing" at the bottom, but she didn't want Annabelle to feel bad. Maybe it was kind of a lie, but lying to protect someone might be okay, she hoped. Her grandma had done that about her dad, hadn't she?

"Well, you deserve it. You have an awesome imagination." Annabelle turned back to close her bedroom door and paused by the chair where Tildy was unzipping her backpack. Annabelle took the Mariah Carey CD from Tildy, pincered between index finger and thumb to minimize her contact.

"My dad gave it to me," Tildy almost whined. It wasn't that she disagreed with Annabelle on the music, she just wanted some sympathy for this little project.

"I get it. I get it." Annabelle grasped the CD more normally as she bumped the mouse to wake the computer. "When you met your dad, did it seem like he was the one in your dream? You know—the one with the guy coming out of your closet."

Tildy had mostly forgotten that dream, but she was sure by now it was not connected to her dad. "I think the dream was before my grandma and I talked about my dad."

"Yeah, but maybe it was like a premonition that you would see your dad. Wasn't it, like, a dark guy? Like your dad?"

"Dark as in shadows. Not dark as in African American."

"Oh. Sorry. That wasn't clear to me."

"I'm surprised you even remember that dream."

"I thought it was cool. And getting a story for class out of a dream was way cool."

"It turned out to be more about ..." She stopped herself. Some part of her felt as if she had already told Annabelle about seeing Jesus, but surely she hadn't. She had definitely tried to tell Grandma, but not Annabelle.

"About what?" Annabelle inserted the CD into the computer. The CD tray rebounded as soon as it closed, sticking its tongue out at them. Annabelle insisted with a second push, and the PC accepted the disc.

"You'll think I'm crazy if I tell you." Even as she said that, Tildy knew Annabelle wouldn't let her get away with it. Some kids would accept her evasion as the end of the conversation, but not Annabelle. Tildy's only chance of not telling her the truth would be to make something else up. But lying about Jesus didn't seem like a good idea.

Annabelle clicked through some software prompts on the screen. Still gripping the mouse, she looked at Tildy. "What? Crazy about what?"

"Okay. Get the ripping started for the CD, and I'll tell you. But you have to promise not to tell anyone else. And you have to promise to still be my friend even if I'm totally nuts."

"Dang. That's a lot of things to promise."

"A.J.?"

"Annabelle. Call me Annabelle. And tell me all about it."

Tildy sat on Annabelle's bed and looked across the room. "Well, that dream was about Jesus. Not about my dad." That was a down payment, like Grandma was always talking about on her house deals. Tildy deposited that much to keep herself from hiding the whole thing from Annabelle.

"Jesus?" Annabelle shuddered as she said it. "Wow. Did you … I mean … that was weird. I just got the creeps, sort of."

"Maybe in a good way?" Tildy strung a hopeful note along the end of her alternate interpretation.

"I don't know." Annabelle glanced at the computer, which seemed to be working on something. Hopefully the MP3 file creation. She turned toward Tildy and just stood there for a second as if she might be afraid to get closer.

Tildy patted the bedspread next to her. "Sit down. I want to tell you a story."

And that's what she did. Tildy skipped "Once upon a time," but she did tell it like a story. At points, it seemed she was getting things out of order, but she gained a sort of momentum that repeatedly pushed her past her second-guessing. There was a definite presence in the room that wanted Tildy to tell her story and not stop for small distractions.

The files finished saving to the hard drive on the computer, and both girls looked when the computer chimed the news. But Tildy was in the middle of her story, the part where Jesus told her what to say to Darla. They both ignored the computer for now.

Tildy impressed herself with the list of evidence she found in her own telling, proving that something real was happening. She would have to call witnesses, of course, if she had to argue this in court, but her own story convinced her that it was worth saying all this to Annabelle.

When she finished and took a deep breath, Tildy waited for a response. She *hoped* for a response. The frozen look on Annabelle's face wasn't promising.

Then her friend looked around the room. "So, do you see him now? Like, right here in my bedroom?"

For just a second, Tildy entertained the possibility that Jesus couldn't show up at Annabelle's house the way he did at Grandma's house, like it was against the house rules. But she suspected Annabelle's parents had never thought to make up such a rule even if they would have been inclined to do so. Which they probably weren't.

In the corner of the room next to Annabelle's closet, Tildy saw a sort of disturbance. She focused there, and Jesus came into view.

Tildy took a deep breath in preparation for describing what she was seeing.

But Annabelle interrupted. "Jesus?" Then she burst into tears.

Tildy had never heard Annabelle cry. She had heard stories of her crying, like when she broke her finger playing soccer. But Tildy had never witnessed anything like this. She looked at Jesus, who was smiling, of course, and then she turned to look at Annabelle. Her friend's face was covered with tears. Her blue eyes where wide and full of something very similar to the shining wonder on Jesus's face. Only then did Tildy grab hold of what was obvious if she just let herself admit it.

Annabelle was seeing Jesus too!

Just stopping herself from swearing—something she hardly ever had to stop herself from doing—Tildy looked at Jesus. "She can see you?"

"Of course she can."

As far as Tildy was concerned, that was the dumbest thing she had ever heard Jesus say. But she let go of that assessment and allowed gurgling laughter to rise out of her chest.

Annabelle interrupted again. "Oh my gosh. He talks!"

That started Tildy cackling—another thing she didn't do often. Something she purposely didn't do. But the look on Annabelle's face compared to the look on Jesus's was way too much. It wasn't that Jesus was so serious. She had seen him look serious, of course. Like, concerned and compassionate. But he wasn't doing that now. He was beaming. It wasn't a jokey grin. It was love. He was just beaming his love at Annabelle.

And Annabelle was bright red. Her blue eyes were standing out in that bright red face. Her whole face was getting puffy. She wasn't mad or sad, surely, but she wasn't beaming her love back at Jesus. And what she said about Jesus talking was hilarious, like she had thought he was just a picture of Jesus or a hologram in the corner.

"He does talk." Tildy's laughter faded fast. She was going to say something funny about Jesus talking, but lost track of what it was.

Like the time the bookshelf fell on top of her when she was little, the significance of what was happening landed on Tildy suddenly. Jesus had shown up in Annabelle's room, and Annabelle could see him. She could see him right in the same place Tildy could see him. And she could hear him too. A giggle tried a comeback at that last thought, but Tildy's giggle was pinned under her shock.

She turned to Jesus. "You're here for Annabelle too?" As that thought graduated to words, she realized part of the weight she felt was regret. Her unique experience with Jesus was no longer unique. Her understanding about why he had appeared to her was getting deleted. At least revised.

"I am always with Annabelle as I am always with you, Tildy. I just chose to show myself to both of you today as a special treat."

For Tildy, the notion of a special treat was full and rich. She expected Annabelle felt the same way. She was pretty sure she had heard Annabelle, or someone in her family, use the phrase. When Tildy's dad brought her that CD, he might have said "special treat." The pie on the way home from the basketball game was one too, though maybe only in Tildy's head. Pacing through this with rapid little mental steps landed Tildy at an uncomfortable place. Was Jesus really saying his showing up to them was just like pie for dessert or a CD that Tildy didn't really like so much?

"The beauty of a special treat is not always the treat itself. The power of it is in the promise. It's knowing that sometimes we get things we don't expect. We even get things we don't deserve." Jesus was using what Tildy thought of as his teaching voice. He was teaching in response to her thoughts.

Unlike some of her least favorite teachers, who used a squeaky, shouting voice for teaching, Jesus had a calming and almost amused tone when he taught. He was apparently excited about what he taught. He was completely convinced it was true. And he didn't seem to need to shout to get it across.

Suddenly Tildy wanted to shout. A *whoopee*. But she became aware of noises in the hall right outside Annabelle's door. A knock.

Annabelle and Tildy turned and looked at each other, their mouths open. Then they looked at Jesus.

"A.J.?" Her mom swung the door open.

The girls swung their heads toward Annabelle's mom, then swung them back to Jesus. He was smiling and holding one finger to his lips.

What did that mean?

Annabelle's mother had a curious scowl on her face.

Tildy looked at Annabelle, who was still red but not crying anymore. Maybe she just looked like she had been laughing really hard.

"Are you okay?" Her mom glanced at Tildy, but focused on Annabelle. She did not focus on Jesus. As in, she clearly didn't notice the strange man in ancient robes standing by the closet door. Annabelle's mom was cool, but she wasn't *that* cool. Where Jesus was concerned, apparently, she was blind.

Had Jesus done something like that at Tildy's house with Grandma? Tildy hadn't been sure that one time when it seemed Grandma might have seen Jesus before he went invisible. But Grandma obviously didn't think she saw anything worth mentioning.

By now, Tildy realized that she and Annabelle were just staring. Not answering. Looking guilty of something. "Sorry. We didn't mean to make so much noise." Tildy elbowed Annabelle.

Annabelle started to reach up to her face but seemed to change her mind. She gave a breathy laugh. "Just goofing around. Sorry."

That seemed to satisfy her mom, who nodded slowly and stepped backward into the hall, bringing the door with her, a lock of blonde hair falling over one eye.

Maybe her mom would talk to Annabelle later about their strange behavior. After the guest was gone. Tildy's grandma might handle the odd situation that way.

Once her mom was gone, Annabelle turned to Jesus.

Tildy did too.

"She couldn't see you." Annabelle kept her voice low, confidential and curious.

"That's right. But she senses my presence in her life many times a day. She was sensing something in here. It confused her because that feeling came with you two acting silly—at least in her eyes."

"Oh." Tildy and Annabelle said that in unison. Then they laughed. But they laughed with hands over mouths. Some things would just be too hard to explain to a grown-up.

Chapter Twenty-Three
Something Hard for Tildy to Recall

That Saturday afternoon united Tildy and Annabelle in a new way. The experience was even more fantastical than Tildy's short story for Mrs. Fredericks. But maybe that was just because she and Annabelle actually believed this story.

Seeing Jesus for herself for those few minutes seemed to be enough to convince Annabelle of the whole thing. "What do you think that was that he did to your grandma?"

"He said he wanted to heal her. And I didn't have to be a saint, or at least a special kind of saint, to help him." Tildy hit the word *help* with its own question mark attached. "But then Grandma said she felt better. No heart problems after that. Though I haven't checked with her lately." Tildy wondered why she hadn't checked. And why hadn't Grandma said anything?

Late that afternoon, a call from her grandma to Annabelle's mom started Tildy on her way home. She said goodbye to Annabelle, whose eyes glowed in a way Tildy had never seen before. She wondered if Annabelle's family would notice. She also wondered if Jesus would start showing up in Annabelle's room after this.

"Hello, Tildy. How was A.J.'s house?" Grandma was wearing a navy blazer and a gray wool skirt. Her winter realtor costume.

"It was good." She almost said *great*, but that might have raised suspicion. "I don't remember if I told you yet. She wants to be called Annabelle now."

"Why's that— Oh, I see. Annabelle's her real first name? I didn't know that."

How could her grandma not know that? Well, how long had Tildy known? She hadn't known Annabelle for long. And just because her grandma had lived in the neighborhood for years, there was no reason she would know what A.J. stood for. This internal dialogue alerted Tildy that she was crabby. And that meant she was tired. The prospect of talking more with her grandma seemed like a heavy lift. She just sighed and headed for her room.

"Did something happen today?" Grandma said it just before Tildy hit the hallway.

"Happen?" Usually if something did happen, that kind of question from Grandma would force Tildy to decide whether to deny what her guardian had mysteriously discerned.

"Yeah. You seem ... tired." Grandma had turned toward the kitchen.

"Actually, it was pretty fun. Maybe I wore myself out having so much fun."

Grandma made a weak noise of recognition.

Tildy didn't turn back to find out what that noise meant. She really *was* tired. Redirecting from her goal of collapsing in her room would take too much energy.

"It was stressful because of the weight of the truth." Jesus was sitting in her desk chair.

Again, his appearance didn't startle her enough to make her scream. But the rush of surprise did wake her up a bit. "Oh. I didn't ..." Tildy was about to say something about not realizing Jesus had left Annabelle's to come here. Even as she stopped herself from saying that, a cranky part of her insisted that it would have made sense in her world.

"Did I start all this by thinking about cutting myself?" She stood in the middle of the room, her door swinging closed behind her. Only then did she wonder if Grandma could hear her.

"She's banging around in the kitchen. Frozen steaks sizzling on the stove will be a good cover. But you should keep your voice down if you don't want her to hear."

"Oh. Okay." Then Tildy wondered if she should feel guilty for trying to hide the fact that Jesus was in her room.

But he went back to her question. "As with everything, I and my Father started all this." He made a one-handed gesture that seemed to include the closet in his answer. "But I was serious when I said I came to help you."

"But it's not like you never do anything like this apart from me, right? You could go and see Annabelle any time whether you were seeing me or not, right?" Exactly what she was asking, what she needed to know, wasn't clear. But it felt big.

"You're wondering about the rules. How unusual this experience is."

"Experience?" It wasn't a word she often used, but it had come up since Jesus came out of her closet.

"I generally don't show up so clearly for most people. But everyone's relationship with me is unique. Look at the Bible. I led Peter out of jail with a rescue angel, but I didn't do it that way for Paul. Same God, same prison system. Different ways of taking care of my own."

Tildy could remember some prison stories from church. That it was Peter who got out of prison with the help of an angel wasn't something she could have answered right in a Bible quiz. But she was willing to learn Bible stories in her bedroom with Jesus.

"You still need to start reading." He glanced toward her Bible with its red cover, where it sat under a pile of books and papers.

"You know right where my Bible is." From where she stood, Tildy could see it. She knew where to look. But it would have taken X-ray vision for Jesus to see it from where he was sitting.

"It's almost as important as knowing where I am."

"Almost?" After that initial adrenaline from Jesus appearing in her chair, Tildy had sunk back into weariness.

"Your Bible is not more important than me, but it is an important way to get to know me."

That seemed a funny thing to say. She blinked at him for a few seconds.

"Save that for later. It will come in handy." Jesus blinked back at her more peacefully. "I can remind you later, if you like."

"If I like? You think I *wouldn't* want you to remind me of important things later in my life?"

"People get busy. People grow up and get focused on things out in the world." He lowered his voice a little. "I am the one sending you all into the world, so I can't blame you entirely."

"Not entirely?"

He grinned. It was a proud grin, like he was pleased with how well she comprehended the things he was saying. But he must already know what she was able to understand. How could he be proud?

"The pride on my face is a reflection. It's a reflection of my Father's pride in you. And it's an image of the pride you should have in yourself." He waited, as if for her to inhale that truth. "You can look to me to tell you what you're worth. In me, you will find a perfect reflection of who you are, Tildy."

"Matilda Marie Hawkins?"

"That's your name. It's a label, not the contents of the package."

"Is *Tildy* more like what's inside?"

"It is, in a way. You have absorbed *Tildy* as your true identity. Truer to you than your full name. In some ways, you see your full name as belonging to your parents and to your family. *Tildy* belongs more particularly to you."

She sat on her bed. "That makes sense, I guess."

"You will discover in your life that people have an amazing capacity to separate things inside their heads and hearts. Some even talk of separating your head from your heart." He waited, as if for her to catch up. "But remember that I am here for your head *and* for your heart. I am here for Tildy and for Matilda and for every part that you haven't even discovered about yourself yet."

She nodded slowly, maybe even solemnly. This seemed like important truth. But she wasn't sure she understood all of it.

"The part of what I'm saying that will make the most sense to you now is that people are able to keep parts of themselves separate from other parts. Take for example knowing that I am with you all the time. Lots of people know that is true, yet very few live as if it were real."

She slid to the top of her bed and pushed her pillow against the scarred wooden headboard. One of those scars was a small collection of letters. "MMH." She had carved her initials with a thumbnail not too long ago.

"You have been living with this kind of divide more clearly than most people over the last few days." He didn't sound mad about that. It was his teaching voice again. He grinned as if he knew she was consoling herself with those thoughts.

She cleared her throat briefly and kept her voice down. "So, I know now that you could show up out of my closet, or just be here sitting in my chair, but I sort of keep that hidden. I mean, I haven't really told my grandma."

"You're not obligated to tell everything to everybody all the time. Wisdom is required to sort that out."

"Is it okay to keep secrets from Grandma?"

"It's best not to, whenever possible. She is responsible for you in many ways. That will change as you get older. It will also change when your mom comes home. And when you get to spend more time with your dad."

A surprising sob burst from Tildy. It almost seemed to burst from her whole face, not just her mouth. She grabbed her face with both hands.

"Yes, your mother is coming home, and pretty soon. And you will get to spend more time with your dad." Clearly he knew why she suddenly broke out crying like that.

Actually, he must have known better than she did. Knowing wasn't a big part of what was happening to her just then. Maybe because of how tired she was, she was *feeling* more than *knowing.* That made her think of what Jesus said about the divide between head and heart.

"All people have the capacity to separate thoughts from feelings. At times it's required to protect people from pain—at least protect them until they have a better opportunity to face the pain."

Somehow she knew he wasn't just talking about people in general. And she wondered what pain she was waiting to face.

In barely more than a whisper, Jesus answered her. "Part of you does remember when your dad tried to take you away."

Tildy's sobbing had stopped, but tears continued to flow. Yet she didn't know what she was sad about. Then she remembered something. In the eyes of her mind, she saw her dad. He was younger. He was nervous, and he was sad. She didn't understand the reasons at the time. But she recognized his sadness now as she looked back. Was Jesus helping her see all this?

"There's a woman over there with that man." Her dad had nodded toward two strangers near a bright sign.

Tildy couldn't even recall now where this was, but it was a bright place. Artificial light. Maybe a mall.

"And she's gonna take you back to your mother."

"Why can't you take me back?" Tildy could hear her own pipy voice. She could almost feel it. Maybe she felt it inside because she still held that question.

She opened her eyes and looked at Jesus. "Why couldn't he take me?"

"Oh, he could have. But he had agreed to let them take you and to not flee or fight. He agreed to all that to keep you from being afraid."

"But I *was* afraid. They were taking me away from my dad." She sniffled hard. "And I knew *he* was afraid. That scared me the most."

Jesus handed her a tissue. "Yes. That's right. But he did the best he could to hide his fear. There are times when adults have to hide things from kids who won't understand what's happening. Child custody is one of those things."

"But it was a mistake, wasn't it? I mean, they kept him from seeing me for all those years." She blew her nose briefly.

"Yes. The judge was harsh. He had little sympathy for an unmarried father, a Black father. And your father had left you and your mom before. That all worked against him. The judge didn't know your dad would never harm you. The lawyers made the judge suspicious of him. So your dad was forbidden. And he couldn't afford a good lawyer who would know how to get that decision reversed."

Tildy realized she was shaking her head. Of course she wasn't denying what Jesus was saying. The hard thing to hear, the hard thing to remember, was that Tildy had sort of known what was happening. And then she had made herself forget.

"You didn't make yourself forget. It was natural to let the hard things get lost in your memory. Pain like that is too much for a six-year-old. Or even an older girl."

"Is eleven old enough?"

"It's old enough for you. And the time is right for your grandma. And for your dad. All those people had to be ready. And your mother had to get out of the way for just a little while."

Tildy blinked her itchy eyes and dabbed at stray tears. A sudden sobriety enveloped her. It was peaceful. It was solid.

"You're feeling the impact of the truth. You're feeling what it's like to bring that old part of yourself in close to who you are now. It's like the six-year-old sitting in that mall has come back to be part of you. Who knew a six-year-old could make you feel stronger?"

She snorted a congested laugh. "You knew."

He just nodded. And smiled.

Chapter Twenty-Four
Trying to Help Her Grandma Believe

"Who were you talking to in there? You didn't even have the phone with you." Grandma was at the end of the hall. She held a spatula in one hand. The look on her face, as if her eyes and mouth were not cooperating with each other, slowed Tildy almost as much as the challenge of the direct question.

Tildy took a deep breath. She forced herself not to close her bedroom door behind her. Jesus was invisible again anyway. "I told you before that I started talking to Jesus more." She questioned her boldness as soon as she let that much out. Maybe she was still tired. Maybe she was mixed up. That six-year-old part of her was probably messing her up.

"Like, praying? To Jesus?"

The way her grandma twined those words into a question full of disbelief reminded Tildy of something. In church they didn't say anything about talking to Jesus as far as she could remember. Doubts about whether she was remembering right made her want to go to church the next morning. That was a first. She squinted one eye. "I really think of it as talking. Like he's a friend that visits me and tells me things." This was cover in case Tildy wasn't supposed to *pray* to Jesus. But it was also a lot closer to how she saw his visits. Prayer had never been this interesting.

Grandma puffed her lips and released a pop of air. "Oh. That sounds good." She turned and led the way to the kitchen table. "And you were telling me something about that when you prayed for my heart condition."

Tildy still didn't remember actually praying in that situation. She was getting hung up now on the definition and practice of prayer. But maybe that was a distraction.

"Yes, it is." That was not a voice, but it was surely communication from her invisible escort, who was apparently accompanying her to the kitchen table.

If she answered that inner voice, would that count as prayer? Wait. She wasn't supposed to get stuck here.

"It was Jesus who told me about your ... palpitations before you said anything about them. And Jesus told me he wanted to heal you."

"He did?" She intoned that question the way she might have to a much younger Tildy telling her about a character in one of her games.

Tildy took a long, slow breath to calm down. Grandma was annoying her. She tried to convince herself that Grandma wasn't doing it on purpose. They stood next to the kitchen table, neither of them moving to be seated.

"Go ahead, Tildy. Tell her everything."

That was definitely not her talking to herself. Why in the world would she tell Grandma everything? No self-respecting sixth grader would say that to herself.

"I was having a really bad day, like I told you before. I was even thinking about ... somehow hurting myself. I was so depressed. And Jesus came into my room so I could really see him and hear him." She laughed. "It happened today at Annabelle's house too. And Annabelle saw him." Tildy didn't mean that as evidence to support her claims. She was just thinking aloud as she recalled how funny it was that Annabelle was impressed that the Jesus in her room actually talked. She snickered until she saw Grandma's tensed-up eyebrows.

"Wait. You were thinking of hurting yourself?"

This was why Tildy didn't want to tell Grandma everything. "I didn't do it. And I'm not gonna do it, ever. Jesus helped me get past it. And he keeps telling me things that make me feel better and better. He was the one who told me I should ask if I could see Dad. I never would have known you would agree to that."

Grandma pulled her chair away from the table, but she still made no move to sit in it. "I was going to contact him and see if he wanted ... I mean, I expected he would want ... I was going to tell you it was okay."

"It's okay, Grandma. I'm not blaming you. It worked out. I know you were trying to protect me. And I know it was scary when Dad tried to take me away. I just remembered some of it now—how the people came to take me away from Dad at the mall, and how sad he was, but how he cooperated so I wouldn't get scared."

Grandma's hand shook where she held the back of her chair.

"Do you wanna sit down, Grandma?"

Without answering, Grandma buckled and landed hard on half the seat. Then she struggled to situate herself more normally on the chair. "Ha." It was a strange laugh. Maybe Grandma had endured an exhausting day like Tildy's.

Tildy's intense day had left her trying to fit too many things together. It was like playing Tetris with pieces coasting in from all four directions.

She scooted her own chair up to the table and reached for the green beans. She was hungry. Grandma had cooked frozen salisbury steaks. They were one of Tildy's favorites. A good brand. And the tater tots were her favorite food entirely.

"Oh, yeah. Your favorites." Grandma's voice sounded as strange as her face had looked before. A laugh seemed to get caught between a sigh and a moan.

But Tildy understood why Grandma was acting so strange. No matter what they taught about praying to God or Jesus, their church definitely didn't teach that girls could see and hear Jesus in their bedrooms. And she was hearing him pretty much everywhere now. Though not all the time.

That reminded her of what Jesus said about most people acting like he wasn't really present. "Do you ever think about how Jesus is really with us all the time?" Tildy speared one of the salisbury steaks and dropped it onto her plate. She was tempted to take two, but she doubted she would really eat two of those broad, flat patties.

Grandma cleared her throat. Then she stared at the tater tots for a few seconds. "I guess I don't think about it very often. But, sure, Jesus is really with us. I mean, we ask him to come into our hearts. And he does. He comes in ..." She had the handle to the green bean spoon between her forefinger and thumb, but she didn't seem to be doing anything except holding it.

"Maybe we can talk about this later. You should probably eat some supper." Tildy thought Grandma's empty stomach was making it harder to focus on what they were talking about. That happened to her sometimes.

"Oh. Thanks." Grandma looked at the beans and started her hand into motion. "No, it's okay. We can talk." But she left the words there as if she had no particular thing she wanted to talk about. When she loaded enough food on her plate to constitute a meal, however, Grandma seemed to arrive back where they had been two minutes ago. "I'm concerned that you were thinking of hurting yourself."

"Yeah, I know. But that was weeks ago. And I'm past that. One of the things that was messing with me was this mean girl at school who was saying nasty things about Mom. But since then, I've found out that girl was just being mean because she's having a really hard time at home." She paused to wonder how things were going at Darla's house. She had considered watching the news in case Darla's dad's crime was famous. But now all she could do was refer the matter to Jesus, the way he had offered before.

"Oh. How did you find out about that girl's home problems?"

These direct questions were really getting Grandma in trouble, but Tildy didn't see it as her job to warn her against it. "Well, really it was Jesus who told me, sort of. He told me something to say to her that would make her stop being so nasty.

And then he helped me really care about what was bothering her even though she was spreading bad rumors about Mom and me."

"What kind of rumors?"

"Sex stuff."

Grandma's eyes flashed. That expression said something akin to "Oh, crap!" but her mouth didn't express the same. She had a tater tot resting on her teeth by now. She was a big advocate of not talking with food in your mouth. Though it was taking her quite a while to actually get food into her mouth tonight. "So ..." Taking in that bite of potato, Grandma chewed vigorously. She chewed and stared at an empty chair across the table. When she swallowed and took a sip of water, she was more animated than at any time in this conversation. "Who's been talking to you about ...? And who's been telling you about Jesus coming to talk to you?"

Curious what that first broken question was supposed to be, Tildy stopped her own chewing. She used a sip of water to get past a bite of salisbury steak. "I, uh, I guess it probably has to do with church. I mean, I don't remember anyone telling me anything like this *exactly*. Though I guess there are those stories where the disciples are, like, hiding, and Jesus just appears in the room, right?"

"Well, sure. That's all in the Bible. But who's been telling you it could happen to you?" Grandma seemed younger, kind of like a college girl trying to figure out all the answers to life and God.

Tildy knew the straight answer to Grandma's last question, but the way Grandma asked it hooked Tildy like the time she was trying to sneak through the neighbor's yard and got her sweater caught on the gate. She tried to pull free. "I really didn't expect it to happen. I didn't ask him to come into my room. Not literally. But he just did it."

And then he did it again. Only this time he was in the kitchen standing behind Grandma.

Tildy looked up at him.

"What are you looking at?" Grandma started to turn, but then kept her eyes locked on Tildy.

"What? Who? It's Jesus."

"How?" Now Grandma turned. But she didn't scream. She must not have seen him.

But there he was.

"How do you know it's Jesus? I don't see anything."

"Annabelle ..." Tildy changed her mind about bringing in corroboration. "I mean, I just thought it looked like him. Like, from the Bible books and from Sunday school. And he talked like him. And he looks at me like that song 'Jesus Loves Me' is real."

"Jesus Loves Me?" Grandma might have been trying to recall the lyrics. Maybe looking for the part where the loving Jesus shows up in the kitchen at dinner time.

Quite without warning, Tildy giggled. She usually didn't giggle even when something was funny. But right there in the kitchen, she started to giggle.

"They call those 'church giggles,' I think." Jesus grinned big.

That Jesus said "I think" struck Tildy as even funnier. Like he didn't know church. He also seemed to be well acquainted with laughs of all sorts. She couldn't stop from laughing harder.

"Tildy, stop that. Are you laughing at me?" Grandma dropped her fork. She started turning to look behind her again, but stopped halfway.

Jesus held up one hand, and that seemed to send calming powers to Tildy.

She slowed her giggles and then stopped. "Sorry, Grandma. It wasn't you so much as Jesus." She took a deep breath. "I guess part of it was nerves. I'm worried what you're gonna think about me if you don't believe me."

"Believe you? How could I possibly believe you?" She had both hands resting on the table, shaking her head.

"Well, there is the healing from the heart arrhythmia." Jesus offered that in a matter-of-fact tone.

"Jesus says you were healed of a heart *a-rhythm-ee-yah*. Or something."

"Heart arrhythmia." Grandma corrected the pronunciation without looking up from where her eyes had landed in the middle of the table. "But how did you know that word? I didn't say it, did I?"

Tildy shook her head.

"Did you look it up on the internet?"

Again, Tildy shook her head.

Jesus intervened again. "You could tell her to try opening her mouth real wide to notice how her jaw pain is gone too. We healed that when we healed her heart."

Tildy wondered who *we* was in that account, but she had work to do—recovering her credibility with her grandma. "Jesus says if you open your mouth real wide, you'll notice the jaw pain is also gone. He healed that at the same time as your heart."

Grandma's hand wandered up to the side of her face. She opened her mouth pretty wide, then wider, then wider than Tildy had ever seen. Grandma's eyebrows drifted to full height. "Well, what do you think about that?"

The dreamy look on her grandma's face started Tildy laughing again. This time it was a normal laugh that she tried to keep concealed under one hand.

Grandma focused on Tildy and smiled. "This is … strange. But I do feel like some of what you're saying makes sense. I mean, I do feel better. And I don't think I told you about my jaw pain." She paused as if waiting for confirmation.

But Tildy wasn't sure what to say. She turned her head side to side slowly.

"So how could you know it was there? And now … now it's all gone. No pain. That's been there for *years*." She was shaking her head a bit more rapidly than Tildy, but all her movements and words were inexact and slow. Dreamlike.

"I just think Jesus did that good stuff for you because he really does love you. And he wanted you to believe that I can really see him."

Grandma smiled with one side of her mouth. She blinked rapidly. "I just don't know."

Tildy looked at Jesus.

He just shrugged.

Chapter Twenty-Five
What the Prayer Group Lady Says

Again, Grandma let the subject drop for the next few days. They didn't go to church that Sunday. Tildy didn't even suggest it.

But on Tuesday night, Grandma did go back to her prayer group. It had been since before Christmas, as far as Tildy could recall. And she couldn't help connecting Grandma's return to prayer group with what Tildy told her about talking to Jesus. A modicum of hope bloomed at that connection, but Tildy didn't actually know what the prayer group ladies would think of her ... experience.

With lots of homework to do, Tildy lost track of Grandma being gone. She often worked on the computer with her grandma in another room, or she worked in her room with Grandma in the family room. So, it was a bit shocking to have Grandma come through the garage door at nine fifteen.

"Oh." Tildy had just reprinted her social studies research paper after finding a mistake in the first sentence. She stood holding it in one hand, staring at Grandma.

"You didn't expect me home so soon?" Grandma said it very gently even if it sounded like a cross between a tease and an accusation.

"Uh, I lost track of time, I guess." Tildy didn't want to admit she'd lost track of Grandma's whereabouts.

"Yeah, it's after nine. You should start getting ready for bed."

"Sure. Right. I just finished printing my report. All set for tomorrow."

"Oh, that's good." Though she sounded somewhat happy about Tildy's accomplishment, the fast fade of Grandma's voice implied distraction.

"Was everything good at prayer meeting?" Tildy knew little about exactly what went on there. Something with praying, obviously. But she wasn't used to Grandma coming home looking distracted or bewildered.

"Good? Sure. It was good to see the ladies. It's been too long." She waved a hand in the air like she was indicating a faraway place in some story she was telling. Another odd move.

"Did something happen?" Then something occurred to Tildy. "Did you tell them about me talking to Jesus?" Maybe the prayer ladies had worked out whether Tildy talking to him in her room counted as prayer. That was their thing, after all.

"No. I didn't say anything in the group." Grandma removed her coat and opened the closet by the front door. She paused to look at Tildy, who had sat back down to log out of the computer.

Tildy turned toward Grandma to check on the reason for that pause.

"I did talk to Patricia, the group leader. Just for a few minutes afterward."

"Oh. You talked to her about me?"

"At first I just asked her a general question about people talking to Jesus and even thinking they can see and hear him." She reached into the closet for a hanger. "I guess she could tell I was asking about someone I knew. She wouldn't let me go until I told her it was you." Reaching into the closet, she loosed a small

206

laugh amongst the coats. "I guess it really made a difference to her."

"It made a difference that it was me who talks to Jesus?"

"She seemed more inclined to ... to actually believe it. She ... I guess she didn't think a kid would make something like that up. And she was saying how Jesus especially encouraged his disciples to bring kids to him." Grandma shook her head. Then she looked down at her black knit scarf. She pulled it from around her neck with one hand.

When Grandma looked at her, Tildy released a breath she had been holding back. She was glad now that she hadn't spent the evening worrying about Grandma telling her friends about Tildy's experience. That would have distracted her from homework.

Maybe Grandma saw that released tension. "So, I guess she believes you. At least she believes something is happening. I didn't give her lots of details. But then, you haven't given me lots." She tipped her head a few degrees to the side before stuffing her scarf in the closet.

"I tried a couple times, but I was worried I was freaking you out."

Grandma closed the closet door. "Well, you were scaring me. I mean, thinking of hurting yourself and then seeing a strange man in your room. It really scared me. But I've thought about it some since then."

"He's really not so strange. I mean, he just shows up at different times, and I'm not even startled. Like, it just seems normal that he would be there all of a sudden." She snickered at the thought. "I guess that's a different kind of normal."

"Strange normal." Grandma gaped her eyes and grinned. She took a deep breath, and her face relaxed. "I still don't know what to think about what you've told me, but at least I'm not so worried about you now."

"That's good. You shouldn't worry. I mean about Jesus and me. It's a good thing. Not something to worry about."

"Ah, but worrying about you is what I do naturally. It's hard to turn it off." Her smile was tired, but it was late. The blankness dulling her eyes was normal this time of night. The old normal.

"I wonder if Jesus is gonna keep showing up so I can see him. I mean, like, forever."

Grandma shook her head as she sauntered into the kitchen. "I guess I wonder that too. I mean, is it something you sort of grow out of?"

Tildy stood at the kitchen door watching her grandma do the usual foraging for water and a snack. "I can pretty much imagine what Jesus would say to that idea." She couldn't help grinning at the thought. "I see him as kind of fun and playful, like he's a big kid. I don't think he expects us to grow out of everything we have as kids."

Now Grandma was nodding as she poured herself milk for a change. She raised the carton to Tildy, who nodded her acceptance. "That sounds like what Patricia would say too. She's a little ... well, odd in her own way. I think she counts part of that oddness as trying to stay childlike. She was saying that stuff about Jesus inviting children, but also about childlikeness being important for all of us." She poured Tildy's milk. "I don't know if I heard her say that before, but it fits with some of her quirks. It seems almost silly how happy she gets when someone shares an answered prayer." Grandma hummed as she turned back to the fridge. "Maybe her strangeness is really normal too."

Tildy had never met Patricia. Her grandma hadn't said much about the prayer group leader. But now Tildy was getting the impression of someone who talked to Jesus quite a bit herself. At least she could imagine that.

And with her imagination accompanying her, Tildy went to bed that night and slept soundly. Though she couldn't recall the dreams exactly, she had a feeling that a question she was waiting to hear answered had been taken care of.

When she awoke in the morning, she wondered if the question was about how Grandma would deal with Tildy's new relationship with Jesus.

That led her to thinking about whether it was right to think of it as a new relationship. Tildy had prayed the salvation prayer years ago. So that was supposed to start everything, as far as she had heard. Or at least as much as she understood. What was this, then?

"A continuation. A deepening. And an answer to a question you didn't know you've been asking ever since you prayed that prayer." Jesus seemed to come out of the closet again, leaning his arm on the dresser as that first time.

"A question? About what?"

"It's a common question for those who pray that prayer or start a relationship with me by whatever means. The question is simply, 'What now?' And my people around the world have a variety of answers. Unfortunately not everyone pursues those answers."

"Like, how would they do that?"

"Well, consider what you were told. They told you that you could invite me into your heart. Did they explain how to communicate with me once I'm in there?"

She pushed herself up from her pillow and sat up, shaking her head. "Not really." In fact, Tildy could look back now and find very little expectation of what she might call a real relationship with this Jesus who was supposed to be living in her heart.

"That's the key, Tildy. A relationship. Every relationship includes communication. And communication with someone who lives in your heart never has to end."

That stirred a different question for Tildy. She scratched between her braids, through her hair covering, as she thought about it. "I've never heard Annabelle talk about having you in her heart."

Jesus smiled. "Their church approaches it differently, but that doesn't mean they can't have a personal relationship. My people just have to accept that I'm real and personal and … real personal." He smiled at his own joke.

She smiled back at him. It was impossible not to be infected by his smile. That was why Tildy knew for sure she would never cut herself. She only had to see that smile, even in her imagination, to feel better.

"And you can talk to me. Keep talking to me even when you can't see me with your eyes. See me in your imagination and listen in your heart."

"Huh. I guess the people in Sunday school didn't say that part. I mean, maybe they thought I was too young to understand it when I asked you in. Listening in my heart makes sense to me now." She pushed her comforter off her lap. "I was thinking last night that I knew how you would answer something Grandma said. That was like listening to you in my heart."

"Exactly. That's exactly what you did. And reading Scripture can be like that too. Once you see the stories about me in there, you'll have a better idea of what I'd say and do in a given situation."

Tildy stood, went to her desk, and dragged her Bible out from under the papers and books. She slid it to the front of the antique white desk and left it there. It was time to get ready for school, but she knew leaving her Bible right there would remind her to start reading it more often. Maybe even every day.

Jesus just smiled at that thought.

Tildy smiled back. The idea that she could make Jesus smile just by thinking good things almost made her giggle. It was still pretty early for giggling. Not even light outside yet.

As usual, Jesus allowed Tildy to focus on her personal chores. But he was never far from her thoughts. He said so many wise and interesting things that she could just think and think on what he had said. She showered, dried, dressed, sprayed conditioner on her braids, packed lunch, ate breakfast, and brushed teeth. Jesus was invisible but never far from her.

"Did they ever tell you in church that you should ask Jesus into your heart?" Tildy and Annabelle were standing by the curb waiting for the bus. The boys were rounding the corner, so Tildy knew their ride would arrive soon.

Annabelle surely wasn't surprised at the question. She had started it, really, by asking for Tildy's latest update from Jesus. "Into my heart? No. Not really. But they did teach us to pray to him and to God and to Mary and such. Those were all, like, *out there*, but they were all listening. I mean, they *are* all listening."

"My grandma's church teaches about asking Jesus into your heart, but Jesus says there are other ways to say it. I'm not even sure where the Bible says the thing about him coming into your heart. But still, he was talking this morning about listening in my heart for what he's saying."

"Listening in your heart?" Annabelle made a show of stretching her ear downward, as if she could listen to her own chest.

Tildy laughed and shoved Annabelle with a mittened hand.

The two brothers arrived at the corner.

"There's the two apostles, Peter and James." She surprised herself with such boldness.

James just shook his head and cast his gaze toward the approaching bus.

Peter grinned at Tildy. That accepting grin felt like compensation for his big brother's usual surliness.

At least that was how Tildy took it. She smiled back at Peter in acceptance of his implied apology. She was offering an apology of her own for blurting the thing about apostles. It was a lot to put on one exchange of smiles, but Tildy thought it was all pretty clear.

As they climbed onto the bus, boys first, Tildy thought about what she was doing. It was as if smiling at Jesus had infected her, made her more inclined to smile at a boy like Peter. But Peter might get ideas about her liking him if she kept smiling like that. She did like Jesus, of course, so she could smile at him all she wanted.

She was smiling at her own thoughts when she sat down. Surely Grandma's prayer group leader was no sillier than Tildy.

"You look like you're telling yourself jokes or something." Annabelle turned to see Tildy's face, stopping the process of pulling her MP3 player out of her backpack.

Glancing around to see if anyone else might have noticed, Tildy forced that grin off her face. Then she gave Annabelle a grimacing apology.

Annabelle leaned in and whispered to Tildy, "Are you listening to Jesus?"

For half a second, Tildy was tempted to pretend she was currently hearing Jesus, like, with a saintly smile on her face. On the other hand, she *had* been thinking about him. "Thinking about his smile, I guess."

Annabelle recoiled and launched her eyebrows up under her fleece hat. Then her mouth bent into an impressed sort of recognition. "Huh. He did have a really nice smile."

Tildy thought, *"Still does."*

Chapter Twenty-Six
Finally Getting to See Her Mom

The news reached Tildy that first week in February, but it was more a promise than a plan when it arrived. Waiting to find out if it would grow from a promise to reality blurred Tildy's attention at school and at home. Her mom was supposed to be getting out of rehab.

"Hopefully." Grandma tagged that onto the news report.

Maybe the rehab center considered it a plan, and Grandma wasn't completely convinced it would come to pass. The small smile she gave Tildy after telling her seemed a little regretful. Was she regretting telling Tildy too early?

Tildy wasn't sure if it was too early to let her know. She didn't like surprises, but she also didn't like waiting. That was a hard combination, of course.

She saw her dad again on the first Friday in February, and they talked over the news about her mother.

"You think she's completely cured?" Tildy poked a french fry at her ketchup and watched her dad for the real answer. Unlike Jesus, grown-ups often said one thing with words and something else with their eyes and tone.

Her dad raised his eyebrows and set his soda cup down. "For most folks, there's no such thing as completely cured from addiction." He sighed and squinted slightly, like he was figuring something out. Something about Tildy. "They say, 'Once an addict, always an addict,' but that doesn't mean people have to keep doing drugs. They can just learn how not to feed their addiction."

"Have you been to rehab?"

Smiling, he shook his head. "No. I actually went to some counseling sessions with your mom though, back in the day. Lots of what the counselor said made sense to me. Maybe it was easier for me to hear because I wasn't caught up in that stuff."

"You went to counseling with her when I was little? Was that so you could help her stop?"

"Kind of. But one thing they're real definite about is that the person who's addicted has to do the work. No one can do it for them. That's part of why I left when you were really small, and why I decided to try and take you away when you were six. I didn't think your mom could do the work." He paused as if wondering whether he could backspace through what he had just said. Then he released a caught breath. "The fact that she's coming out of this rehabilitation program means she did the work, and they expect she's ready to keep on doing it."

That was the first time Tildy thought his face disagreed with his words. "So, we can't really be sure she can do it."

"Right." He squinted slightly at her. "I try to sound positive, and I will always sound positive around her, but as you get older, you'll figure out how this works for you. You gotta be clear that you can't fix her. And you're not to blame for anything she does." He lowered his smooth forehead toward her and wrinkled it with a lift of his eyebrows. "You understand what I'm saying?"

She nodded, but her nodding head was acting more certain than the thoughts inside it.

"Your grandma and I will be here for you even if something goes wrong with your mom. But while she's with you, you should enjoy her. Get along with her and try to understand what she's going through."

"And Jesus is with me too." Tildy was fiddling with the straw in her drink cup. They hadn't been to church together yet. She wasn't sure what her dad would think about Jesus being with her.

"That is very true." His face was plain, not excited, not disagreeing with his own words. "That's one of the steps for recovery too. Relying on a higher power. And, of course, there is no higher power than Jesus." His voice had a little sing-song recitation in it, like he was sharing someone else's truth, one he *hoped* was true.

Her dad's words bolstered Tildy's confidence. That she couldn't fully count on her mom had always been hard to accept. Having her dad added back into her life felt like a new drawer of hope. And then there was Jesus.

At home on Saturday morning, Jesus stood near her bed. "Just be yourself, and trust me with your mom. That's really the way to go with everyone you know and meet. You can't change people. Only I can. And I can only do it with their cooperation. So that leaves you free to be a kid for a few more years."

"After that?" She was sitting at her desk sorting her music files on her MP3 player.

Jesus sat on her bed and leaned back against the headboard like she usually did. "After that it gets more complicated because you start taking on responsibility for caring for and providing for other people. But it's still the same core truth. You can offer, but it's up to others to decide to receive or not. That's just like what I face all the time."

Tildy let the MP3 player rest on her social studies book. "That sounds discouraging."

"I'm never without courage. Neither should you be. You will only be discouraged when you take responsibility for others. Taking on tasks you cannot complete is a sure road to discouragement. I *know* people, so I'm not surprised when they do what is consistent with their individual nature. I always hope for the best. And I keep offering all I have to give."

"Well, please offer all that to my mom. She's gonna need it."

"Yes. I'll do that. And you keep turning that job over to me. Then you'll avoid lots of discouragement."

"But not all of it?"

His smile didn't fade even as he turned his head slightly left and then right.

Tildy remembered that moment the rest of that Saturday.

That afternoon, she told Ms. Sullivan her mom was coming home.

"Oh, that's good. And she's gonna live with your grandma for a while? I mean, both of you will?"

Tildy pulled another silver pushpin out of the canvas frame. "Yeah. I guess we'll keep living with Grandma for a while, at least. I haven't really talked to her about that." She had finished stapling the canvas to that big frame where Ms. Sullivan had stretched it over the course of the week. With the last of the pushpins out, the staples keeping the canvas tight, Tildy snapped the center of the oatmeal-colored surface with her middle finger. It thumped like a drum stuffed with blankets. She had heard that sound at school the other day when they moved instruments off the auditorium stage.

Ms. Sullivan smiled at Tildy. "That's a good test of the stretching. Sounds just right."

"And a good test in case someone wants to play drums on it?"

Ms. Sullivan laughed. "I've had lots of strange requests, but not that one ... yet."

"You might consider it. A new line of art works." Tildy grinned at her teacher.

Ms. Sullivan was like Jesus in the purity of her smile.

On Sunday, Tildy had to force herself to eat breakfast. Her grandma was sitting at the kitchen table sipping coffee and reading the Sunday paper. She hadn't turned the page for as long as Tildy had been in the room.

Frozen waffles were the only thing Tildy could talk herself into making and eating.

Grandma didn't say anything about Tildy toasting the waffles. Maybe that was because it was Sunday. Or maybe because Grandma was staring into the unknown future and not really at that newspaper.

It was a special day. A day for a special treat. Hopefully.

It took Tildy a lot longer than usual to eat the two waffles, smeared with margarine and soaked in syrup.

Grandma did offer a disapproving tilt of the head at all that syrup. Tildy had overdone it by accident.

After she cleaned up the kitchen and got dressed, her grandma left to pick up Mom.

Tildy started straightening her room. When everything was in order—better than any day she could remember—she headed back to the kitchen. She was still scrubbing at the sink when she heard the car pull up the driveway.

She dropped the sponge and turned the water on to wash the bleach smell from her hands. The liquid soap smelled like oranges. That was way better than Comet. She scrubbed until her hands were red. She probably should have been wearing those big yellow gloves from under the sink, but she wasn't thinking perfectly straight this morning.

The door from the garage opened with a bump, a whish and a babble of voices. Women's voices. Familiar voices.

Tildy started to scamper away from those sounds and then stopped. Where was she going? Running away? She turned back to the little hall from the garage. And there stood her mom.

She was smiling generously. That in itself was different. At least different from the way she was when she visited on Christmas.

"Tildy!" She dropped her backpack against the wall and rushed to grab her girl.

Tildy felt like a little kid all of a sudden. She wanted nothing more than that hug from her mom. Her mom's smell wasn't the same, but the sound of her crying was as much a part of Tildy as her own breathing. Those arms were the ones Tildy had felt the most in her life. The other adults were much less likely to hold her than her mom had always been.

Only when wrapped in those arms did Tildy taste how much she missed being touched. Her head was higher on her mom's chest, she noted. She could just see over her mom's shoulder. And there was her grandma, grinning sideways and forgetting to close the door from the garage. At least she forgot for a while.

The sound of that door clumping shut seemed to awaken all three of them back to normality. Her mom backed up and took Tildy's face in her hands. She smiled her lemon-slice smile, showing lots of teeth as always. And Tildy realized what she had noticed about the smell. No cigarette smoke. At least lots less than she was used to.

"You quit smoking?"

Her mom snorted and looked over her shoulder at Grandma. "Her nose still works, I guess."

Grandma laughed, slipping past them with a suitcase in one hand.

Tildy regretted saying that about the cigarettes. At least she hadn't said anything directly about how her mother smelled different. That would have been rude, by this family's standards. Even with that little rudeness, this greeting was much more satisfying than Christmas had been. But Tildy knew this was much more than a visit, the promise of more than a single day.

"What have you been up to? Made any changes to your room?"

The first thing Tildy thought of was the man installed in her closet, but she didn't dig into that thought even long enough to start laughing. "Come see. I don't think it's changed so much, but I did clean it up."

Without thinking, Tildy took her mother's hand and led her down the hall. She could hear her mom breathing excitedly, a smile plastered on her face.

"I see you did clean up. Very impressive." She sounded genuinely impressed, no hint of sarcasm.

"I listen to more music on my MP3 player these days. But you got me that player, so you know about that. Oh, Grandma got me a clock radio a couple months ago."

They stood together in the door. From there, Tildy could see a pink sock poking out from under the bed. She let go of her mother's hand and scooped up that sock. She took two long strides to her closet and aimed the sock at her dirty clothes bin. Only startling slightly this time, she stopped when she saw Jesus standing in there. He moved aside to reveal the clothes bin. She snuffled a laugh at him. Or maybe at herself for being a girl who could find Jesus standing in her closet and not totally freak out.

Knowing he was there kept a grin on Tildy's face even more than having her mom back. She wasn't sure she should compare those two things, but she decided not to feel guilty either way.

By the time they were sitting at the kitchen table for grilled cheese sandwiches, her mom had unpacked her stuff into her old room and helped Grandma move some things out to the family room and some to her own bedroom. One filing cabinet would stay in the second bedroom as it always had. It was much too heavy for them to move on a casual Sunday.

"So, I guess you're not going to church these days." Tildy's mom leaned back in her seat as *her* mom slid a crispy sandwich onto her plate for Sunday lunch.

"Well, I went to prayer group the last couple weeks, but we haven't made it out of the house on a Sunday for a while. Gets to be a habit to just take the morning off. I usually have work in the afternoon, of course."

"You been staying home on your own, Tildy?" Her mom was leaned back in her chair, hands resting next to her plate.

"Sometimes. Sometimes I go to Annabelle's house for the afternoon."

"Annabelle? Who's that?"

"Oh, A.J. wants to be called by her real name these days." Tildy's sandwich landed on her plate as she pushed half a dozen dill slices off her fork. Grandma refused to cook the pickles in, but she didn't object to Tildy having them on her plate.

"She does? Well, I guess you girls are getting older. A.J. was sort of a boy's name anyway."

"That's what she said. Though she was worried that Annabelle sounded too prissy or something."

"Prissy?"

"Something." Tildy crunched into her sandwich and recalled that A.J. had said something about the name being too *White*. She didn't want to mention that in front of her mom and grandma.

"No prayers?" Grandma was sliding into her chair.

"Oops." Tildy apologized with her mouth full.

Her mom just bobbed her eyebrows as she chewed a bite of her own sandwich.

"Mind if I pray?" Grandma said it evenly, not in anger.

"Of course. Sorry I forgot. The grilled cheese is really yummy." Tildy had always loved her grandma's grilled cheese sandwiches—one of the few things she cooked that didn't come out of the freezer.

"Okay." Grandma reached one hand for Tildy, who wiped hers on a napkin before taking that hand. And she reached her other hand toward Mom.

The three of them sat linked like that for a few seconds before Grandma started her usual mealtime prayer. Before the *amen*, however, she added, "And thank you for bringing us all back together, and for being here in the midst of us."

Two new notes. Had Tildy influenced that last part with her experience with Jesus? Well, Jesus had really done it, but Tildy was glad to hear Grandma acknowledge the invisible person in the room.

Tildy resisted snickering at that thought, compelled toward another bite of that grilled cheese sandwich.

Chapter Twenty-Seven
Trying to Find Her Balance Again

Monday with her mom in the house was unreal. Leaving the house seemed wrong, but Tildy went through the motions anyway. Most of the time at school, she wondered what her mother was doing. Was she at home the whole day? Was she looking online for a job? Did she go to one of those meetings she was supposed to do every week, or even every day?

Annabelle put up with Tildy wondering aloud on the bus and in the halls at school. More than once, her friend did the sort of "Mm-hmm" Tildy was used to hearing from her grandma.

Tildy assumed she was annoying Annabelle. She did pause a couple times to appreciate her friend's patience.

By Tuesday, Tildy was ready to try to embrace the new normal. It turned out the new normal was just as cold as the old normal—nine degrees when she left the house. She hadn't seen her mother that morning, but she knew it was too early to expect hugs from Mom. Grandma had patted her on the back and wished her well as usual.

And, as usual, Annabelle arrived at the bus stop about the same time as Tildy. When the boys arrived, Tildy raised her head and spotted the bus turning onto the street. Very normal.

"Was your mom looking for a job yesterday?" Annabelle was dancing from one foot to the other, bouncing her knees. The topic of conversation was probably not important. She was just trying to get her mind off the cold, most likely.

Tildy was relieved that Annabelle had been the first to mention her mom. "I think she was looking on the internet. I think you can see, like, want ads on there."

"My uncle found a job on a website that just does that—getting people jobs. It's a whole deal." Annabelle stopped bopping and watched the bus sail to its rest at the curb, great curls of vapor wafting around them like an old movie scene at a train station.

The boys let them get on first. Tildy had unintentionally blocked them out. No more basketball in gym, she had to get her practice wherever she could.

"You guys doing gymnastics in gym now?" Tildy was following Annabelle closely.

Annabelle nodded enthusiastically. "I can actually do a handstand for more than a second now."

Looking for commiseration for having to switch from basketball, her favorite, to gymnastics, her least favorite, Tildy was talking to the wrong person. She let it drop, though she *was* impressed about the handstand.

She probably had about half her mind on school that morning. At least until art class. Ms. Sullivan was sitting on the front table with her feet dangling, pink satin ballerina slippers on her feet. She was so cool.

"Hello, Tildy. Hello, Annabelle. How is the world treating you these days?" The class was less than half full, students still streaming in.

Tildy led the way to a front table, which she had adopted the third week of class with only a little complaining from Annabelle. "My mom's home, so that's ... something." Tildy didn't intend to say that, but she kept her voice down and probably wasn't heard by any of the other students.

"Everything okay?"

"Hard to tell. Too early, I think." Tildy could feel Annabelle staring at her. Maybe Annabelle was surprised to hear her saying so much to a teacher. She only knew about Tildy's special relationship with Ms. Sullivan from afar. Tildy hadn't shared much about how they talked when she worked in the studio.

"Well, I know you have your grandma and your dad. And I'm sure Annabelle is a sturdy support. But feel free to come and talk when you need to. Remember, I've been through something similar." Ms. Sullivan's voice was low and soothing until she looked up and greeted the next bunch of students who herded into the room.

As others settled into their seats, Tildy got a brave little smile from Annabelle. She seemed quite satisfied with being a sturdy support. After breaking from that best-friend moment, Tildy thought she felt a calming rub between her shoulder blades. Annabelle wouldn't do that, but Jesus certainly would.

Not until afternoon study hall did Tildy surrender fully to the weight of her worries about her mom. She sat staring at her English reading, seeing not a word of it. Sitting at the library table alone, she sat up straighter when she felt something like an arm wrapping around her shoulders.

"It's heavy because it's not your load."

"Huh?" She looked around to see if anyone had heard her respond to her invisible study partner.

"The burden you feel when you stop to think about your mom. The weight in your chest. It seems heavy to you because you were never meant to lift it. It would make as much sense for you to carry the bus home from school as carrying the weight of your mother's problems."

Tildy snorted an airy laugh and shook her head for a second before recalling where she was. She inhaled deeply and tried to let Jesus's words go as deep as that breath.

"That's a good thing to do. Deep breath. Let it out." He seemed to be chuckling in a satisfied way. *"And take Ms. Sullivan up on her offer. You can also go to the school counselor. Mrs. Knapp deals with these sorts of troubles every day."*

"That seems like a lot of work."

"Actually, it is. It will take discipline and effort. But the work of dumping the burden is the work you are supposed to be doing. The effort will not be wasted."

On Wednesday, Tildy heard from Jesus again, this time in the most unlikely of places. The gym. On the balance beam. She was walking heel to toe with a student spotting her on each side when a thought slipped in.

"Balance takes work and relaxation."

Had Mr. Enriquez said that before? Probably not. It sounded too mystical for him.

Tildy did the turn at the end of the beam, her weight on the balls of her feet, only a slight wobble.

"Awesome. I wish I could do it like that." Darla was one of her spotters.

Tildy grinned.

The teacher's assistant congratulated her and told her to give up the beam to Darla. "Tildy, you stay and spot for her, please."

Tildy nodded as she watched Darla put one foot on the beam and then hesitate. "Just think of it this way—balance takes both work and relaxation."

Darla looked confused for a second. Then she tipped her head. She anchored a hand on Tildy's shoulder and pushed herself up, both feet wobbling on the beam. "Work and relax."

"It's a balance." Tildy almost felt like she was saying it in unison with Jesus, but she had to ignore that thought to keep from laughing. Not a good idea to laugh while Darla was waving her hands to stay on the beam.

After class, Darla walked with her to the locker room. "That was pretty good, Tildy. I'm gonna keep that in mind. Work and relax."

"I didn't invent it. A wise teacher told me that one. I'm trying to do that with my ... home situation."

Darla took a deep breath. "Uh, yeah. I'll have to think about doing it there too."

Tildy had finally surrendered to the urge to look up Darla's father on the internet. First, she had to remember what their last name was. Eventually she did find a story in a Chicago paper about a conviction and jail time for the commodities trader.

When they reached the locker room, Tildy patted Darla on the back very briefly and sent a prayer heavenward for her and her family. Then she stretched past where she could be confident of her balance. "Feel free to talk about it with me. And the counselors are real good here too. At least that's what I hear."

Darla blinked fast and only glanced at Tildy. "I still feel so bad about the things I was saying about you at the beginning of the semester."

Tildy grinned. The grin grew as she thought about her response. "I seriously forgot all about that. You and I have, like, real-life stuff to deal with. That was just ... kid stuff, really." Maybe she had overstated her forgiveness, but she decided not to get tangled in trying to fix that.

Nodding very rapidly, Darla peeled off and headed to her locker.

Tildy assumed Darla couldn't say anything because she was about to cry. A couple sniffles and a little sting to her own eyes slowed Tildy. Then she was back to being normal.

"Maybe normal has changed for you, Tildy."

As she quietly snickered at that thought, she appreciated that Jesus said *maybe*. He was being generous.

"Do *your* work and relax." She muttered it to herself. This time, it felt like *she* was the voice of Jesus. At least for herself.

Chapter Twenty-Eight
Tildy in the Closet with Jesus

Spring finally arrived, blooming and growing with summer clearly in mind. As Tildy's sixth-grade year slowed to an end, so too did her mother's recovery. Mom went out with some friends one Friday night and didn't come home by Saturday morning.

Tildy's first hint of trouble was the sound of her grandma sniffling. Grandma was in her bedroom, maybe with the door open. Tildy's door was open a few inches, but she stayed in bed. She couldn't explain how she knew what her grandma was sniffling about. She just knew. But, as she lay in bed thinking about it, she realized she didn't know everything. What had happened? Had her mom called? Was she hurt? In jail?

The time her mom was arrested had only come clear to Tildy weeks later. Her grandma had given a generic explanation when she went to pick up her daughter from ... somewhere.

Tildy wanted to know more this time. But she also wanted to talk to Jesus about it. She hadn't seen him very often over the past couple months. She felt his touches at times, and his thoughts often got mixed into hers. But there had been few appearances, even after the time she tried to get her mom to let her pray for healing.

Now she thought of those times when he had sat by her bed and talked in low tones. How had she gotten him to do that? Of course she hadn't done anything. He just showed up. Where was he now?

Her grandma shuffled past her door, interrupting that thought.

Tildy pushed back the covers and forced herself to sit up. She looked at the birthday card on her dresser. From her dad. She had celebrated with him last night. Her actual birthday was tomorrow. Just her and Grandma and Mom. That was the plan. That had been the plan. She sucked in a huge breath and let it out. It was a protest sigh, but she didn't know yet what she was protesting.

Only stopping at the bathroom because she couldn't wait, she hurried to the kitchen where Grandma sat at the kitchen table. No coffee. No sign of breakfast.

Tildy thought to offer to make Grandma coffee, but she had never actually done that before. She skipped the offer. "What happened?"

Grandma looked up from her hands, folded in front of her. Something in her face flipped before she answered, like a second lens over her eyes. "Your mom didn't come home last night."

Tildy had guessed that part. "Do you know where she is?"

"Not precisely. She left a ... confusing message on my phone." She turned toward the window.

"And? What did she say?" Tildy wanted to soften her words as soon as she said them. She stepped next to Grandma and put a hand on her shoulder.

Grandma glanced up at her and released a sigh. Maybe it was a protesting sigh too. "Well, it was hard to tell. She was obviously ... impaired." She snorted. "Obviously using again."

Like all those times Tildy had discovered Jesus in unexpected places, she wasn't startled by this news. She had known it, somehow. "Do we have to go get her?"

Grandma blinked and raised her eyes toward Tildy's face. "Oh, Tildy. You don't have to rescue your mother. Neither of us have to do that." She wrapped an arm around Tildy's waist and pulled her close.

It was a little awkward hugging Grandma like that, but Tildy pressed her hand on Grandma's opposite shoulder to keep from falling into her lap. "I know. It's not my burden to carry. I was just ... wondering." Where was Jesus right now?

"Yes. We get to wonder. But worrying will make us old before our time." Grandma allowed a very short chuckle, then sobered immediately. "I expect she'll come home when she can. And I expect she'll ... Well, we'll just see."

Tildy wondered if Grandma had been going to a counselor. She sounded just like Dad. And she sounded like she had been listening to Mrs. Knapp at school. Tildy had discovered it was much better to use study hall to talk to the school counselor than to stare at a textbook, worrying.

Somehow she and Grandma unwound themselves from each other and had their breakfast. Tildy wasn't really trying to get away with something when she toasted two waffles. It just seemed easy. And a bit comforting.

Grandma had her coffee and a piece of toast. She finished eating before she got another call on her cell phone. She stood and left the room as she answered. Her hissing whispers told Tildy who was calling.

Tildy still wanted more details. She wanted to know what to expect. That much seemed fair, didn't it?

Not until Tildy was dressed for soccer and sitting at the end of her bed did Grandma come to her door with news.

"She says ... your mother says ... she's not coming home. Not for a while, anyway." Her voice was quavering, a much older voice than belonged to Tildy's young grandma.

For a second, Tildy wondered if she was going to make it to the soccer game. She stopped herself from glancing at the clock radio. But that jump from the very bad news about her mom to worrying about the soccer game made her stomach turn over.

Grandma looked at Tildy's uniform and her gym bag next to her on the bed. "You think you can still play soccer? Maybe I shouldn't have told you till after the game."

It felt like Grandma was allowing Tildy behind the curtain to see how the play was produced. She felt a little bad for Grandma because she suspected she had not meant to show Tildy so much.

"Annabelle's coming to pick me up. I can still go." The answer was out of a dream, part of Tildy's mind that ran with little effort. Could she play soccer out of that dream?

As it turned out, she could slip her mother's problems into a pocket like the one in the door of her grandma's car. Really today was just like when her mom had been in rehab. Tildy worried, but she tucked that away and went on with her life.

Annabelle had talked Tildy into joining her recreation-league soccer team this spring. It wasn't as bad as Tildy had feared. She got to play goalkeeper. She got to use her hands for about half her time on the field. And she turned out to be a pretty good goalkeeper, as good as any of the boys on the team.

She saved three goals that day, though none of them were very hard. And she didn't allow any. They won the game three to one. All that was good, including Annabelle's goal.

On the ride home, she leaned toward Annabelle in the back seat. "I think my mom's in trouble again. She says she's not coming home."

Annabelle's dad, the coach of their team, was playing sports radio and talking to Annabelle's brother in the front seat. He probably didn't hear what Tildy said.

"Wait. When did you hear about this?" Annabelle held her water bottle in her lap, her mouth hanging open, a small drop of water poised on the tip of her bottom lip.

"Before soccer. Grandma almost talked me into not going, but that wouldn't have helped."

"So she's in rehab again?"

"I wish. No. She's with some friends, I think."

"And not coming home?"

Of course that blew Annabelle's mind. Her family wasn't perfect—Tildy had overheard some arguments—but they all stayed inside the boundaries. Boundaries as clear as the soccer field lines. And they stayed together. Annabelle would have no idea what it was like to have a family so broken and scattered. But at least she was trying.

Tildy leaned her head back on the seat. She was sweaty and itchy. She was done with soccer for another Saturday, and she was hoping to get done with worrying about her mother sometime soon.

After her shower and a banana in the kitchen—still too early for lunch—Tildy wandered back toward her bedroom. Grandma had left a note on the table. After a rush of excitement, Tildy read it to find the usual. Grandma had a showing. She would be gone for a couple hours. Tildy working at Ms. Sullivan's studio would happen this afternoon. Her grandma would call and let the teacher know her schedule. That was taken care of.

Back in her room, Tildy stared at her desk. Not much to do there. Homework was thinning at the end of the year. She was caught up on her reading. There were some discussion questions in science, but she couldn't persuade herself to sit down and finish those.

She glanced at her closet. Where was Jesus?

Of course he was inside her. That was the *right* answer.

She paused and tried to still her thoughts for a few seconds. Then she did something she had never attempted before. She climbed into her closet, pushing her laundry bin to one side, plowing shoes and fallen clothes ahead of it. She settled atop the fuzzy slippers she never wore and a fleece sweater that was too small for her. A soft place to sit, at least for a little while. She thought about closing the closet door, but that seemed too claustrophobic. Folding her legs beneath her, she leaned against the back wall of the closet.

"Jesus, you know I'm worried, of course. You know all about it. You even know where my mom is and what she's doing. Do you know what she needs?" She shook her head at herself, pushing the hem of one of her dresses away from her face.

"*Thanks for making the effort, Tildy.*" It wasn't his actual voice. But it was him. His words. She was pretty sure.

"The effort? You mean, like, climbing into the closet?"

He might have laughed at that. A welcoming and friendly laugh. "*Yes, dear. Sometimes you have to climb over a few things and push a few things aside to find space to meet with me. It happens.*"

"*It happens?*" She tried to imagine other people climbing into their closets. Ms. Sullivan. Her dad. Her grandma. The prayer group lady she had met recently. Actually, Tildy could imagine *that* lady having a dedicated place in her closet just for meeting with Jesus. Tildy smiled at the thought.

"*Your mother is in my hands, remember?*"

Tildy indulged a relaxing sigh, grateful for Jesus getting to the point. But he always got to the point. He just brought other things with him along the way.

"*You're getting so good at understanding me. You just need to take time to listen.*"

"Not just when my mom disappears?"

"*Right. Even when things are going well. Talk to me like a friend. You don't just talk to Annabelle when everything's messed up.*"

"Am I just hearing you in my head?"

"*Yes. That's a good way to think of it. In your head and in your heart. This is how it will be with us most of the time.*"

Though seeing and feeling him next to her had been spectacular, she appreciated knowing what to expect. Jesus's promises were things she could plan on.

"*I can be as close and available to you as you want. Anytime.*" It felt like he was pushing past her musing. Going deeper, somehow. "*I am here as surely as you are here, Tildy.*" His voice had changed. It was more solid.

Audible? Maybe not. But closer. Deeper.

Then she felt his presence more palpably. He was beside her. He was inside her. He was even behind her, as solid as that wall.

231

Jesus had her back. And he was filling that closet. He was even reaching beyond her little closet, beyond that dark space smelling of her laundry and her shoes. He was going as deep as she could imagine a feeling being. And he was reaching out. He was stretching his hands, extending his power out to the world around her. Even out to her mom, wherever she was.

Then Tildy broke open. Tears poured out. She sobbed out of sadness. She wept relief. She cried out of satisfaction that Jesus was so close. And she stayed in that closet for a long time. How long? She didn't know. She wiped away the tears with an old T-shirt and sniffled hard.

However long it lasted, all those tears left her exhausted.

"Will you always be in my closet?"

Jesus chuckled, or so it seemed. *"Will you always be in here?"*

She snickered right back at him.

"If you come in here to meet with me, I will meet with you. But our meetings will be unpredictable. I am the author of the unexpected, even though I made the world on which the first expectations were built. The devil's breakage and disappointment need not be the only unexpected things that come to you—if you will meet with me."

Hearing a long speech like that assured Tildy she wasn't just speaking to herself.

"That wasn't such a long speech." He seemed to fake being offended.

She laughed at him again. "Okay. Was it, like, a sermon, then?"

"Sure, the famous Sermon in the Closet."

Tildy laughed in her closet, though probably not as long as she had cried in there. And the refreshment of both gave her the courage to climb out of that little refuge and face another new normal.

There, in the middle of her room, she was quite sure she still heard Jesus laughing. Or maybe it wasn't hearing him so much as feeling his joy and his freedom. She just hoped she could keep all of that in her life and in her heart forever.

Chapter Twenty-Nine
About That Guy on the Bus

Tildy slipped her smartphone into her jacket pocket, reminding herself she put it there so she wouldn't panic later when she couldn't find it. At twenty-five, she wasn't supposed to be worried about a failing memory, but her preoccupation with her presentation in class today was adding decades to her life.

"Does this bus go downtown?" A small boy was looking at her. He had huge eyes and a baby-doll mouth about the size of his eyes. He was holding the hand of a woman who was talking on her phone with her arm wrapped around a yellow pole. There were a couple seats available, but the woman on the phone didn't seem to notice. She didn't seem to be paying attention to the boy either.

Tildy smiled at him. "Yes, it does. Are you going to school downtown?"

"No. I don't go to school yet. I stay with my grandma." He looked up at the woman on the phone. She didn't look a day over forty. Maybe she wasn't.

"Oh, I see."

"You going to … work?" He squinted just a little as if sizing her up.

"No. I'm going to school."

"Aren't you too old for school?"

She grinned. "Graduate school. It's school for old people."

The woman was off the phone now. She looked at Tildy. "What are you studying?"

"Art curation. Like working in a museum."

"Oh, yeah? Where do you study that?"

"I'm at the University of Chicago."

"Oh, that's fine. Your momma must be very proud of you."

Tildy took a deep breath. "She was. She passed on a few years ago, but she was very proud of me."

"Oh. I'm sorry."

Tildy waved one hand very briefly. "My grandmas are both still alive. And my dad. He brags on me all the time." She grinned to allow the woman permission to forgive herself, if she was willing to accept it.

Letting her eyes drift toward the front of the bus, Tildy noticed a man twisting in his seat, apparently agitated. Then she noticed the man who was talking to him. He was dressed very strangely, even for the eclectic Rogers Park neighborhood.

And then that strangely dressed man cast the briefest glance in Tildy's direction.

Was that ...? She had stopped breathing. Was that *Jesus*, riding on a CTA bus?

She shook that absurd notion away and glanced at the woman with the little boy. She was saying something to Tildy again. Tildy had missed part of it.

"... so good when you can get that kind of support." The woman slowed and tipped her head toward Tildy.

Tildy focused on her again. "I have been blessed with lots of support of all kinds. Parents, grandparents, teachers, mentors." She looked toward the front of the bus again. "And I believe in Jesus, and believe he's been with me all along the way." She had never talked like that to a stranger on the bus. It just tumbled out.

"Amen. Ain't that the truth? The very best kinda truth."

Tildy and that young grandmother exchanged grins. And Tildy knew she would call one of her own grandmas to see how she was doing when she got off the bus.

Then she watched those two men near the front of the bus again. If that one wasn't Jesus, then he was doing a pretty good ... She couldn't even finish the thought. An expanding warmth up her back nearly lifted her off the seat. It seemed to come with a rising urge to run to the front of the bus and touch that man. To embrace him, even.

The young grandmother turned her head as if following Tildy's gaping stare. Others were looking too. They were all glaring suspiciously at the nervous man with the round shoulders and the tousled, dark hair. They were looking at him like he was crazy.

That was when it occurred to Tildy that others might not be seeing *two* men up there. She looked at the woman with her arm still wrapped around the pole. "Strange." Tildy nodded toward those two men.

The woman shrugged. "It takes all kinds." She shook her head. "Though sometimes I see somebody who looks pretty normal talking to themselves, only to find out they have one of them earbuds in their ear. Talking on their phone."

Tildy recalled the first time she had made that mistake, walking on her college campus and seeing a professor talking to no one, no phone in his hand. She turned her attention back to the two men—or maybe just one man—near the front of the bus.

The guy whose back was to her still seemed tense, but he wasn't talking to the man facing him anymore.

A clear look at the smiling face of that other man nearly toppled Tildy onto her knees.

He returned her attention as if he could feel what was stirring her from nearly a whole bus length away.

She put a hand over her mouth to hold in the laughter. How long had it been since she'd giggled? How long had it been since she'd actually seen Jesus? The whole Jesus. There was that time when she was praying for a friend in college, and she thought she actually saw Jesus's hand. At least the outline, for a second. But here he was. As real as when he came out of her closet like he was haunting her childhood bedroom. As real as when he sat next to her bed and talked her to sleep.

Tears filled her eyes. What was she supposed to do now? Should she go up there and talk to him? But what if no one else was seeing him? She would look pretty crazy talking to an empty bench.

That grandma got busy on her phone and was ignoring Tildy, for which she was grateful. Tildy was surely acting as crazy and distracted as the pudgy guy in the tan coat.

The bus slowed to a stop, a transfer stop. And Jesus seemed to remind that guy to get off there.

Tildy almost laughed aloud at the idea of Jesus as a guide to the Chicago Transit Authority. But she knew there was more going on with that guy. More than Jesus showing him where to get off the bus.

Her internal speculations stopped just before that guy got off.

Jesus looked right at her. And she heard his voice in her head very clearly. *"Say a prayer for this guy, Tildy. He needs my help."*

She chuckled softly before rebuking herself for not thinking of praying already. She nodded at Jesus as he hustled off at the stop, the man with him staggering after. *"Bless him, Jesus. Just like you've done for me over and over."* She swiped a tear off her cheek.

Tildy smiled out the window at the two men now waiting at the transfer stop.

Jesus waved at her, and she clamped her hand over her mouth.

Then she returned to praying for the disheveled man and whatever struggle he was facing. *"Help him to receive what you're offering."* It felt like an inspired prayer. As much as any she had prayed in all her life.

Want to read more?

The Seeing Jesus Series

Book 1 - *Seeing Jesus*: Philly Thompson lives alone with his cat, Irving, in a one-bedroom apartment in Chicago. He worries about his weight, frets about his job, longs to get back with his ex-girlfriend, and wishes his ma would stop nagging him. To you and me, a pretty average guy. To Jesus, the raw material for a miracle ... or two.

When this ordinary guy stumbles into an extraordinary experience, everything seems possible, except staying stuck in that same dull life. Seeing and hearing Jesus right beside him rocks Philly's world and reaches beyond him to his coworkers, his girlfriends and his family. Too bad no one else can see or hear Jesus there. Will Philly be rejected yet again? Will they just decide that he's crazier than they imagined? Or will they let Philly's contact with the Divine lift them out of their suffering and light their lives with hope?

Book 2 - *Hearing Jesus*: Gladys Hight lives alone in a cozy little house in southeastern Wisconsin. Occasionally, her family has heard her speaking with Harry, her husband, who died four years ago. When she assumes she's alone in the house one Sunday, a stranger suddenly appears and begins talking to her as if he has known her forever. Despite discovering an unexpected man in her house, Gladys is not frightened, though she does wonder anew if she's losing her marbles. Complicating her self-doubt is the fact that the man smiling at her in her hallway looks just as she imagines Jesus would. Further, she discovers that no one else can see him or hear him as she can.

Though she had never wished for such a rare experience, nor even imagined such a thing possible, nothing in all her life impacts Gladys more profoundly than actually seeing and hearing Jesus.

Book 3 - *Sharing Jesus*: What could be better than marrying your soulmate, with whom you can share the rest of your life? Sharing

Jesus with that person.

Kayla and Jason have been married for three months when she begins to hear a disembodied voice. After Jason contemplates putting her away quietly, for her approaching insanity, he hears it too.

What follows is the story of two people meeting Jesus, in a visceral and life-changing way, and doing it as a couple, newly married and still forming the fringes and foundations of their dreams--together and separately.

Book 4 - *Finding Jesus*: This fourth book in the SEEING JESUS series, introduces Karl Meyer, whose retirement becomes a lonely prospect when his wife leaves him and his dog dies. Such losses might test one's sanity. That's what Karl assumed was happening when he began to hear noises, and then voices, in his old house. Though dizzying at times, what follows fills Karl's home with beloved companions and hope for the future.

Book 5 - *Holding Jesus*: Trudy Jensen has been caring for other people for over twenty years, their broken hearts, broken lives and broken relationships. Now she's thinking about her own relationships, particularly with men. Should she try online dating? What if one of her counselling clients found her online?

Even as she stalls over these questions she meets an intriguing man. Does she recognize him? Is he only friendly and not really dangerous? Is he who he claims to be?

Accompany Trudy as she wakes to a smiling face, cries on a reliable shoulder and discovers that God is real in her daily life.

Book 6 - *Hosting Jesus*: Philly Thompson once met Jesus on a city bus. After that extraordinary visit, Philly's life didn't go back to being ordinary. The intervening years, however, have been more tragic than magic. In that time, he lost loved ones, lost another job, and lost much of his faith. Jesus didn't promise him a story filled with magic. But he did offer himself, a continued connection with Jesus, his dearest friend.

That friend is talking to Philly again, and inviting him back into conversation and back into helping people in need. By now, Philly has settled into a new life full of hope and possibilities. Will it be full of Jesus? How can he include Jesus in his life again?

See more and **sign up for your newsletter** at our **web site**:
https://www.jeffreymcclainjones.com/

Amazon Author Page: https://www.amazon.com/Jeffrey-McClain-Jones/e/B00AEXAIlC/ref=dp_byline_cont_pop_ebooks_1

Facebook: https://www.facebook.com/jeffreymcclainjones

Printed in Great Britain
by Amazon